CITY OF SOULS

SOUL COURT ASCENSION BOOK ONE

MEL HARDING-SHAW

CORUSCATE PRESS

Cover design by Alerim

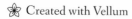 Created with Vellum

To my wingpeople.

CHAPTER 1
HEL

Hel hesitated on the threshold of the forge she was leaving, assessing her options. The bag of copper cuffs she'd just collected hung heavy on her back and the vibration from her smartwatch reminded her she was seven minutes shy of losing the bonus for fast delivery. The unreasonable deadline was a fucking crock because this package was going straight to her boss at the courier headquarters and she knew he wouldn't be able to give them out until shift change anyway. Veer left and take the safer, slower route overshadowed by the buildings and causeways of the city proper? Or cut through the dead zone of the waterfront and get that bonus? She glanced down at her watch and the graphic showing her indenture debt flashed, taunting her with the opportunity of another incremental step closer to independence.

"You're fast for a human, but it's not worth the risk, sweetheart. Keep that beautiful body safe," Wayland called from behind her.

Hel glanced over her shoulder at the smith, her fingers

absently stroking the cold metal of the baton with its concealed blades that was strapped to her thigh. Wayland was as annoyingly attractive as most elementals. The strength it took to hold their sweeping wings clear of the ground and manoeuvre in flight gave them a base-level muscle definition that wasn't remotely fair, and Wayland's physique was even more sculpted from his work at the forge. His feathers were a deep grey that bore a remarkable resemblance to the steel he worked and the same colour was mirrored in eyes framed with gentle laugh lines. For an elemental, he was bearable. His bulging muscles did nothing for her, though. She was stronger than a human, too, not that he knew that. Big deal. Despite her disinterest, his flirting still sparked an ache deep inside her that she quickly squashed. Even if he hadn't been an elemental, he wasn't worth the risk. Loneliness was survivable. Being discovered because she'd let her guard down and drawn attention to herself was not.

Hel shot him an aggressive grin over her shoulder as she stepped out into the fading sunlight and spun toward the dead zone without bothering to respond.

As she pushed herself into a ground-eating run to make up time, her eyes scanned the sky above the nearby shoreline for threats. The humans had built a large chunk of their city on land reclaimed from the sea, and they'd paid for it when the Melding hit. The merging of two realities and the resulting earthquakes had reverted the shoreline back to where nature intended and left the twisted wreckage of high-rise buildings scattered in the shallows of the harbour like half-buried zombies clawing out of a watery architectural graveyard.

Out where she was, past the edge of the city's safe zone,

the rubble had been shifted to create a kind of breakwater that doubled as a barrier against the ocean's predators that found a safe haven in the harbour. She was careful to keep close to the buildings looming to her left, away from the uneven edge where cracked asphalt gave way to sandy beach. Boarded-up windows loomed above her. Most of these buildings closest to the water were empty, part of a defensive barrier, but at least they had warded foundations that should keep her safe from any creatures coming up through the earth beneath her.

A flicker of shadow overhead had her flinching closer to the wall. Hel swore to herself as she searched her surroundings for the cause and failed to find it. Yanking her baton from its sheath, she put on a burst of speed.

Despite the danger, she revelled in the sensation of her feet pounding on the ground and the sharp wind blowing off the harbour that whipped her hair back from her face. In these moments of absolute focus with muscles straining she could almost forget everything else. All the loneliness, the constant fear of discovery, the grind of working day after day to clear her debt. It all faded to the background.

Her destination was one of the many elemental structures scattered through the city. A building grown from the rock of its foundations, sculpted and reinforced with pure elemental power and nestled in the shadow of the iconic Soul Tower. The tower itself was already visible in the distance ahead of her. Its soaring circular façade of twenty-nine stories topped with a crown of nine radiating metal posts was impossible to miss. The humans used to call it the Majestic Centre and it was the tallest building in the city, tall enough that it should've succumbed to aerial attack long ago. Instead, the elementals had saved it from destruction in the first hours after the Melding, reinforcing every pane of glass with the impossibly strong and intricate metalwork only their magic could produce until it looked like a soaring sculpture of leadlight stained glass. At night, the coloured lights that tipped those posts made it look like jewels on its crown. Under attack, the entire building would light up like a beacon of death magic.

Thinking of the unique necromancy wielded by the elemental lord of the City of Souls did nothing to ease the anxiety that stray shadow had sparked and her discomfit only grew as she approached the most exposed section of her route. Before the Melding sank so much infrastructure into the sea, five multi-lane roads had formed a broad intersection at her location. There was no cover.

A flash of colour to her right had her launching into a sprint towards the shelter of the abandoned hotel that was still too far ahead. The movement had come from across the lapping waters of the ocean near the looming silhouette of the old museum that formed a sand-coloured island a block or two offshore. Hel slowed her momentum to check what she was up against even as every cell in her body was screaming at her to run. The light from the setting sun glinted off a burnished gold form suspended below the kind of sweeping wingspan needed to keep a body that size airborne.

The creature was small for one of the griffins that nested on Matiu Island in the harbour's centre, probably one of the juveniles. The older griffins knew to steer clear of the city's defences. She let out a breath and forced her shoulders to relax. She could work with this. She couldn't outrun even a juvenile, but it wasn't old enough to have fully honed its predatory technique. It wasn't flying death yet.

The distraction of watching the incoming predator sent her stumbling on the damaged road and she sprawled forward, twisting her body to avoid damaging the package on her back as her knees took the brunt of her weight. She scrambled back to her feet, cursing herself for the stupid mistake. The incursion of the beach and water in this part of the city made the uneven road far too dangerous to run on while looking in the other direction. There was a reason it was called the dead zone, even if attacks were less common now the city's defences were so well coordinated.

The young griffin was closing in as she took off again, her movement sparking its instinct to chase. She ran faster, mentally calculating velocity and the seconds until it would strike as she tightened her grip on her weapon. She wasn't going to make it to cover. The backdraft of the griffin's wings buffeted her as she finally spun to confront it, already raising her weapon to strike as she foiled its attack position by leaping toward it. She'd timed it perfectly, interrupting its lunge before it could use its dive to pin her to the ground with wickedly sharp lion claws. The griffin's hooked beak gaped wide as it snapped at her, and she used her twisting momentum to put her whole body behind a strike that smashed her heavy metal baton into its face.

Her fingers numbed at the vibrating impact, the resounding crack quickly followed by an ear-piercing shriek and a rush of air that knocked her to the ground as the poor creature beat a fast retreat. She winced in sympathy. It wasn't the griffin's fault Hel looked like prey, and she was pretty sure its beak had split beneath the blow. Hopefully it hadn't splintered.

She groaned as she dragged herself back upright and glanced at her watch. Thirty seconds to the deadline. There was no way she was going to make it. She may as well have taken the long way round and saved herself the extra bruises. It took far more effort than it should've done to force her aching knees back into a jog.

By the time she made it back to the courier headquarters, the adrenaline rush of her run-in with the griffin was fading along with the last of the daylight. She could feel the fabric of her skinny black jeans pulling at the grazes on her knees where the blood had dried on it. At least she hadn't put a hole in the thick denim. Her outfit was one of the few concessions she'd wrangled from the company that had purchased her debt twelve years ago. They had a uniform, but it was designed for the winged elementals that dominated the profession. They'd let her pick her own version of the black-on-black ensemble. Black jeans, leather boots that protected her lower legs but flexible enough to run in, black tank top, and black leather jacket. Tidy jeans were a luxury as far from the main trade routes as they were, and if she'd damaged them then the cost of replacing them would have been added to her debt. It wouldn't be the first time. They knew she wouldn't stick around once it was repaid and they took great pleasure in finding ways to delay the day she left.

Hel stroked the weapon at her side to calm her angry thoughts. As an indentured 'employee', she shouldn't have been trusted with a weapon at all. But her thirteen-year-old self had refused to be parted from her last connection to the woman who raised her, the woman who'd trained her to defend herself. If they'd realised how strong she was or that the baton contained two wickedly sharp blades,

6

each the length of her forearm, they probably would've taken it off her. Instead, the elemental head of the couriers, Ryker, had found it endearing and let her keep it. She'd been careful not to give them any reason to take it. Any scraps she got into with the other couriers, she settled hand to hand, making sure to pull her punches and speed so no one suspected she wasn't as human as she appeared. It helped that no one in this world would conceive of a person who wasn't either human or elemental. Despite her care, she'd seen the hidden curiosity in their faces when she'd clocked up the early delivery bonuses time and again, even when the city was beset by swarms of predators. It was a delicate balancing act—being competent enough to get the bonuses but not so competent they started looking into why.

"Missed your bonus today, hot stuff," Ryker said with a smirk as she walked into his office and dropped the bag of cuffs onto his desk with a clunk.

"I live to please," Hel said, bitterness slipping into her voice.

Ryker's gaze dropped to the scrapes on her hands. "Did you run into some trouble? You know you need to get checked out if you got an injury on the job."

Hel rolled her eyes. "So you can add another medic bill to my debt again?" She'd only just repaid the bill for her replacement contraceptive implant. Not that she was likely to make use of it.

Ryker's deep burgundy feathers ruffled in irritation and his jaw tensed in that way he seemed to reserve just for her. He'd had a lot of opportunities to perfect it. He had the kind of classically handsome face and unflappable demeanour that allowed him to blend into any setting and there was nothing she loved more than making him lose the control he so valued.

"Believe it or not I'd prefer not to come in tomorrow and find you've bled out during the night because you're too stubborn to ask for help," he snapped. "You're not a damn child anymore. Show some maturity."

Hel shoved away from the desk to leave, but his grip closed around her wrist, jerking her to a stop.

"I just tripped. I'm fine," she muttered through gritted teeth. What was his problem?

He took another moment to search her eyes for any sign she was lying, then released her. "Come grab one of these cuffs before you head out tomorrow," he said.

"What for? Why can't I just grab one now?"

"Lord Bastion's got us chasing a bounty. He's stopping by shortly to magic these. This is elemental business. Tell anyone and I won't be able to save you, not that you've ever had a problem keeping quiet. The job's volunteer only and has to fit around our other duties. I assume you're keen to throw yourself at extra money like usual."

Hel hid her surprise at being included in whatever this was. They must be desperate. "Who's the bounty?" she asked.

"He's looking for a ... creature. Tentacles, wings, horns, and don't even ask me what's going on with its jaw—too many sections and lots of sharp teeth. It's intelligent and carnivorous, so don't drop your guard if you see it and whatever you do, do NOT kill it. All we need to do is get one of these cuffs on it so Lord Bastion can track it down."

"If he's throwing magic around to make these cuffs for us, wouldn't it be easier to just track it himself with his power?"

"Too hard to track. The creature's lair is in a pocket

dimension no one can reach. It only comes to our world to feed."

Hel felt a tingling thrill at the information. She'd never heard of a creature like this. It must be travelling by portal, but that kind of magic was all but unheard of in their world. The elementals might not be able to track it, but she had a special affinity to anything that involved portals, not that she could ever admit it. She passed as human and humans didn't have magic. Could she risk using her power a little to help win the hunt? Maybe if the pay was good enough. A passive search shouldn't draw any attention. "So, what? I'm supposed to wander around hoping I stumble across a hungry predator?"

"Yes. If you want the bonus before one of the guys gets there first."

Hel narrowed her eyes at his smug tone. He loved manipulating her into doing what he wanted and he knew he'd reeled her in. "How many guys are looking? And what kind of bonus?"

"I doubt anyone's going to pass up the opportunity, so all of us. Across every city we have a base in around the world. Triple hazard pay to the winner. Nothing for the rest."

Hel lost her words for a moment. This creature must be next-level important. Even with the company's cut, that would put a major dent in her debt. "Wait. So, we don't even know if it'll come here?"

"Why? You got something better to do?"

Hel rolled her eyes and flipped him off as she stalked to the door. He knew damn well she didn't. Between Wayland's flirting and Ryker's taunts, the loneliness that was usually no more than a zephyr of grey across her life was threatening to break into a howling gale-force storm.

Ryker's chuckle followed her across the room, and she added a glare over her shoulder for good measure as she yanked the door open. For the second time that day, she was caught looking in the wrong direction. Sparks of energy shot through her body as she careened into a very solid, very muscled chest. One that made her body respond in every way Wayland's hadn't earlier in the day. She tried to side-step around whoever it was but of course he'd flared out his damn wings for balance when she crashed into him and her move left her brushing up rudely against his primaries. The contact with his soft feathers sent more sparks across her skin, sparks that sang a siren's call to her power in a way she'd never felt before.

She cleared her throat and stepped back from the black wing that filled her vision. Black. Fuck. There was only one elemental with wings that colour, and she'd successfully avoided coming to his notice for twelve years. The last thing she needed was the lord of the entire damn city learning who she was or paying any kind of attention to her. Especially when he basically 'owned' her after funding the purchase of her indenture debt for the couriers all those years ago. Though she doubted he even knew who she was. She pushed down a surge of loathing.

"Sorry," she muttered, glancing up at his face as she finally managed to successfully step around him when he tucked his wings tight against his back.

She almost stumbled again when their eyes met and she fell into their depths. His iris was impossibly black, the same darkness as his wings that were more the absence of light than an actual colour. The thinnest line of silver ringed his pupil, matching the sparks of magic dancing across his wing surface. Death magic. The same sparks she could still feel twining through her power like a caress.

Lord Bastion was frowning slightly as if he couldn't make sense of the weird interaction of their power. He was probably wondering why his magic was responding to a human who shouldn't have any. Meanwhile, her hussy magic was trying to send sparks of itself to sink into him in return. That would definitely give her away. Annoyance surged inside her again and she took a deep breath, locking down her control. It took physical effort to break their eye contact and leave. The tingling warmth down her back told her he stared after her until she ducked around a corner out of sight.

When she finally reached her bedroom upstairs, she kicked the door shut and didn't bother taking off her boots before falling back on the aging springs of her twin bed. The streetlight outside her window flicked on as she stared up at the ceiling and she watched the blue-white light catch on the thin cobwebs that stretched across it. She really needed to grab a broom and get rid of them. Closing her eyes, she tried to breathe deep but, even in the darkness, the walls felt like they were shrinking closer.

Unable to rest on the lumpy mattress a second longer, she dropped to the ground and started working her way through strength exercises before moving on to practising strikes with the baton. When that still didn't alleviate the claustrophobic sense of being exposed, she hunted down a late dinner in the communal kitchen before retreating back to bed to read. Her eyes skimmed the same paragraph over and over on repeat, never taking it in. She sighed in disgust and put the book away.

Usually, she kept her head down, avoiding being seen. But every few months she needed to blow off some steam and release the pressure. This was definitely one of those times. She didn't have many clothes that weren't uniform standard, but she changed into a fitted leather cropped corset, unbraiding her long black hair and twisting it into a messy up-do with tendrils hanging down to frame her face. A deep red lipstick she'd discovered while hiding in an abandoned store five years back completed the look.

By the time she'd finished, she could've been any other twenty-something club goer. She'd blend right in and, hopefully, no one would even notice her in the crowd. Her watch display had turned red a while back as if she didn't already know it was past her curfew but it was unlikely anyone would be monitoring the GPS right then. She smiled at the chance to stick it to Ryker and wedged her window open, sliding out onto the awning underneath before flipping herself over the edge to drop down to the pavement. If only getting up again would be as easy. That was future Hel's problem, though.

She paused halfway down the street in the shadow of a doorway at the sound of wings overhead, waiting for whichever of the couriers was heading out on a job to pass. By their unspoken code developed over the years, they would give her shit and try to block her if they caught her leaving, but would look the other way if they ran into each other at the club. Well, anyone but Ryker. She'd never figured out exactly why, but she suspected the rest of them had started feeling guilty about the whole indenture thing once she'd been around a while. Unlike her, the rest of the couriers had come to this remote outpost of civilisation by choice for the hazard pay when Ryker had shifted their headquarters here. Hel had been a last-minute addition, indentured with Lord Bastion's financing to make up numbers when it turned out even hazard pay couldn't tempt enough elementals to work for a ruthless patricidal necromancer. She'd been stuck here ever since.

Proximity to that creepy necromancy aside and despite its name, the nightclub known as The Crypt on one of the lower levels of Soul Tower was the safest and most crowded nightlife in the city. The wards on the building were impenetrable and the anonymity of a heaving crowd was exactly what she needed to pretend she wasn't alone. When the courier was out of sight, she hurried on, eager to lose herself.

Her skin tingled at the sense of exposure as she entered the soaring atrium of the tower, overlooked by walkways and balconies. A wall of one-way mirrored windows two stories up concealed whoever was in the guard control room. The atrium was topped with a patchwork glass ceiling that gifted a view of shards of night sky, but Hel was more focused on marking the shadowy forms of the armed sentries standing near the encircling balustrades shrouded in bougainvillea. She jogged up the defunct escalators framed by twin ramps of flowing water features and round to the tighter stairwell that led up to the club as quickly as she could.

As she took the stairs two at a time, the bass vibrations of the music filled the air and set her body thrumming. All she wanted was to move and forget. The bouncer at the unassuming door to The Crypt was an elemental whose eyes drifted up her body as she came into view. He flared his chocolate brown wings a little in the enclosed space just as she reached him and she resisted raising an eyebrow at the attention-grabbing move that also happened to mean she couldn't get past without brushing up against him.

"Haven't seen you for a while, beautiful. Save a dance for me?"

"Nice try, Silas." She smiled to take the sting out of the rejection as she slid past him into the heat and noise of the club. She'd had to flirt with him a little to avoid giving up her weapon at the door when she first started coming but she didn't want to lead him on. She didn't sleep with elementals. Ever. Especially black-winged elementals with a body that set her aflame and magic that made her soul shiver.

CHAPTER 2
BAST

B ast stood on the VIP balcony of The Crypt and looked down at the heaving mass of people on the dance floor. Before the Melding, elementals would never have danced in such an enclosed space. When they let loose, it would've been outdoors with the whole sky as their playground in sprawling street parties on the roofs and bridgeways of their cities.

Bast kept his face a neutral mask as he watched on, all too conscious of the wary glances thrown in his direction. Usually, people were better at hiding their fear of his unique power. This reaction was the price of appearing ruthless enough to keep his city out of the courts' crosshairs. The saboteur they'd found earlier in the week had required him to send a strong message. The recording of the criminal's fall from the roof of Soul Tower, flailing in the city's winds as he tried and failed to slow his descent with only one functioning wing, had quickly gone viral on social media. The impact with the curved glass archway that covered the building's entrance had left the man's body a crumpled mess that reminded Bast of a monarch butterfly he'd once watched emerge from its cocoon only to become a ragged tangle when caught by the wind, wings still damp. He'd almost felt guilty about returning the shattered body to the Air Court alive. Lady Aliya had little patience for failure.

Blinking back the remembered images, he forced himself to refocus on the people below. Elementals rubbing shoulders with humans, uncaring of the sweaty bodies pressed up against their feathers. It might not be the freedom of flight, but the reverberation of the music against the walls and the undercurrent of simple joy in surviving another day, another week, was its own kind of intoxication. The invisible barriers between the human and elemental citizens of the City of Souls eroded more every year, and it was nowhere more visible than here where partners were just as likely to pair off across species as stick to their own kind. The partnership of city leaders had worked hard to build that trust, although he suspected it was the playing hard that had made the most difference.

An arm wrapped around him and passed him a tumbler of whiskey and he tipped his chin in thanks to the human he'd bound to him with magic the day they chose each other as brothers. Ra squeezed his shoulder before releasing him to take a sip of his drink. He'd always been that way from the first day they'd met, drawing him out of the darkness with his unashamedly open affection. Ra's nickname was perfect for him. While it'd started out as nothing more than the shortening of a name Ra had made Bast swear never to reveal, the meaning had evolved the day his friend started shortening Bastion to Bast, joking that their namesakes now shared a pantheon—deities of the Sun and Protection. Ra's irreverent brightness was absolutely a ray of fucking sunshine; whether Bast could live up to the whole protection thing remained to be seen. Bast's younger self hadn't known quite what to make of a man who was willing to not just befriend but hug someone known as a monster to his own people. Now, Ra was one of the three people in the world Bast would drag back from beyond the veil if he died.

A flash of familiar dark hair on the dancefloor below them caught his eye and his curious friend craned his neck to see who he was watching. The woman he'd run into outside Ryker's office was totally lost in the music. She looked like a warrior. Dangerous. Exquisite. He could still picture her wide green eyes as she stared at him. They were coloured darkest jade, or pounamu as the city's humans would call it, and contained a raft of emotions but not one shred of fear. It was that lack of fear that had held him stunned so long. Well, that and the strange sensation of his magic trying to jump straight to foreplay with a woman of a non-magical species who wouldn't even be able to feel it. If he concentrated, he could almost believe her intoxicating scent was drifting up to him where he stood on the balcony—night-blooming jasmine cut through with metallic steel from the weapons she shouldn't have been allowed to bring into his club.

Her sleek black hair spun out from her body as she danced, whipping around her like gravity had given up containing her energy. The subtle curve of her well-defined biceps as her arms raised above her head showed she was stronger than her slender frame would suggest. She'd have to be to work with the couriers. As a small space cleared around her, he could see the rhythmic sway of her hips sheathed in tight black jeans had entranced men and women alike around her. Her lips curved in pleasure as she threw back her head and she was oblivious to them all, oblivious to him. He couldn't look away.

Ra leaned closer, his teasing voice whispering in his ear. "See something you like?"

Bast shoved him away. "I told you. I'm taking a break from all that. I need to focus on securing my place with the courts before Tyson gets the balls to start something again."

"So, you won't mind if I go play with her then?"

Bast was caught by surprise at the possessive surge through him and the low growl of his words slipped out before he could catch them. "You could have literally *any* other person here. Find someone else."

Ra cracked up laughing, the rich sound carrying across the loud music and turning heads towards them. "'Taking a break'. Sure, bro."

Bast glared at him and took a long drink of whiskey, relishing the smooth burn of the liquor down his throat. Ra had been his wingman, friend, and family since the day Bast had flown into the city mere hours after the realities had collapsed, melding their two Earths into one. He couldn't have hidden his interest in the woman below from the man who knew him better than anyone if he'd tried, but he was well aware who she would likely choose between them if given the option. His objectively gorgeous friend who was always ready with an easy-going smile had a major advantage over him—he was human and charming. Safe. Women threw themselves at Bast, but only for his status and the thrill of the danger he represented, the fear he inspired. He had no interest in them. The woman hadn't thrown herself at him in anything but the literal sense. And she hadn't been afraid.

That power everyone feared in him was impossible to hide, shouted to the world through the unique black wings that rested behind him absorbing the flashing lights of the club and appearing to be made from shadow. He pulled them in tighter, concealing the flashes of shining silver magic that drifted across their inner surface. The eerie light was pulsing in time to the music as if the dead souls whose power had been trapped by his feathers wanted to let loose.

The vibration of the satellite phone in Bast's pocket distracted him before he could decide whether to pursue his prey down to the dance floor. He checked the display and saw it was Morrigan, the captain of the elemental scouts. She'd only be calling him at this time of night if it was something she couldn't handle herself. He left his glass on one of the bar tables and quickly shifted to the back of the balcony and out into a quieter hallway with Ra trailing along behind him. The music dropped to a distant thrum as they shut the door.

"What's up?" he asked.

"The scouts have reported an anomaly by the old Civic Square. Two dead bodies nearby. Human. Looks like they've had their throats torn out by something. And the pyramid just offshore has something weird going on. Something magic."

"What kind of magic? Are we under attack?" Bast snapped out.

"Whatever it is, it's not elemental. The water around it is disturbed and there's a darkness wreathing up from underneath. I don't know how else to describe it."

"Fuck. Don't go near it. Form a perimeter and get another team hunting whatever predator took the humans out. I'll be there in five."

"Thanks, Bast."

Bast was already striding to the exit when Ra reached out and grabbed his shoulder. "Can I do anything?" he asked.

Bast shook his head. "No. I think the contagion has finally reached us. It had to happen eventually. The Earth Court's been dealing with outbreaks for months."

Ra flinched, his voice dropping to a murmur, as if that might make it less real. "Damn. I was hoping we might be isolated enough to avoid it. Be careful. Don't take any stupid risks."

"I promise nothing. It's killing the world. My power comes from death. I'm sure there's something I can do."

Ra sighed and pulled him into a tight hug. "If you die, I'll kill you."

THE OLD CIVIC Square was so close to Soul Tower that Bast felt he'd barely snapped out his wings to catch the ubiquitous winds of the city before he was circling the glass-tipped pyramid looming over the encroaching seawater that filled the square.

Between the buildings on three sides and the raised area the pyramid rested on, the square itself looked like some sort of giant reflection pool. At least the water was shallow enough not to hide any dangerous predators this close to the urban shoreline. The pyramid itself was one of those rare structures that had appeared in similar form in both realities before the Melding. In the elemental world, it had been a monument to the fallen that doubled as a defensive position —beauty, memory and aggression combined. In the human world, it had merely been a design quirk above a space that had long since succumbed to earthquakes and the encroaching ocean. Now, the pyramid was a mix of elemental and human design that nestled down close to the water level.

Four of the city's scouts hovered a safe distance away from the pyramid, watching the water warily as it appeared to lean away from the pyramid like it was reluctant to wash up against its sides. The darkness Morrigan had mentioned was barely visible with the limited light from the stars, a testament to the elemental captain's sharp eyesight. It looked like tendrils of black fog were drifting up from the brickwork in the narrow path that split through the middle of the pyramid's structure.

He knew from his discussions with the Earth Lord Mica, the only elemental ruler who voluntarily spoke to him, that the darkness would slowly seep in all directions. And wherever it spread, there would be death. In Mica's lands, spots of darkness like this formed pools that stretched up from farmland like stalagmites. Any birds that passed through the columns never re-emerged. He'd watched the footage of them dropping from sight, presumably suffocating in the dense blackness the eye couldn't penetrate. The only positive was that the contagion spread so slowly Mica could clear the land around them with barriers of earth and magic wards to keep his people safe. For now, at least.

Morrigan broke off from her perimeter position and came to a hover to Bast's left, her deep brown skin and dappled azure and dark grey wings appearing shadowy in the night sky. "It's the contagion, isn't it? Can you do anything?"

Bast dropped lower, conscious of the captain's presence close behind him, a silent promise of her help if it was needed. He'd secured her and her scouts' loyalty years before when he stabilised the city. Despite their fear of his power, they were his people—loyal to the bone and fiercely proud of his dark reputation that kept their city from being subsumed into one of the court's territories.

Bast hovered just above the point of the pyramid and stretched his awareness out toward the nexus of his power, calling on the souls from this sector of the city for their help. The brightly flaring silver sparks across the inside of his wings reflected in the glass just below him. He waited until he was overflowing with power before sinking his focus down toward the darkness. A whisper made of hundreds of strands of voices sounded in his mind—*Careful. It is more than death. Even we couldn't bring you back to life from that,* the souls warned him.

How can I contain it? he asked the whispers of the dead in his mind. So many had died in the city during the Melding and its aftermath that even twenty-five years later the power they channelled to him there was like white-water rapids crashing through his body. It helped that the souls had all lingered in the space between life and death his magic sprang from, protecting their families, their descendants. Sometimes one would speak to him, sometimes many. Today, all he felt was their emotion in response—fear. He had to try, though. It was too near the city. They couldn't afford to let it spread. Who knew how the consuming darkness would respond to such a meal.

Going on instinct, he formed his power into a torrent of silver flames to burn out the infection. The darkness surged away from every fiery missile he sent at it, spreading itself further across the ground and sending the seawater crashing in waves toward the surrounding buildings. He cursed as he realised he was making it worse, not better. He focused harder, sinking deep into his magic to feel what'd caused the reaction. He sent out a smaller lick of flame, forcing himself to concentrate on the sensory feedback from his power despite the sickening sensation the contagion incited. As the blackness surged again in response, he realised his flame wasn't actually making contact with it. Almost like the contagion couldn't touch it. Curious.

He stopped his assault and frowned down at the black fog that had stretched and reformed in the narrow space below him. Ripples were forming in the nearest pool of darkness where a single drop was stretching up towards him from its middle as if it would try to pierce his body. Lord Mica had warned him that the darkness had latched onto the wards he'd set around it; the contagion seeming to adopt them as a shell that stretched alongside its growth instead of limiting it. The Earth Lord's wards had helped keep unsuspecting people and animals out of the contagion, but couldn't contain its spread. Something about the way the darkness had avoided Bast's flames made him want to test his own version, though.

He let his power cascade out until it formed a wide sphere, fully encasing the darkness. It was a classic shield, not all that different from the kind a normal elemental mage would make. But, as he forced the sphere of his power to contract and condense, he saw the darkness pull in on itself as if its power and his were magnets of the same polarity, repelling each other. The contagion might be more than death, but apparently it was still related enough to his unique death magic to have this reaction. He refused to think about what that said about him, focusing instead on crushing that darkness into a smaller and smaller space. His chest heaved and he gasped for breath with the effort it took to tighten his hold until the fog was no bigger than a skull. The pressure of the hungry roiling darkness was immense by the time he was finished and he hoped it couldn't continue to grow in the absence of anything feeding it. His ward wouldn't last if it did. Only time would tell.

Breathing a silent thanks for the contagion's location, distant enough from any occupied buildings and next to exactly the kind of structure he needed, he anchored his ward to the twisting vines of mage-crafted metalwork that stretched up the pyramid's sides. He wasn't sure he could've held the darkness back long enough for Zee, their magical engineer, to come and construct something he could hang the magic from if it hadn't already been there. Once the anchor had stabilised the sphere, he sliced off his connection to the construct and left it to do its thing. He could sense the warm approval of the souls whose power he'd drawn on. They entrusted him with the gift of their magic because he protected what had once been theirs. Their city, their family, their home.

Stand watch over the darkness, please. His thoughts felt sluggish with exhaustion as he pushed the command to the collection of souls that focused on this sector of the city and made a mental note to update the database Ra had made for him to keep track of the responsibilities of each group of the dead. They didn't have the benefit of a sentient stronghold to keep them safe like the elemental courts did. The City of Souls was too young and its ley lines too few to form the kind of consciousness that would've protected its people. In a world where belief shaped reality, Bast's ability to recruit and precisely manage thousands of souls to maintain a stable vision of the city was the only reason they could thrive. It was their most closely guarded secret. The painstaking work of sectioning the souls into units that each held a carefully curated memory of the city had taken the better part of three years and countless hours of negotiation between the human and elemental leaders of the city.

Bast was so lost in rambling memory he hadn't noticed his vision dimming. As his feet brushed on the rough side of the pyramid, he realised he'd been slowly losing altitude, dazed from the mental effort of containing the contagion. Belatedly, he tried to beat his wings and felt the muscles of his back cramp tight and seize up just before the Captain dropped in front to bodily haul him back into the safety of the air.

"Thanks," Bast muttered, as Morrigan released him high enough that he could coast back to his suite at Soul Tower.

"Is it fixed?" the gruff woman asked.

"It's contained for now. You'll need to put a sentry there around the clock. Don't let anyone near it."

"Will do. Right after I make sure you don't drop out of the sky on the way home. No way am I risking having to explain to Ana why you ended up as roadkill. The woman's terrifying."

Bast had just enough energy to smirk at the reference to his fierce tower manager who bossed them all around despite being human and short enough that she didn't even reach his shoulder. Then he angled toward the crown of lights that circled his penthouse apartment and dropped down onto the wide balcony that stretched out from his living area. He stumbled as he landed, almost falling to his knees before catching himself on the wall.

"Let me know if you want some remedial flying lessons!" Morrigan teased as she swept back toward the pyramid.

He flicked a rude gesture at her retreating back and staggered inside followed by the fading sounds of her irreverent laughter.

BAST WOKE with a groan the next morning as Ana shoved his boots off the end of the couch. All he could remember of his fading dream was the image of deep green eyes and the seductive scent of jasmine.

"Auē! Bast! I swear to the dead if you've got tarseal on the couch again, no court would convict me for my reaction."

Bast scrubbed a hand over his face and grunted what he hoped sounded like an apology as he staggered upright and headed toward a hot shower and clean clothes.

His wings were still dripping when he emerged ten minutes later, leaving two trails of water along the hardwood floors that he knew he'd catch hell for. A steaming mug of kawakawa tea spiked with a mild magical stimulant was sitting next to his computer when he dropped into the chair in his study. The peppery brew was one of the city's major local exports, made by a human who harvested the leaves and an elemental with just enough magic to imbue them into a suitable replacement for the too-expensive coffee they only imported to impress visiting dignitaries. He smiled as he took a sip. Ana might pretend to be a hard-arse, but she was the closest thing to a mother he had. By the time his computer chimed with an incoming call, the hot drink had revived him enough to put on the elemental lord mask that kept their city undisturbed.

"Mica, to what do I owe the pleasure?" Bast inspected the Earth Lord's image as he spoke. Smudges of darkness under his eyes marred the smooth bronze of his skin that hailed from the edges of his territory in the Middle East and subtle lines of stress pinched his face. He purposely didn't use Mica's title, as if they were the same rank in truth and his city hadn't just commandeered the term lord for him. If Mica was annoyed by the lack, he hid it behind a perfect veneer of civility. He was that way every time they spoke— poker-faced and shrewd. The other rulers were far more volatile. Bast's half-brother Tyson the Fire Lord probably would've launched an attack as soon as his unadorned name left Bast's lips.

"Good morning, Bastion. Are you well?" Mica's tone carried the slightest hint of reproof for his attempt at avoiding social pleasantries.

Bast didn't need pleasantries. He just needed the same respect as the rest of the elemental rulers. "We had our first brush with the contagion last night," he said, instead of answering the question.

"Do you need any help?"

Bast raised his eyebrows in surprise despite himself. He hadn't expected any offers of assistance, even from the relatively easy-going Earth Lord, who Ra described as the elemental equivalent of Switzerland. Not that the old human political divides had existed for the last two decades. They'd all been subsumed by the courts.

"Don't look so surprised. If this thing spreads, we will all suffer the consequences. If you can't keep your people safe, I can have someone come and ward it."

Bast let his face lose any hint of emotion at the conde-scension thinly veiled behind the Earth Lord's words. He almost wished he could gloat about the fact he was the only elemental who could contain the contagion, but it was better to play his cards closer to his chest for now. "I'm perfectly capable of keeping my people safe. If I wasn't, Tyson would have burned this city to the ground years ago. Now, was there a reason you disturbed my morning?"

Mica sighed. "I apologise Bastion. I didn't mean it like that. It was a genuine offer. Look, quite honestly, we need your help. The contagion is spreading. No one knows how to eliminate it. We need access to our histories to search for answers, but the Archivist has been holed up in their dimension for years and none of us have had any luck finding them. Tir must be hunting somewhere isolated enough to stay below the radar. Somewhere like your city. With your *unique* power, maybe you'd have better luck finding them than we have."

Bast leaned back and considered what he could extract from this situation. He'd known they needed to search the Archives. That's why he'd already set the couriers a bounty to hunt down the Archivist with the cuffs he'd magicked. Now he just needed to give himself some room to negotiate.

"If I help you, I want a seat on the Council."

Mica was shaking his head before he'd even finished the sentence. "Bastion, please. You know that's not going to happen. Lord Tyson would veto it as soon as I raised the motion. Lady Aliya almost certainly would as well and Lady Nerida would probably just abstain. I know you have always denied being responsible, but there is no denying your father's corpse danced in that courtyard the day he died. We all saw it. The Council will not admit someone who murdered one of its own members."

Bast rolled his eyes. Even if he'd killed his father, which he hadn't, he would hardly be the first on the council to have murdered one of their own if they let him join. "So, I'm just supposed to become your errand boy? Run and fetch Tir and then hide back in my isolated city so none of you have to deal with me?"

"If we don't stop the contagion, your city will fall just the same as ours," Mica replied. He must have been tired because Bast could hear the slightest edge of temper in his words. The Earth Lord was centuries old and renowned for his composure.

Bast glared at him in silence, biding his time. The play for a council seat had just been a starting bid so he could get what he really wanted, access to the four rulers on his own turf. He'd known Mica wouldn't go for it, but it was still frustrating that he wouldn't even consider it. Bast's territory was more stable than any of the courts and his unique magic should've been respected instead of reviled. The rulers of the four courts would never voluntarily share their power, but with a bit of luck he could wrest something almost as satisfying from this arrangement—vengeance. One of them had framed him for his father's death and he may never have better leverage to try and figure out who it was.

"Fine. Then I want to at least host the next council session here with a non-voting seat. I can't help if I don't know what I'm facing."

"Lord Tyson will hate that."

"You've always been very convincing. So, convince him," Bast said, hanging up before the Earth Lord could reply.

Mica's text came through mere hours after they finished

the call. *If you can prove you can find Tir, the council agrees to you hosting the session.*

Bast's heart raced as he read the message. The couriers had never let him down. They'd get the proof. And if they didn't, he was sure they could figure out how to manufacture some between them. He replied, *I'll have it to you within the week.*

CHAPTER 3
HEL

The cuff Hel had picked up from Ryker first thing in the morning thrummed with power in her belt pouch as she stepped out onto the street. She resisted the urge to stroke it. It was a pale echo of what she'd felt standing next to Lord Bastion, but it still resonated against her magic in a way that was disconcertingly pleasant.

Shaking off the temptation, Hel stretched her magical sense out to the edges of her range in the hopes of finding a trace of the creature Ryker had set them hunting. Usually, her awareness of the connections between worlds was background noise that didn't focus much further than a few blocks around her, but when she concentrated she could reach a radius of a couple hours' travel. It was a drain on her energy levels, but not as distracting as it had been in the early days post-Melding when the constant clash of worlds that caused the reality fluctuations had been like knives stabbing into every inch of her skin.

An immediate sickening sensation against her power caught her by surprise, close enough that she would've felt it earlier if she hadn't been so distracted by the cuff's enticing magic. She let the nauseating pull carry her the short distance to the old Civic Square, pausing in the shadow of a green wall as she spied the scouts keeping a discreet watch on the area. The last thing she needed was to draw attention to herself.

As she let her senses drift to concentrate on the pyramid just off-shore, she filtered through the sensations bombarding her and realised there were two distinct strands. One was the unknown nauseating sense of darkness that had drawn her there in the first place, but the other was the fading echo of an all-too-familiar portal signature that left her heart racing and her arms covered in goose-bumps despite the warm leather of her jacket. It had been years since her father's hounds had been so close to her. She wondered what had drawn them to the City of Souls. Had she done something to give herself away or were they just extending their search pattern, having failed to find her in the Earth Lord's territory where she'd almost been caught in her childhood?

Her instincts screamed at her to flee the city but if Ryker's people started hunting her as well, there was little chance she would get clear and she would lose the little freedom she had that could mean the difference between survival and death. She was about to ease herself away from the square when a pick-up truck pulled up nearby, a mound hidden by a tarpaulin in the back.

The scout on the nearest building dropped to the ground between them and the driver shifted the tarpaulin to reveal the motionless dead form of one of her father's hellhounds in the bed of the truck. Technically Amira, the woman who raised her, had told her they were called starhounds, but to her they'd always personified death and torment. Pony-sized with thick black fur often matted with blood, their eyes burned with an internal flame and their hinged venomous fangs were so long they curved below their bottom jaw when extended.

She sunk to a crouch as relief flooded through her that this one was no longer alive to track her. The hounds generally hunted alone unless they found something of interest and called for the pack. She was probably safe for now, but she needed to keep her senses stretched wide. She'd grown complacent thinking they'd lost her trail.

That renewed determination to exert her power to search her surroundings was how she felt the disturbance of a portal forming on the edge of the city in the early evening two days later. She was spinning and running towards the focal point of the sensation before she consciously processed what it was. Even from this distance, maybe five minutes' run away if she was gauging it correctly, she could tell it was not one of her father's. This one felt more personal somehow, a cool liquid shadow slipping into the city that left a phantom taste like fine whiskey on her tongue. It was nothing like the vast molten heat of her father's portals and it wasn't at all what she imagined the creature described by Ryker might create. Given she wasn't aware of anyone else in the world who could portal, the chances were high it was the target she was hunting.

As she pounded up Lambton Quay, the few humans braving the more direct routes of the streets rather than the criss-crossing covered causeways the elementals had grown moved out of her way to let her past. At least there were some advantages to her courier uniform. As the buzz of the portal against her senses grew ahead of her, she felt a shiver of fear. She had an awful suspicion she knew where the creature had decided to hunt, and it was not somewhere anyone in their right mind would enter.

Her hunch was confirmed when she reached the end of the Quay and felt a tug in her chest pulling her up past the soaring cenotaph streaked green with copper toward the distinctive circular building beyond it. One of the many human couriers who hadn't lasted longer than a month had explained to her that the horseman looking down from his high perch was rising above blood and conflict to find heavenly peace. She'd jokingly teased him about falling for Lady Aliya's 'angelic' PR campaign and the conversation had ended awkwardly when she'd realised he actually had. He'd left not long after, chasing a view of the Court of Air's floating stronghold the Lady's followers whispered was like Heaven. She shook her head again at the foolishness. There was no peace to be had in the sky, especially in Aotearoa where winged predators gravitated to breed.

Hel's feet slowed subconsciously as she crossed closer to the brutalist hive-shaped building ahead that used to house the now long-defunct human Government of Aotearoa. Hel forced herself to take the stairs two at a time, shoving away her nervousness. This side of the multi-tiered circular building had sunk into the ground a little courtesy of the wyrms that had burrowed up through its foundations to feast on its occupants shortly after the Melding. It had taken time for the elementals to ward all the vulnerable human buildings against attack. The bunker beneath it had been full of humans responding to the crisis when it had succumbed, none of whom realised what a tempting meal they would make for the giant earth dragons that travelled the islands' fault-lines. The entirety of the human country's leadership had been taken out in under an hour, leaving a vacuum for the few surviving cities in Aotearoa to form their own governance alongside the elementals they depended on to stay safe. She'd heard the building was now a hollow shell thanks to the predators' blind destruction, but no one was stupid enough to enter it, so she'd never seen it for herself.

Hel eyed the looming façade warily as she approached. There was a lip of concrete within jumping reach that would allow her to drag herself up to what used to be a circumference of triple-height windows and was now blank open space. It wasn't the wyrms she was worried about. They'd tunnelled back out toward the Wellington Fault years ago once the city's defences had been refortified. It was the creatures that'd moved in afterward using those same tunnels that were the problem.

Back before the Melding, the building had been called the Beehive for its shape, but it was now known as the Spiderhive for the nest of winged giant spiders, or arachdryn, that had settled in the abandoned space. Lord Bastion had warded the building to keep them from using the city as their hunting ground, but no one could keep the arachdryn out altogether and the nocturnal creatures used the wyrm's tunnels to hunt in the old botanical gardens and bushy hillsides on the northern edge of the city. Mostly they caught livestock and small winged predators, but only because no one was stupid enough to spend any time out in the forests surrounding the city at night.

Hel forced herself to focus again and hunted for the sensation of the portal. It wasn't far away; the creature must have stuck to the outer edges of the Spiderhive. Sensible. Even if you were bad-ass enough to eat winged spider monsters, you still didn't want to be caught surrounded in an enclosed space. Especially when the prey you were hunting could crawl on the roof. If her senses were accurate, she should be able to reach the portal point by hauling herself up on the ledge and circling to the left. Still, she hesitated. She was right on the edges of the wards that kept the arachdryn contained. A prickle like pins and needles stroked across her skin from the necromantic magic used to create them. She should be able to cross it. It was only designed to keep the arachdryn in, not to keep anyone out. There was no point wasting magic when no one would be stupid enough to try and get in. No one except her. Was she really going to do this just for a chance at that bonus? The familiar rage as she glanced at the debt display on her smartwatch said yes.

Hel swore to herself and jumped up to catch the ledge and haul herself up. The pins-and-needles sensation of the ward flared like each needle had turned white-hot as she crossed its threshold before subsiding as she rolled onto the floor and back to her feet. She shook her arms out as she scanned the ceiling high above her and the curved walls stretching away on either side. Thick webbing stretched along its length, but there was no movement in the shadows and the webs didn't block the passageway, designed to store live prey rather than catch it. Now that she was past the ward, the wafting scent of decomposing flesh made her stomach heave. She took shallow breaths through her mouth and jogged carefully around the curved passage in the direction of the portal. She was hoping the nocturnal arachdryn were still sleeping in the depths of the building avoiding this causeway that was open to the elements and sunshine. If only the sun wasn't setting. The sooner she got out of here the better. Although she was starting to rethink getting anywhere near this creature if it was scary enough to take on an arachdryn nest.

When she'd set out, it had been the cusp of evening with street lights just starting to come on. There were no lights in this abandoned hell-hole and, as the sun dipped below the horizon, the pools of shadow around her were growing steadily darker. She stretched every sense wide, hoping to catch any hint of movement before the darkness drew the arachdryn out to become a threat. Her boots barely made a sound on the grimy wooden floor and she kept to the outer edges of the building, hoping the nearby wards would be another deterrent.

She'd made it as far as a half-collapsed stairwell when she noticed a hint of something in the shadows closest to the wall, a darker patch of black on black. She froze in place and strained her eyes as she tried to see. As quietly as she could, she crept closer to the inner wall of the passage, hugging close to the fat wooden-clad pillar she'd paused by without touching the sticky threads coating it. When she could finally make out the scene before her, it took her brain a moment to process. An arachdryn as big as a cow was twitching on its back; a hunched figure feeding from it near its head. Two strong hands held snapping mandibles clear of the feeding creature's body and each of the arachdryn's legs, covered in tiny spines that stung like the native ongaonga nettles, had been wrenched out straight by sinuous tentacles writhing from the hunter's head like hair.

Hel watched for another few seconds, trying to gauge exactly how stupid it would be to approach. As she crept closer, the creature remained oblivious to her, its view blocked by the giant furred body of its prey. The copper cuff Ryker had given her was a cool weight in her fingers as she fished it from her pocket at the same time she drew her baton from her thigh sheath. She wished she had another hand free so she could've twisted the weapon open into its two concealed blades. If she was going to fight something with tentacles, she wanted to be able to cut herself free. She'd be fine, though. All she needed to do was slap the cuff on its wrist and run away. How hard could it be?

Every instinct was screaming at her to start running and forget the bounty. For once, she ignored it. Her life was an endless series of risk assessments and cautionary actions to keep herself hidden and safe, but this job would fast-forward her freedom by months. It was worth the risk. She dropped into a crouch and slunk closer to the arachdryn's head. It seemed to be nearing the end of its death throes, its legs relaxing and curling inward. The creature wouldn't be distracted much longer. It was now or never. Before she could re-think, she lunged forward and locked the cuff around its wrist.

The creature's tentacled head jerked away from the arachdryn's body as soon as the metal touched its skin and a screech of pure fury ricocheted through the building so loudly Hel's bones started to ache. She scrambled backward and fell hard on her tailbone, barely noticing the new stabbing pain against the agony of the creature's voice. As its scream faded, she heard a thump of flesh on wood as something hit the ground. She couldn't look away to see what had caused it, because her eyes were caught on the creature's face. Horns swept up from its forehead and its ears were pointed, almost delicate. A tri-hinged jaw gaped open revealing rows of razor-sharp teeth still dripping with arachdryn blood. Despite all that, and the strangely elegant tentacles sweeping from its scalp instead of hair, it had an otherwise humanish face and form. That wasn't what held her transfixed though. It was its eyes, swirling with pinpricks of coloured light like a nebula and tightened in a way that spoke of exhausted hurt. She knew that look. It was the look of a predator turned prey. It was the look she saw every day in the mirror.

"I'm sorry," she whispered.

The creature's eyes widened in surprise and it released its prey, moving impossibly quickly back to the safety of its portal that was all but invisible at the top of the stairwell. The undulating movement of its floor-length tentacles behind it screened its body from view and before she knew it, the portal had winked out of existence and Hel was alone in the passageway next to the, thankfully, dead arachdryn.

She swallowed hard and lurched to her feet, glancing down to where the strange thumping noise had come from seconds earlier. Lying on the ground next to the withering arachdryn carcass was the twitching hand of the creature, severed at the wrist. Hel stared at it blankly, the copper cuff still attached to it glinting in the dim light. She could swear the creature hadn't had a weapon to amputate its limb. It had fallen off much like a skink's tail could. Her stomach churned at the thought before her pragmatic side took over. At least she had proof she'd found the creature. Maybe they'd give her part of the fee. She'd managed to get the cuff on it after all. It wasn't her fault the damn thing detached its own hand to get it off.

Swinging her courier pack off her back, she managed to get the hand into it without touching it. The blood dripping from the stump had already slowed to a sluggish trickle. It was time to get out of there. She headed straight toward the three-story empty windowpanes. Even in this higher section of the building, she should be able to make the jump down to the ground. The sooner there was a ward between her and the arachdryn again, the better. The short jog back to the concrete ledge was punctuated by the tell-tale distant clicking of spider claws on concrete. She moved faster. She was already reaching down to grasp the ledge as she emerged into the night, but as she tried to swing her body out into open space, she was stopped by a smooth barrier of solid air.

"Fuck," she whispered. She'd thought the ward was keyed to keep the arachdryn in. It wasn't. It was keyed to keep *everything* in.

A rustling sounded from behind her and spun to face it. Clusters of glinting red points shone in the darkness. Spider eyes. A lot of spider eyes. Far too many. And they were creeping closer. They seemed cautious after the threat of the creature who'd now left, but that wouldn't last long. Hel's head spun back and forth, looking at the safety of the pavement only one impassable step away and then back to the incoming horde of predators. She was out of options.

She'd only ever made a portal once in her life. She'd been thirteen years old and not long after her only friend and her guardian were both dead as a result. Her father's hounds could track her portals the same way she could track the creature's. It didn't matter. The choice between dead now and dead later was no choice at all. Maybe the hounds that traced her would emerge inside the Spiderhive and get eaten. One could always hope.

As the first spiny leg reached out to tap her cheek, she yanked her power to herself and split the air open behind her, her magic flashing plasma blue in the darkness like the hottest of suns. She didn't need to go far. In fact, the less distance she went, the harder it would be to track and the more likely her hunters would end up stuck in the Spiderhive wards. She threw herself backward through the rift in space she'd created just deep enough to breach the ward and was already slamming it closed as she hurtled down to the pavement. Twisted in the air, she tucked her shoulder to avoid the worst of the impact. Her roll left her lying winded on her back just in time for the arachdryn leg severed by her closing portal to fall on her face. She choked back a scream and flung the leg away, the stinging rash from its spines already spreading across her cheek and palm where she'd touched it.

Groaning, she staggered to her feet. She needed to get as far away as possible from the portal site before the hounds came sniffing. Her abused body fought against her demands as she dragged it into a sprint, not caring she was moving faster than a human should. Distance was what mattered now and most humans kept to the causeways once night fell anyway. The streets should be clear. Hopefully no one would notice.

The sting on her cheek grew sharper as a gust of ice-cold wind hit it. She groaned again as she felt her face swell. There was no way she could hide it. If the hounds didn't catch her on the way back, Ryker was going to kill her anyway for being so reckless.

She slowed her run once she was out of sight of the Spiderhive and by the time the courier headquarters was visible ahead of her she was walking, despite the need to get inside to safety. Every muscle ached from her fall and she suspected the venom from the arachdryn spines wasn't helping. It left her lethargic and in a foul mood as well as making her skin itch like crazy. She barely noticed the other couriers shifting out of her way as she stalked into the building toward Ryker's office, but they noticed her. Ryker's eyes traced the rash across her face as she kicked the door shut behind her. Before he could rip into her and make her visit the medic, she swung her bag off her back and dumped the sluggishly bleeding severed hand in the middle of his dark oak desk.

Her eyes stayed trained on the hand rather than Ryker as she waited for his response. Now that she wasn't running for her life, she could see that each finger ended in a pointed claw that looked like it'd been retractable when it had still been connected to the rest of its body. She poked at one absently as she waited for Ryker to explode at her and watched it shift into the nailbed under the pressure.

"What the fuck, Hel?"

That wasn't good. His voice was quiet and even despite swearing. You could always tell he was really mad when he sounded that calm. She forced herself to look up at his face and held her expression motionless. "I cuffed that creature, but its hand fell off."

"It's hand just ... fell off?" Ryker repeated, slowly.

"Yup. I didn't touch it except to slap the cuff on."

"And where were you when its hand was falling off?"

"Standing in front of it."

"Where *exactly* were you standing?"

Hel swallowed and looked back down at the creepy talons again. It was less stressful than watching Ryker. "On the edge of the Spiderhive."

Ryker dropped his face into his hands and rubbed his temples. "And how did you get *out* of the Spiderhive? I assume you were inside given you look like an arachdryn gave you a love tap."

She took a calming breath to stall as she scrambled for an explanation that would keep her magic hidden. "The creature ran as soon as it dropped its hand. The portal must have messed up the warding and I managed to slip out. The arachdryn didn't follow so I guess I got lucky with the timing." There. That wasn't even a lie. She hadn't said which portal had messed up the warding.

"And what was your plan if you didn't get lucky with the timing of the ward failure that you couldn't possibly have anticipated?"

Hel shrugged and Ryker swore under his breath and stalked around to her side of the desk to grab both her shoulders. "Do we have to have this conversation every fucking week? I get that you feel trapped but it's not worth risking your life just to pay off a bit of debt. If you ever thought about something other than getting free for more than a second, you might notice you have a safe place to sleep, work that you're good at, and a bunch of elementals who are all rather fond of your heart still beating. I need to call this in to Lord Bastion. Sit down and shut up until he gets here."

Hel blinked after him as he wrenched the office door open and turned around to glare at her until she sat herself down on the hard visitor's chair. Apparently he didn't want her listening in to his conversation. This mess just got better and better. The last thing she needed was another run-in with the disconcerting necromancer. She'd already drawn far too much attention to herself and there were too many loose ends to try and hide. Her brain wasn't functioning properly though, still struggling from her injuries and the unfamiliar exhaustion of using her power.

Her aching muscles had stiffened and the coppery scent of the creature's blood had permeated through the office by the time the door opened again. Hel jumped to her feet, pivoting toward the sound, and froze as Lord Bastion swept into the room ahead of Ryker. He must've been at an event or something because he was wearing a tailored black suit and a collared white linen shirt. Or maybe he always looked like he'd just stepped off a damn catwalk. His shoulder-length black hair was swept back from his face in a messy tie, probably to keep it out of the way on the short flight to the building because it was too casual for the rest of his fashionable appearance. She'd been too distracted by his eyes the other day to take in much else but now she avoided them, not wanting to get caught again.

It wasn't until she saw his lips lifting in a smirk that she realised she was blocking his way and had been watching him too long. Her shoulders tensed in annoyance and she shifted to lean against the wall. Two sets of wings made for cramped quarters in the modest office.

Lord Bastion rested back against Ryker's desk, perching on its edge as he watched her with a singular focus. She'd heard he was a playboy. He was definitely as arrogant as all the rest of them. She ignored the infuriating tingle of her body's unwelcome response to his inspection. Even if she didn't hate everything he was, no way would she go there with an elemental. It was far safer to stick to humans. Or no one. No one had been her preferred option for a while.

"Ryker tells me you found the Archivist in the Spider-hive?" he finally said.

His voice was low and smooth and it was totally unfair that he could send shivers up her spine with that alone. She tilted her head in acknowledgement rather than bothering to speak and forced her sluggish mind to focus. His question had revealed more than he'd meant it to. She'd thought there was too much intelligence in the creature's eyes for this to be purely a monster hunt and if it, or rather *they*, were some kind of Archivist that was definitely the case. What had the poor thing done to deserve being hunted this way?

"How did you find it?" Lord Bastion asked.

Shit. She'd been so busy explaining getting out of the Spiderhive to Ryker that she hadn't planned a story to explain finding the creature. She rested her hand on her weapon, using its familiar weight against her leg to ground herself and ignoring Ryker's warning glare at the threat that could be read into the movement. Amira, the woman who'd raised her, had prepared her for these types of questions. The elementals knew some rare humans could sense the power from the ley lines the elementals used, but they kept that fact hidden. If she was vague enough, she should be able to pass herself off as an unwitting magical radar.

Hel shrugged and let her cheeks flush as if she was embarrassed to be caught acting illogically. "Sometimes I just get a hunch and follow it. It's saved my life before. This time, it led me to your Archivist."

"She's the only human who's ever managed to consistently stay out of danger in our line of work," Ryker chimed in.

Hel glared at him and forced her knuckles to relax where they'd turned white from her grip on her baton. The bastard knew she didn't like this kind of attention. He could've kept his mouth shut.

"Is that so?" Lord Bastion asked, tilting his head to the side to look her over again as if he might see some visible sign of the magic sense she was pretending not to know about.

Fuck it. No amount of money was worth subjecting herself to this man's appraisal and she had zero interest in helping him with a damn thing. She needed to shut this down fast. "If that's all, I'll leave you two to your meeting," she said, already walking to the door.

"That's not all, Ms..." Lord Bastion's voice snapped out from behind her.

"She just goes by Helaine or Hel. No surname. She's been with us since she was thirteen. She still acts that age half the time," Ryker explained, his voice every bit as infuriated as Lord Bastion's at her rudeness.

Well, that answered that then. His money had purchased her debt, trapping her in indenture. Her whole life with the couriers she'd been told there was nowhere she could run or hide that Lord Bastion's army of invisible souls wouldn't be able to find her, and she was so inconsequential that *he didn't even know who she was*. Not that that would stop Bastion hunting her down like property if Ryker ever reported her missing. Hel turned back with her hand on the door handle and forced her sweetest smile onto her face. "I apologise. What else did you need?" she said, adopting a saccharine tone she hoped would placate her interrogator as much as its hidden sarcasm would rile up Ryker even more.

Lord Bastion's frown deepened and he stood up to approach her, pausing within arm's reach. She resisted the urge to punch him as he reached out and touched a finger to her chin to make her meet his eyes. "I would like to hear the full story of how you came to possess that hand from your own lips," he said, his eyes flicking to said lips for the briefest of moments as he spoke.

Hel kept her breathing even, suppressing any signs of her anger and the need to shove him away to avoid his disconcerting nearness. "Of course. Please, sit down," she said, keeping her sweet-girl act in place and gesturing to the chair behind him in the hopes he'd back off.

He smiled and dropped his hand. "No. I'd rather we were more comfortable. We'll talk over dinner. My penthouse in an hour," he said, before sliding past her and out the door.

Hel's jaw dropped and she forgot there was anyone else in the room until Ryker's laughter jerked her out of her confused state of shock.

"Serves you right for all the shit you've pulled today," Ryker said.

"Fuck you," she shot back. And fuck the man who hadn't even bothered to pretend she had a choice because he owned her. And fuck his creepy necromancy that could stalk her to make sure she complied.

CHAPTER 4
HEL

For the second night in the space of a week, Hel stepped foot into the imposing entryway of Soul Tower. Only this time, there was a human waiting to greet her. She couldn't blend into the anonymity of a throng of club-goers tonight. It felt like a lifetime of doing everything she could to hide in plain sight was under threat and every cell in her body was screaming at her to run while she still could. She knew it was already too late, though. It'd probably been too late the second she collided with Bastion in Ryker's office. He hadn't just noticed her, he'd *seen* her.

The man waiting for her held his hand out to shake hers as she approached him at the base of the second set of flowing water features that flanked the two non-functioning escalators. His curious gaze scanned her from head to toe as if he was trying to figure out what about her had caught his lord's interest. He looked exactly like what she expected of someone who spent his life in the inner circle of the city's ruler. A little too attractive. A lot too calculating. Too every-thing. Dangerous. His perfectly styled blond hair swept to the side framing a face of beautifully sharp angles. He wasn't much taller than her and his build was lean but his tightly tailored suit showed off every defined muscle. She knew who he was before he spoke. Rumour had it he and Lord Bastion were like brothers. He was known for being the life of every party and he'd been the driving force behind starting the nightclub in the tower.

"Welcome to Soul Tower, Helaine. I'm Ra. I'll take you up to see him, now." He held her hand a moment too long, a practised charming smile on his face.

"Whatever. Let's just get this over with," Hel snapped, pulling her hand away and striding ahead of him up the stairs even though she hated leaving her back vulnerable to anyone.

She was forced to wait for him at the elevators and it was all she could do not to snarl when he gestured in a gentlemanly fashion for her to precede him into the lift.

"Tough crowd," he murmured as they stood facing the centre elevator's doors that were uniquely framed in a thin line of shining black obsidian. "This elevator is reserved for Bast's use. It's the only one with access to his penthouse."

Hel rolled her eyes. Of course it was. She ignored the way her stomach dropped as they passed floor after floor heading up to the twenty-ninth storey. She forced herself to breathe deep and calm her racing heart. Maybe there was still a way out. If she was rude enough to make Bastion lose interest, things could go back to normal and she wouldn't risk pinging the radar of her father's hunters.

They were both silent as Ra let her into the home of the necromancer Lord of the City of Souls and took her leather jacket for her. The thump of her boots on the parquet flooring almost made her wince. She would've taken them off if it wouldn't leave her feeling vulnerable. Absently, she stroked the weapon by her side. There was no reason to feel that way.

When they emerged from the hallway into the open-plan living space Bastion was waiting there, leaning casually against the polished stone of the breakfast bar with a glass of whiskey in his hand. The sleeves of his tailored business shirt were rolled to his elbows, exposing muscled forearms. Hel's breath hitched before she caught herself. Damn him. Why couldn't he look as cold as his reputation? Even the dark shadow of his furled wings that should've looked chilling just left her remembering how soft his feathers had felt against her skin.

Bastion was inspecting her every bit as closely as she had him, his eyes lingering on her face and then her collarbones where they were exposed by the black singlet she was wearing. If she'd known Ra was going to take her leather jacket off her, she'd have worn something less revealing.

"Well, I can tell I'm the third wheel here," Ra's dry voice said from behind her.

Fuck. How long had they been standing there staring at each other?

"That will be all thank you, Ra," Bastion said, sharing a smirk with his friend in a way that made Hel's blood boil. Arrogant bastard.

Her breath caught as Bastion stepped closer and tilted her chin up with one finger, a slight frown creasing his brow as he peered at her cheek where she'd been injured by the arachdryn spines.

"The redness is almost gone already. Even mild arachdryn stings usually take a human days to heal," he said.

Hel kept her expression neutral as her heart rate accelerated from adrenaline. Her healing speed was similar to an elemental, far faster than a human, but there was no way she could give that away. "It barely touched me," she lied, jerking her face free from Bastion's soft touch and stepping back to give herself some breathing room.

Forcing her eyes away from the infuriating elemental before her, Hel scanned the room more thoroughly, habit making her note each exit and potential weapon. She couldn't help but make her way closer to the curved floor-to-ceiling windows as she finally processed the stunning panoramic view of the city criss-crossed with the latticework of magical elemental metal that encased the building. She shivered a little as the shadowy silhouette of the metal vines reminded her of the arachdryn webbing in the Spiderhive.

"Drink?" Bastion asked.

Hel hesitated, but what harm could it do? At least he wasn't still asking about her face. She needed something to make this less painful. "Sure."

She glanced back over her shoulder and watched as Bastion refilled his glass and poured another before joining her. Below them, the soaring shadows of elementals in flight glided over the twinkling lights of the buildings that surrounded them. Once he'd passed her a crystal glass, Bastion dimmed the interior lights throwing the night-time cityscape into sharp relief. As high up the tower as they were, the poles that gave the building its crown were still almost invisible in the darkness and the globes of light at their tips seemed to be suspended shining spheres in the air just ahead of them.

"It's a stunning view," Hel offered.

"Yes, it is," Bastion replied, but when she looked back at him she saw he was watching her, not the city.

The unwelcome warmth that filled her sent her magic spiralling toward his and she clamped down on it again, holding it close before it could twine around him like some sort of desperate cat. What was wrong with her? She didn't want any part of her touching any part of him, especially the raw intimacy of their powers brushing together. Hel cleared her throat and searched for a distraction from the intensity that had grown between them. This meeting was getting off track. The dining table nearby was laden with food and she figured the sooner they moved on to that part of the evening, the sooner it would be over. She needed out.

"You didn't have to go to this trouble," Hel said, knowing she sounded rude and not caring as she gestured at the spread.

"But I wanted to."

"And I guess you always get what you want."

"Pretty much." Bastion smiled and his eyes dropped to her lips before flicking back to her face. *Creep*, she thought. Ignoring the fact she'd done the same to him.

His movements were annoyingly graceful as he pulled a chair out for her. "Please. Have a seat."

Hel perched at the head of the long glass table, poised to jump to her feet if needed. She'd been hunted too long to let her guard down and everything about this night was setting off alarms for her. She'd assumed Bastion would take the other end of the table like some historical lord, or maybe hoped was a better word. Instead, he sat to her right and started serving her cuts of medium-rare steak and crispy roast potatoes. They were both silent as he poured them glasses of red wine.

"So, how did you come to work for the couriers?" he asked, and the question was exactly what Hel needed to find

her equilibrium because it filled her with rage. Her indenture was so meaningless to him he didn't even remember
purchasing it. She was just an anonymous line of property
on his balance sheet under assets.

Hel took a breath while she fought for self-control. "You
bought me for them."

Bastion frowned. "What?"

Hel's gaze returned to her food as she gave her quiet,
clipped explanation. If she couldn't avoid his attention, she
could at least make sure he knew exactly what he'd done to
her. "My guardian was killed when I was thirteen. The local
militia decided to charge me for the associated property
damage, medical care, funeral, and the five years of board
and food I'd need while I was still a minor. The couriers
were about to move headquarters here to take up the
contract with you. They purchased my debt on your behalf
and then happily added moving costs, uniforms, and training. It's been twelve years and I still haven't made a dent
in it."

Bastion looked angry at being called out. Good. Maybe
now he'd drop the pretence of hospitality. "I had no idea," he
said, finally.

Hel shrugged. "You're an elemental and a necromancer.
What do you care?"

The gentle play of their magic against each other that
Hel hadn't noticed had slipped from her control turned
jagged as she watched his anger transform to something
darker. Something in what she'd just said had hit a nerve. Or
perhaps it was the derision she hadn't been able to keep from
her tone.

"What the fuck is that supposed to mean?" he almost
snarled. "And the term is soulweaver, not necromancer. The

courts branded me that so people would think I defiled their corpses when they died. That's not how my power works, nor would the souls let me get away with it."

Hel ignored the question, deciding the fastest way out of there was to give him the explanation he wanted so she could leave. His anger was a good thing. Hopefully he wouldn't test her so deeply and she could get away with hiding her magic under the deception of pretending to have a sense of the ley lines the elementals used. It should be easier to fool him given he was the only elemental in existence *without* that kind of magic because of his necromancy. "You wanted to know how I got the creature's hand. I was on Lambton Quay when I had a feeling I needed to head north. The feeling drew me to the Spiderhive, so I went to investigate. Your 'archivist' was feeding on an arachdryn when I arrived. I cuffed it. Its arm fell off. It portalled away and I got out of there. Story done. Can I go now?" she said.

Bastion's wings trembled where they hung behind him as if he was resisting the urge to spread them wide to intimidate her. "No. You can't. Describe the feeling for me."

Hel blinked slowly, wondering how much she could fudge it. Vague would be best. "I don't know. I was thinking about how Ryker described the Archivist and it just felt like the earth was pulling me north," she said.

Bastion frowned again. "The thing is, Helaine, the Archivist is cunning. They've evaded us for years. They chose to hunt in the Spiderhive because the warding on the building blocks any feelings like you describe. That's why no elementals came flying. Is there anything else you can tell me about what you felt? Any small detail could make a difference."

Well, fuck. That wasn't good. Anything else she said was

just going to risk exposing herself even more. "No," she snapped.

Bastion looked like he didn't believe her, but he didn't keep pressing. "I'm going to need you to work with me to find them again. The elemental rulers are arriving for the council sessions in a week. They'll be here for a fortnight. I need to produce the Archivist before they leave. This could change your life. You'd have the whole council in your debt. You could even attend the ball, make some powerful friends," he said, his earlier anger hidden as his voice turned soft and cajoling.

Nausea roiled in her stomach and Hel could barely hold her food down. There would be no faster way to die on the fangs of her father's hounds than to make a spectacle of herself like that. The council sessions were where the most important decisions for their world were made and they were always surrounded by a slew of media and PR broadcasts around the globe, especially the annual ball. She'd be exposed in no time. And there was no way she could risk the courts' rulers realising she had power a human shouldn't have. Her indenture would be nothing compared to what she'd face at their hands.

"Not interested," she said, hoping Bastion didn't notice the panic threading into her voice.

Bastion was quiet for a moment and she forced herself to ignore him and take another bite of her food.

"It wasn't a request. There's a contagion spreading around the world that could cause more destruction than the Melding. It's only my power that's keeping the city safe right now and I don't know how long that will last. The other courts don't even have that option. The Archivist is our only hope of figuring out how to stop it and you're the only one who's managed to track them. You *will* do this."

Hel remembered the sickening feel of the darkness contained in the old Civic Square and swallowed hard—it had felt like death not just for people and animals, but for their world, their whole reality. She had her own problems, though. "Or what? You're going to throw me off a building like you did that other guy? Good luck with that. Still not interested. If you're so powerful, I'm sure you can figure something out."

Bastion shoved his chair back with a screech and strode away from the table. It wasn't just his wings that were vibrating with anger now, but his entire presence that had swelled to fill the room. His power was immense and she was drowning in the sensation of him. It shouldn't have felt good. Maybe taunting him hadn't been her best idea.

"If you're so selfish that you won't stretch yourself to help save millions of people then maybe I can convince you with something you actually care about. Money. Help me track the Archivist and I'll wipe your debt." His voice dripped with disgust and he hadn't bothered turning around from where he was standing back by the windows looking out over the city again.

Hel froze in place, her heart pounding. He was offering her freedom years earlier than she could've hoped to achieve it, but there was no way she could take him up on it. Freedom was worthless if it meant exposing herself to be killed by her hunters. She'd felt the strength of Bastion's power containing the contagion at the old Civic Square. The city would do just fine without her and she was sure they'd find another option. Not that she could explain any of that to him even if she'd wanted to. Which she didn't. She didn't owe him an explanation and there was no reason she should care that he was disgusted with her for her refusal. Her indenture contract set out the terms of her service, and she had every right to refuse to alter them. One of the few rights she had. She shoved aside the squirming discomfort she didn't want to feel and stood up from the table, heading for the door. "I'd rather stay in debt than take money from the man who bought me like property. The answer's no. I'll see myself out."

Hel always made sure she had multiple exits and she'd quietly explored the public levels of the tower enough while visiting The Crypt that it was no exception. Knowing Bastion would likely tell the guards to stop her leaving, she ran to the elevator as soon as she was out of his sight and got off five storeys above the arch of glass that covered the building's entryway, slipping through the darkened reception rooms until she was out on a small semi-circular balcony. From there, all she had to do was use the twisting metal that covered the building to climb down to the archway before creeping across the adjacent roofs to make her way back down to street level. It wouldn't have worked if the shielding in the metal had been activated, and she knew she didn't have much time before the alarm on the door brought a guard to investigate. She'd only get away with that trick once, but it was worth it to get clear.

There was no way she could go to bed with the combination of anger and fear coursing through her system, so instead she snuck back into headquarters to borrow one of the short swords from the courier's armoury and made her way to the abandoned parking building she'd discovered years ago when she'd been exploring Opera House Lane. The couriers either didn't know about, or turned a blind eye, to her weapons practice there. They probably figured there wasn't much trouble a teenager could teach herself with the sword. What they didn't know was that her guardian had placed her first practice sword in her hand at the age of three. Amira might have died ten years later, but that had been plenty of time to lay the groundwork so Hel could keep her skills sharp alone.

The abandoned carpark structure on the edge of the dead zone was impossible to get to from the seaward side. It was only accessible through an exposed external stairway at the blocked end of a laneway that had been decorated with fairy lights by some optimistic person who thought it might push back the darkness of their new world.

The building had no lighting and the vacant maze of concrete was rife with exposed rusty reinforcing bars jutting out from the walls. It was still standing after countless earthquakes, though, so she figured it must be structurally sound. Gaps in the roof and walls let in just enough ambient glow for Hel to navigate the shards of crumbling concrete that littered the space. Her inhuman eyesight was the only thing that let her safely traverse what was essentially one giant tripping hazard.

Slipping through the darkness, she made her way up to the third floor where she'd cleared a practice circle for herself. The soft sound of the blade slipping from its sheath as she drew it calmed her thoughts and, breathing deep, she lost herself to the familiar patterns of her training. The short sword she wielded was one favoured by elementals—lightweight, double-bladed for ease of slashing in flight, and one-handed to allow for a dagger or gun in the other hand depending on your preference. She revelled in the sensation of perfect balance as she used her twisting momentum to add power to a strike before smoothly shifting into a block. The swish of the blade cutting the air was music to her soul, the only noise filling the space as she moved on silent feet and controlled her breathing in a way a human couldn't have. Her lung capacity far exceeded theirs.

Hel was mid-way through a sweeping diagonal downward slash when the barest hint of movement by a column had her pivoting toward the threat, sending one of her tiny concealed throwing daggers into the darkness before she'd even fully processed the presence.

Bastion jerked to the side just in time to avoid the blade spinning toward his face. "That's the third time you've been rude to me tonight. There won't be a fourth," he said.

Hel froze mid-way through lunging toward him as she processed exactly who she'd attacked. Fuck. Not good. The brief thrill of fear changed to anger as she caught the glint of his eyes inspecting her body from the shadows.

She shoved the sword into the scabbard hanging from her waist. "Eyes up, Mister."

Bastion smirked and cocked his head, searching her face as if it might reveal how she could tell what he'd been looking at in the darkness that surrounded them. "It's 'my lord' to you."

Hel rolled her eyes and went to retrieve the dagger that had clattered to the ground behind him. "How'd you find me?" she asked. If he'd got the codes to track her smartwatch from Ryker that was going to be a pain.

"Our conversation wasn't finished," Bastion said, ignoring her question like she'd ignored his earlier.

"It was for me."

"What will it take for you to get over yourself and help? Shall I show you what the contagion is capable of? There's an outbreak right here in the city. We could take one of your friends over there and see what happens when they touch it." And there it was. The infamous ruthlessness he'd been hiding with his attempt at being charming earlier in the evening.

"Too bad for you, I don't have any friends," Hel muttered.

She felt a grim satisfaction as she watched his jaw tense as he gritted his teeth in annoyance, but it shattered with his next words.

"I can make your life very difficult, Helaine. I can take back your indenture debt from the couriers and make you mine. I can put your face all over the news as our potential saviour and destroy that anonymity you cling to. You can help me willingly, or you can lose control. The choice is yours but I'll get what I want either way."

Her eyes widened in panic. How had he figured out her need to stay hidden? Her stomach dropped as realisation struck. Fucking Ryker. How much had he told Bastion about her? How many of her secrets had he found out over the years and never let on?

She was opening her mouth to tell him to go fuck himself when the entire north wall of the parking building exploded inward at them. Hel sensed as much as saw Bastion drawing his weapon as she unsheathed her sword and turned to face the iridescent blue-green head of a dragon that was lunging its hand-length fangs at the necromancer. The beautiful creature was struggling to drag its body through the wreckage of the wall, desperate to reach him. As Bastion spun his body to the right to avoid its snapping jaws, Hel saw its eyes were swirling with black and glowing orange like a lava flow—a tell-tale sign of the Fire

Court's magic at play influencing the predator. Elementals were flashy that way.

The poor dragon seemed a little stunned from crashing head-first into reinforced concrete. Hel watched in surprise as Bastion sheathed his sword instead of attacking it. He darted forward, launching himself up onto the dragon's head where he grasped its horns to stay out of reach of those vicious teeth and any fire. She felt the surge of his death magic filling the air, sending shivers across her skin that she wished she could say were unpleasant. He didn't seem to be using his power to kill the creature. Apparently he had a soft spot for them, too. That didn't mean he was a good person.

Some sixth sense made her look away from the giant threat in front of her and peer into the shadows to her left. The artificially altered magic light of the dragon's eyes had cast a soft orange glow on the rough concrete floor that was mirrored in the red-orange wings of the silent elemental stalking closer through the darkness. That wing colour said the woman was a high-ranking member of the Fire Court with enough magic to have taken on her lord's colours. Everyone knew there was no love lost between the Fire Court and Lord Bastion, who'd killed their last lord, his father. She was clearly an assassin. Hel was momentarily caught by surprise at the surge of protectiveness she felt. If anyone was going to kill Bastion, it would be her. This bitch could fuck right off. She was moving before she'd even finished the thought, her speed catching the elemental killer by surprise. The assassin hesitated just long enough for Hel to close the distance between them.

Hel didn't give the woman a chance to launch a magical attack. She drew her baton with her left hand even as she slashed down with the sword in her other, her strike missing as it whistled through the space the assassin had been half a breath before. As she twisted to avoid the woman's return attack, the knowledge sunk into her that this was going to end in one of their deaths. The other courts might tacitly ignore these attempts on Bastion's life, but they still needed to keep up appearances. She wasn't going to leave behind a witness. The knowledge was freeing. There was no need to pretend she was limited to a human's strength and speed in this fight and the calculating confusion on the elemental's face said she'd already clocked there was something unnatural about Hel.

The woman fought with one weapon, using her other hand to strike out in punches as fast as Hel's defence. Time lost meaning as attack blurred to defence and back in a flurry of movement. A blow caught Hel in the ribs and she twisted out of reach, wincing in pain.

The roar of the dragon, too close for comfort, distracted both of them from their dance of death. Hel risked a glance sideways to see Bastion soaring through the air as the creature threw him off before trying to wrench its huge body out of the hole in the building's side. He must've managed to break the compulsion on it.

A flash of fiery magic seared past her toward the still airborne necromancer and Hel swung back toward the assassin, cursing herself for her inattention. The woman's face was twisted into a snarl as she prepared to send another bolt of power at the man whose body Hel had just heard thump to the ground somewhere behind her. Taking advantage of the assassin's momentary distraction, she silently slipped beneath her guard. The woman's eyes widened as she realised a moment too late that she'd overextended herself to target her mark. Hel focused every drop of her true strength and speed into the strike that sent her blade slicing through the woman's neck in a perfectly clean strike even Amira would have praised her for.

Bastion's groan from nearby drew her attention back to the infuriating death mage as he flipped back to his feet just in time for the woman's decapitated head to roll to a stop at them. Her now-headless body crumpled to the floor.

Hel stood with the corpse between them, twisted red-orange wings forming a pool of feathers on the stark grey of the concrete as she bent down to wipe the blood from her blade on the elemental's shirt. She could feel a bruise rising on her cheekbone from a punch she hadn't noticed in the heat of the moment and the tickling drip of blood from thin scrapes down her biceps where she'd been a little too slow to avoid the attacker's blades.

"Oops," she said, as she took in Bastion's glare, hoping he'd been too busy with the dragon to notice her inhuman abilities.

"It's hard to question a dead assassin," Bastion growled.

"You're welcome," Hel replied, before spinning on her heel to leave.

"I'm not done with you," he called after her, his voice echoing off the concrete walls.

She gave him a middle-finger salute as she walked away, leaving him to deal with the still thrashing dragon.

She didn't owe him a damn thing.

CHAPTER 5
HEL

Hel stormed along the laneway that led from the parking building, letting her anger burn away the pain from her injuries. Arrogant prick and his threats. Why had she even helped him? There was a moment as she'd watched the assassin approach when she could have just stepped to the side. But no, she couldn't stand by and watch someone else be hunted like she was. She'd had to go and attack the killer. She hadn't been just any elemental either. Fuck. What if she was a member of the Fire Lord's actual family? Would he come after her?

Hel groaned to herself and turned away from the direction that would take her home, heading toward the outer edges of the city. She needed to think. Slipping through the familiar streets, she kept her body concealed from the skies behind awnings and make-shift passageways formed from magicked metal and the rubble of damaged buildings. Her destination was another abandoned building, this one the old Embassy cinema that would have been snapped up if it didn't border the wilds past the city's safe zone. People were slowly venturing out this far as the population rebounded, but there were still more vacant buildings than occupied. Someone would probably snap up this one soon. Until then, it was one of many hideaways she came to when she needed to escape the eyes of the couriers.

Curved staircases swept up either side of the atrium as she ducked in the door. A circular hole in the ceiling above gave her a view up to the next level. Part of the wrought-iron balustrade that used to enclose the hole overhead was lying on the tiny white mosaic tiles of the floor to her right where someone, or some*thing*, had violently fallen through it. Cracked and grimy wall tiles hugged the walls. She'd polished one clean to see its colour once—a deep purple. In the darkness, it was all shades of black.

Hel went straight ahead through a passageway rather than upstairs and found herself in what used to be a windowless bar nestled in the depths of the cinema. No light reached there, but she could still see every empty chair clearly as if they were patiently waiting for someone to return. She threw herself down on one of them and immediately winced at the twinge from her ribs. The damn assassin must have bruised them. She pinched her fingers on the bridge of her nose and let out a long sigh. It was decision time. 'Lord' Bastion wasn't going to take no for an answer, but no amount of money was worth that risk. She'd thrown any excuse her panicking brain could think of at him in the vain hope he'd back off and it had only made him more determined. She could play his game or she could run. Either way, her life was never going to be the same. She leaned back against the wall and closed her eyes as her thoughts spiralled.

The vibration of her watch against her wrist woke her with a start hours later. It was flashing red in the darkness.

Fuck. If she didn't report in, Ryker would use the tracer in it to send someone to retrieve her. She hauled her phone out of the secure case hanging on her belt and saw she'd missed three calls while she'd slept, the perils of her accelerated healing. She should've gone back to headquarters. It wasn't safe to lose consciousness like that in an unguarded location. She shook her head at her stupidity and called Ryker.

"Where the fuck are you, Hel?" he snapped as soon as he answered.

"I'm out. Am I not allowed out anymore?"

"You walked out on the lord of our city, got into a fight and killed someone, walked out on the lord *again*, ignored all my calls, and now it's dawn and you still haven't come home. So, no. You're not allowed out right now."

Hel winced as his voice increased in volume to a yell and rubbed her tired face. Then she winced again because her face was still swollen and bruised from the night before. "I'm sorry. I fell asleep. I'll be back soon," she mumbled.

"Please tell me you fell asleep in someone's bed and you're not in an abandoned building somewhere?"

Hel shut her eyes again. "I'll be back soon."

"You really pissed him off, Hel. He's reclaimed your debt. You're to report to him at Soul Tower by midday."

Hel hung up and stared blankly into the shadows. Bastion's threat from the night before played through her mind on repeat. *I can buy your indenture debt and make you mine. I can put your face all over the news...*

The grey light of an overcast morning filtered through the windows above the entry doors when she limped back out into the atrium of the cinema. She sat on the bottom steps of one of the stairwells, wishing she had some of the stimulant kawakawa tea as she waited for her brain to finish waking up. Her stomach felt weighted down with lead. If she didn't know better, she'd say Ryker was giving her a chance to run with his heads up. She knew he'd send her straight back to Bastion if she returned home, though. Would Bastion really put her image all over the news? She shook her head at her wishful thinking. He'd already followed through on the first part of his threat, so of course he would.

Her father's people didn't know what she looked like and his hounds didn't have her scent. It was one of her main advantages in staying free from them all these years and why she was so careful to keep herself hidden. Her guardian had shapeshifted her to appear human when she was a baby and now it was the only body she'd ever known, the body she was stuck with when her guardian died. Neither she nor her father had ever seen her true form.

If Bastion put her face on the news so soon after the portal she'd rashly made the other day, it would only be a matter of time before her hunters connected the dots and identified her. And if Lord Bastion or the rulers of the other courts realised she had power they could exploit they'd be almost as bad. She could run, but once her likeness was released she'd have nowhere to hide. She was well and truly stuck. The only option she had was to take back what little control Bastion had left open to her and use it to keep herself safe. The bastard had known exactly what he was doing when he made that threat. She was royally screwed.

Hel snuck back into her bedroom through the window when she finally returned home and took a long hot shower before replacing the sword she'd borrowed in the armoury. Ryker was leaning in the doorway when she turned around.

"I thought you might finally make a run for it," he said,

and the words sounded almost kind. Had he been giving her a chance after all?

Hel's shoulders stiffened. "Yeah, well. The bastard didn't exactly leave me any choice."

Ryker frowned. "Don't call him that. It's bad enough he gets that shit from the elemental families. He's kept this city safe as long as you've been alive. Show some respect."

Hel shrugged and looked away. She was too tired to start a fight with her boss.

"What made you decide to return?"

Hel looked back at the man who'd guided her life throughout her teenage years. His deep burgundy wings contrasted against the cream of the walls and those familiar piercing dark tanzanite eyes held hers. He was too smart not to have figured out she was hiding from something. She may as well tell him the truth. "He threatened to put my face all over the news," she said flatly.

Hel watched as Ryker shifted slightly on his feet. She knew him, knew his mannerisms. That was a flash of guilt. "You told him how to trap me," she whispered, surprised at the ache of betrayal stabbing through her chest.

Ryker sighed and dropped his head. "I didn't mean to. He was clever about it."

Hel shrugged again. "It's fine. You're an elemental. He's your lord. That's what you do."

Ryker reached out to her as she tried to push past him. "That's not what happened, Hel. He's not a bad person. He won't hurt you. And the way you two were looking at each other, maybe this will be a good thing."

"Whatever," she said and shoved past him out into the hallway.

HEL MADE a point of being ten minutes late to Soul Tower.
He might have trapped her into helping him find the stupid
Archivist so he could find a cure for this contagion, but that
didn't mean she was going to follow his orders. She paused in
the doorway to Bastion's study and took a moment to process
the sight of him sitting behind a huge desk made of obsidian
polished to a mirrored sheen. Behind him, the tower's
panoramic view of the city was on full display. There was no
meal this time. He was all business.

Bastion ignored her while he finished reading something
on his computer screen. Even half-hidden behind his desk,
his sheer physicality was overwhelming. He was wearing
another collared button-up shirt, black like his wings this
time, although no dye could come close to replicating the
absence of light that was Bastion's feathers. His shirt hugged
every powerful muscle she'd watched straining against the
dragon the previous night. If he was injured at all, she
couldn't see it. His black hair hung loose around his shoulders and that enticing stubble spread like a shadow below
high cheekbones and around his soft lips, the lower one
slightly fuller. She mentally shook herself and forced her
eyes back to the view. What the hell was wrong with her?
She hated this guy, but every time she saw him she was thoroughly distracted by his presence. It's not like she even
needed to breathe all that often, so why was she struggling to
keep her breathing steady? She concentrated on the distant
shapes of griffins wheeling over the harbour.

"I thought I'd have to send a search party out, Helaine."

Ugh. Even his voice made her shiver. All deep and arrogant. Bastard. But she needed to bend or he would break her. "You were right. I don't want to lose control. But once I find your Archivist, you'll wipe my debt in full and transport me to one of the other continents."

Bastion leaned back in his chair and his wings opened slightly behind him. "You want to leave Aotearoa?"

"If I was anywhere else, I could've run. I'm cornered here. I want out." Hel frowned as Bastion started shaking his head.

"That wasn't the deal and you don't have any leverage. Find the Archivist and I wipe your debt. Anything else is your problem," he said.

Her lips tightened as she held back the tirade fighting to escape them and resisted the urge to turn around and storm out again. She knew damn well he had no intention of letting her go when this arrangement was over. There wasn't a lot she could do about it, though. "Fine. Where do we start?"

Bastion smiled and pushed a sheaf of papers over the desk to her. "This is your new contract. Sign it."

"Why do we need a contract? Just call it a job for the couriers."

"I reclaimed your debt. You don't work for them anymore. You're mine."

Hel's hands fisted by her sides at the suggestion she was fucking property. "I saved your life. By my reckoning, you should owe me."

Bastion let out a laugh. "I'm a soulweaver, Helaine. This city is my stronghold, my power base. Even if I'd died, my souls here would never have let me cross the veil. They would have brought me back. You saved nothing."

Hel shivered and tried to tell herself it wasn't fear. She'd heard rumours that Bastion was more immortal than most of his kind but it was one thing to hear it whispered on a street corner and quite another to have the man himself explain it as if it was casual conversation. "If you own my debt then why do we need a contract?"

"Because I'm not arguing with you every time you decide you don't want to do something for me. You sign now, and if you breach it there will be consequences."

Hel stalked forward and threw herself into the chair to read the damn contract. She was swearing under her breath before she got past the first paragraph. If she ran, the contract term would extend one year past her debt repayment date for each day she was absent. If she refused an order, the contract term would extend. If she was openly disrespectful of Bastion in front of others, the contract term would extend. Then she reached the last item under 'summary of duties' and shoved herself to her feet, yanking her baton from its holster at her thigh as she did so. Her vision narrowed in rage until all she could see was Bastion's face from which she fully intended to knock the smirking smile.

"I wouldn't, Helaine," Bastion said softly in warning. He hadn't shifted a muscle despite the fact she was ready to lunge over the desk at him.

Hel took deep shaking breaths until the rest of the room started to come back into focus and shoved the baton back into its sheath. "Why the fuck does this say I have to pretend to be your lover for the next month?"

"As I told you before, the elemental rulers are coming to the city next week to hold council. I promised to deliver the Archivist to them during their visit. You don't seem to want to draw attention to yourself, so you need an excuse no one will question for you to be here."

Hel knew this misdirection was just what she needed to

keep her power hidden from the courts, but every part of her rejected it. "Why can't I just pretend I'm your fucking servant? It's not that far from the truth."

Bastion frowned at her comment but continued to explain in a too patient voice. "It's their business to know everything about their enemies. They know the names and faces of everyone I trust. They won't believe for a second you've waltzed into my inner circle as an employee, but it wouldn't be the first time a whirlwind romance brought someone close to power. Plus, you're human. Anyone serving the Council during their stay will have to be elemental."

"I'm still not buying it. There must be another way."

"How much time was there between when you first got the feeling drawing you to the Archivist and when the creature fled?"

"Not much. Maybe ten minutes," Hel said, grudgingly.

"If you get that feeling again, I need to be able to abandon the council meeting and take you there immediately without causing offence or inviting scrutiny. An urgent call from my lover can be explained away. And, frankly, I don't trust you as far as I can drop you. This way, you know all it will take is a word from me and your photo will be everywhere. The world loves a good romantic scandal. The gossip sites will be all over it. The only way you will keep your privacy is by staying in the tower where my people and my power can control any media and by sticking to the contract."

Hel narrowed her eyes suspiciously. "Are you sure there's not another reason?"

"Why? Do you think I'm after something? I assure you I have no difficulty finding people to warm my bed and I prefer them to be willing. The alternative is that I tell the council you have the power to track the Archivist and that's why I'm keeping you close. That will certainly make you the focus of their attention and I expect they'd attempt to kidnap you so they can avoid me altogether."

Hel stared at him. She could sense there was something more to this ridiculous suggestion, but he wasn't going to tell her what it was. Elemental rulers always had a dozen reasons for anything they did. "What exactly does pretending to be your lover entail?" she ground out.

"You'll stay in the spare room of my penthouse. When we're with anyone other than my main advisor Ra or the Tower Manager Ana, you'll have to pretend to like me."

"And what will you be doing?"

Bastion's smirk widened. "I suppose I'll have to pretend to like you as well."

Hel rolled her eyes. "There has to be another way. I'm not doing it."

Bastion pulled out his phone and snapped a photo of her.

"What the fuck are you doing?"

Bastion glanced over at her. "I needed a photo to send to the news sites."

The taste of metallic blood filled her mouth as she broke the skin on her lip biting it to keep from screaming at him. "Fine. But, no kissing. No groping," she hissed.

"Helaine, you live in this city so I'm sure you know my reputation. There's a reason I have a nightclub in my tower and it sure as fuck isn't to behave. No one is going to believe I'm with you if we don't touch."

The sensation she'd been having of control slipping through her fingers was fast becoming more an avalanche smothering her. Hel squeezed her eyes shut. How had it come to this? She should have run when she had the chance. "Fine. No groping. No tongue. You let me go the second the Archivist is found. If you disrespect me, I will pin your fucking balls to the nearest hard surface," she said through gritted teeth.

Bastion laughed, seemingly genuinely amused by her statement. "Deal."

Hel scrawled her signature across the contract so hard she almost ripped the paper.

"Excellent. Here's an access card to the tower and the penthouse. You will use my private elevator. The fewer of my people you talk to, the less chance they'll figure anything out. If you run off, I'll take the card back and you'll be stuck here, so don't even think about it. Plus, I can't control whether people take photos of you outside of the Tower. Now, do you know how to use your senses to search for the Archivist? Do you need training?"

"I managed just fine last time. Trust me, I'm not going to take any longer finding them than I have to."

"I need to know if it was a fluke or if you can consciously do it, Helaine."

Hel stared at him with no expression on her face. What to say without giving away the level of control she had and how different her magic was from what he understood? "I take my freedom seriously. I've got it under control. If the Archivist appears anywhere inside the city at any time, I will know."

Bastion looked like he couldn't decide whether to be impressed, doubtful, or suspicious. It was a good time to change the subject before he asked too many questions. "I need to get my stuff from home," Hel said.

"Your room already has everything you'll need. You can't

wear your uniform here. You're mine now. You need to look the part."

"I'm *pretending* to be yours."

"No, Helaine. You're mine. You signed the contract. Get used to it."

Hel swiped the access card off the desk and stormed out.

Bastion's apartment looked different during the day, more homely. Of course, it probably helped that a middle-aged Māori woman with silvered hair was bustling around in the kitchen preparing food while an elemental girl bounced up and down on the couch. They both looked up at the sound of her access card letting her in.

"Tēnā koe! You must be Helaine," the woman said, walking towards her with a smile and her hands outstretched in welcome.

Before she knew it, Hel was being hugged by both the woman and the girl. She froze in place, not sure how to deal with the affection. Even her guardian had never hugged her and the couriers certainly hadn't.

"I'm Ana, Manager of the Tower, and this is my daughter Kaia."

"Nice to meet you. Just call me Hel. Everyone who isn't pissed at me does," she finally managed to respond.

Ana laughed. "Alright, Hel. Are you hungry? Come sit down and I'll make you a sandwich."

"Isn't that a little beneath the Manager of Soul Tower?" Hel asked, not quite able to let her frustration go to be polite. She was genuinely curious, though. The Tower wasn't just a home and nightclub, it housed the meetings of the city's ruling partnership, and had floors of hydroponics that fed not just the Tower's occupants, but many others when supplies dried up in emergencies. And who knew what secrets the rest of the building held? It was the hub of the city and Lord Bastion's power base. She was a little surprised he'd entrusted its management to a human. It didn't match what she knew of Elemental snobbery at all.

Ana arched an eyebrow, smile still in place but silently calling her out for her rudeness. "Bast is family. I'd do anything for him and he asked me to keep an eye on you. I'm already making my daughter lunch, so it's no extra work." The subtle warning in her tone was obvious. She was loyal to Bastion and Hel better not make any trouble.

Hel walked to the dining table on auto-pilot and quickly found herself with an excited eleven year old staring at her in fascination. The girl had her mum's skin colouring, but her wings were unusual for an elemental child. Children's wings were usually pastel pale, only growing into their vibrancy as they hit puberty or when they shifted to the colour of their court if they had enough magic to need training. The inner surface of Kaia's wings was a normal soft cream, but the outer surface already had a decent scattering of iridescent electric blue feathers among the softer aquamarine. She looked a lot like the kōtare kingfishers that perched on stray wires on the outskirts of the city, as if her wings couldn't help but reflect her connection to the fauna of the land.

"Mum says you get to do a big acting performance with Uncle Basti and I get to keep it a secret," she finally squealed.

Hel's mouth dropped open. Uncle Basti? What the? "Ummm ... yeah, I guess," she finally croaked.

Ana smiled as she brought two sandwiches made of thick

home-baked rēwena bread to the table. "Kaia, you know he doesn't like you using that name."

Kaia only giggled in response. "How long are you staying? What's that weapon on your leg? Will you have time to play with me?" She barely paused between her sentences and Hel couldn't help but smile at the girl's energy.

"I'm staying for a few weeks. My weapon is a modified baton, which is basically a big stick. Stick fighting has a lot of similarities with sword fighting if you've ever tried that. And I have no idea what I'll be doing here, so I don't know what time I will or won't have."

The door opened again as Hel bit into the soft fluffy bread of the sandwich and the same guy who'd shown her up the night before walked in—Ra. His collared shirt was open at the neck and half untucked from his skinny black jeans. Grey eyes met hers as he joined her at the table.

"Afternoon, Helaine. I see Bast finally managed to win you over."

"It's just Hel. And if I had any choice in the matter, I wouldn't be here," Hel muttered and then focused on eating.

Ra sighed and ran his hand through his blond hair. "He didn't have any choice, either."

Hel couldn't hold back her snort. Whatever.

"I'll let you get settled in the penthouse today. Then we'll need to spend the rest of the week briefing you on what to expect with the council."

Hel nodded, but she was already thinking about how she could get out of there faster. She didn't want to spend one minute longer in this place than she had to. As soon as she was alone, she'd start seeing if she could stretch out her search any further than it already was. That's if she hadn't already scared the Archivist away from the city when she'd made them lose part of a limb. She wondered how long it would take to grow back and how often they needed to feed.

Ana showed her the room she'd be staying in when she finished lunch. It was three times the size of her room back at headquarters and the bed was king-size. Her window looked out over the city towards the old stadium to the northeast and there was a comfy two-seater couch beneath it with a sculptural art deco floor lamp nearby. It all screamed money and power. The en-suite bathroom even had a bath, something she hadn't had access to since sometime in her distant childhood when her guardian was still alive. She peered into the drawers and wardrobes and found an assortment of clothes including dresses, colourful silk shirts, jeans, and a wrapped garment that looked like it might be a freaking ball-gown. How had he known what size she was? And how arrogant was he to get all this assuming she would even come?

She clicked her neck as tension spread through her. She needed out. Needed to breathe fresh air and be moving. She strode down the corridor toward the large deck off the living room. It was set behind the penthouse and sheltered on three sides from the wind. Clearing the outdoor furniture to the edges of the space, she dropped down onto the black tiled deck to start doing push-ups. If she didn't let out this frustration, she was going to explode. When the ache in her arm muscles failed to dull her burning anger, she launched into an hour of drills with the baton. With every rush of air her strikes created, she imagined smacking a certain black-winged arrogant bastard. She was conscious of Ana coming to check on her from time to time, but she ignored the kind woman. By the time she was done, she was drenched in sweat and finally capable of looking around herself without shaking in rage.

"You're pretty good at that," Bastion said from the sliding door to the lounge where he was leaning. How long had he been watching her and how had she not noticed him?

"Lucky for you. You'd be dead if I wasn't. Even if it wouldn't have stuck," Hel snapped back.

Bastion was silent for a while as she stretched. "True. Any sign of the Archivist yet?"

Hel swallowed a frustrated growl. "Trust me. You'll be the first to know. That's my ticket out of here."

"Thank you, Hel," he said, presumably because Ana had told him to stop using her full name.

When she looked up again, he was gone. An unnatural chill sent goose-bumps shivering across her skin as she stood panting on the deck. She looked up at the twisting elemental metalwork that formed a lattice over the building. In times of attack, it became an impenetrable shield. According to the elementals she'd spoken to, that outer structure held a vast reservoir of dead souls for Bastion's use. Were they watching her now, too? Waiting for her to try and escape so they could warn their master or strike her down? She hurried back inside wondering if she was fooling herself to think she'd ever get free.

CHAPTER 6
BAST

Bast stood in the shadows and studied the sleeping face of the woman he'd manipulated into invading his space. She was lying on her side facing the door, facing him. The defined muscles of her biceps reminded him of Morrigan and the female scouts. The kind of muscles you got from regular weapons practice rather than the gym. She should've looked peaceful, but even like this he could still see the anger and strength she wrapped around herself as if that alone could keep her hidden. It was there in the angle of her stubborn jaw and the way one hand rested beneath her pillow on the dagger she'd concealed there. If she knew what he was considering, he had no doubt she would be trying to stab him with it.

Everything rested on her ability to track the Archivist— she was the only chance to find the cure to the contagion he could still sense like a plague on reality from where he had contained it two blocks away, and the Archivist was the only reason the elemental rulers had agreed to come to his city. He couldn't live as he had been any longer. He needed to know who'd framed him for killing his father, who'd made his corpse dance in the streets until every accusing eye had turned to the bastard necromancer son they all knew about but no one ever acknowledged. Not until the day they decided he was a murderer. Then they'd been all too willing to acknowledge his parentage. All too willing to allow his half-brother Lord Tyson to send his assassins to chase him across the world when Bast was no more than fifteen. He'd lost his childhood that day.

He couldn't risk losing Hel and he knew she'd run the moment she saw an opportunity. She'd run off every time they'd met, after all. Where most people wanted to befriend him for his power despite their fear, she'd shown no hint of fear but hadn't been able to get out of there fast enough. There was no way he'd let it happen again. There was no need to inspect any further all the reasons he didn't want to let her go. The less they acknowledged the draw between them, the better. She might not have the same fear he was used to seeing, but she had the same disgust. He could hear it in her voice. For a moment when they'd first met he'd thought she might be different, but she was just as bigoted against his soulweaving as everyone else. For some reason, he felt that like a betrayal. As if the fact she was making his power thrum inside him by her mere proximity meant she owed him more. Not to mention the effect she was having on other parts of his body. It was infuriating. *She* was infuriating.

He needed her help and if there were a few extra enticements to hold her close, that didn't make what he was about to do any less necessary. A tendril of guilt whispered through him as he reached for his power and let it drift over her body, lulling her into a deeper sleep. He watched the silver mist stroking down her throat where he could just make out her pulse in the darkness and felt a moment of envy before scoffing at himself. Ridiculous. To be envious of his own power touching her.

He circled round to the other side of the bed and stepped closer, pushing aside the whispering guilt. There were other ways to track her if she ran. Ways she wouldn't have even noticed. Placing his mark on someone like he had with Ra and Ana was nothing like the invasiveness of a mating bond—few elementals voluntarily entered that kind of co-dependence, least of all someone with power as dangerous as his—but it still created a level of connection he knew Hel would hate him for. This way would be more convincing to the council, though. It would make them believe their sham relationship, and it wasn't without benefit to her. His mark would open a conduit between his power and her body. She would heal faster, live longer, age slower. Still in his forties, he was too young to know how powerful his marks would prove to be. He'd only placed two. One on Ra and one on Ana. It was too soon to know how much extra life he'd given them, but Ra hadn't aged a day in the years since his mark was placed, despite now being fifty.

He leaned over the unconscious woman and tugged the sheet lower, baring the smooth curve of her shoulders. When he brushed the wild mass of her pitch-black hair away from her face, he had to clench his fist tight to resist the urge to let his fingers stroke down her cheekbone. Why the fuck did he still have this driving need to touch her when she made no effort to hide her disdain for his power? Power he'd only ever used to keep the city she lived in safe. The city she couldn't be bothered lifting a finger to save without being forced to, despite all he'd offered. What kind of selfish fucking person let their bigotry justify refusing to do something that would literally save not just their life, but everyone else's too? He might be using the situation to manipulate the rulers into coming to him, but he would've helped them even if he hadn't wanted to find his father's real killer. Unlike Hel, who was happy to ignore the threat of death in their backyard. Was she completely without honour?

He ground his teeth as anger swept through him again, but his hand remained gentle as he swept her hair further across the pillow to bare her back to him. He was careful to ensure he never so much as brushed a fingertip against her too alluring skin. Her breaths seemed impossibly slow as she lay there. The beautiful line of her spine barely moved as she inhaled and exhaled with long pauses between. Bast frowned and then mentally shook himself. He wasn't there to drown in the image of her reclined on his sheets.

His hand drifted between her shoulder blades and hovered a hairsbreadth from her skin. Reaching out to the souls around him, he let them feel his intent rather than vocalising it. He was surprised at the eager rush of power down his arms like they had been straining to reach for her already and had finally been let free. There was no hesitation from the dead, no testing his motives as they so often did, despite his lingering guilt. Power arced through every cell of his body, flowing down his arms and fingers into the woman lying below him, sinking into her soul-deep.

The black lines of his mark grew across her back and stretched around until they appeared like a tattoo of stylised wings. Only if you looked closer, this tattoo was an endlessly shifting stream of darkness that perfectly matched the absence of light of his feathers. Hidden in the depths of that inky blackness were glimpses of the silver power that came from the countless souls that had been lost in this city. His mark spread from the tips of her shoulders down to the small of her back, sweeping around the enticing dip of her waist so the bottom edges would be visible on both sides of her tightly muscled abdomen like she was enfolded in his wings. It was far larger than he'd ever made one before—his power responding to his subconscious need to *claim*.

Bast smiled in satisfaction even as he swayed in exhaustion and felt his vision narrowing and darkening. She was his, and now everyone who saw her would know it. She could never hide from him again and he wouldn't be forced to watch as her beauty and strength succumbed to age. He blinked at those last thoughts and pulled them back. It wasn't about that. He just needed to keep track of her for a few months. He would remove the mark when they were done. He could imagine Ra's scoffing response to his denial.

He gently pulled the sheet back up over her shoulders and watched her for one more breath before turning away. The drain on his power and the exposure of the new connection left him staggering across the room with every nerve feeling like it had been bared to the world. It took all his control to silently leave rather than collapse on the bed with Hel and spoon his aching body around hers. He fell into his bed with a hint of a smile as he lost the fight to remain conscious. She'd be fuming when she noticed what he'd done. Her eyes would spark and she would stroke her weapons as she failed to hide her need for violence. He couldn't wait.

"WHAT's your take on where the families will be at next week?" Bast asked Ra the next morning.

Ra turned back to him and pushed one of the teas he'd been making across the benchtop. "Aliya, our Lady of Air, is riding high on this cult she's managed to create for herself. If I didn't know better I'd say she was starting to believe her own hype with the amount of propaganda coming out from Air Court. She's outright calling her stronghold Heaven and her people are pushing hard on the 'miracles' they've been performing. She's already turning the contagion to her advantage. They're pitching it as the end-times and the Air Court as humanity's saviours."

"She's saying she can save them from the contagion? Has she found a cure?"

Ra grimaced in disgust. "No. She's saying she's an angel who can save their souls when they die. I wouldn't be surprised if she's not even interested in a cure, given the power she's twisting from the situation. And her flying stronghold isn't likely to be affected until the contagion is widespread, since she doesn't need to let it land."

Bast rolled his eyes. "Typical court bullshit. At least we know Mica and the Earth Court will be keen to find a cure. He wouldn't have reached out to me if he wasn't desperate. What about Nerida?"

"The Water Court is still more focused on cleaning the oceans than anything else. She's another one who probably won't see the effects of the contagion in her territory until it's too late unless it changes its pattern of contamination. It's been years since Lady Nerida bothered bringing her floating stronghold into a port."

"She still blames you humans for the destruction of the oceans she's responsible for. Which is fair enough, but saving the ocean is pointless if the entire world succumbs to this contagion. Plus, she's still holding a grudge about my illustrious father setting part of her territory on fire before the Melding. It'll take time to make her see past her grievances and come out of her isolation."

Ra snorted in derision. "Whatever. She's got responsibilities and she's shoving her head in the sand to ignore them."

"Then you will have to help me charm her into looking up."

"Like you charmed Hel?" Ra smirked.

"Shut up. What about my dear brother? Anything new to report?" Ra might not be connected to the elemental courts directly in any way, but his ability to search and manipulate information meant he often knew developments even before the elemental spies they had in the courts could report back to them. To the rest of the world, Ra appeared to be nothing more than the marketing manager for the City of Souls, carefully manipulating Bast's image to combat the efforts of the courts to turn the populace against him. The reality was that he was so much more. He was family, his most trusted advisor and intrinsic to the partnership of humans and elementals that kept the city safe.

"Same old. Still wants to kill you. Seems he's decided to amp up the assassins again, but you already know that. Try not to get dead."

Ra's look of concern belied his casual statement. Bast reached out to squeeze his shoulder in understanding, and that was the point at which a screech of rage came from his guest's ensuite.

Ra raised an eyebrow in question as Bast hid a grin behind another sip of tea. His friend didn't have long to wait for an explanation. Hel emerged into the living area with hair dripping wet, wrapped in nothing but a black towel, and stormed toward Bast.

"You bastard! You branded me?! I'm not fucking *property*, dickhead!"

Bast ignored Ra's sharply indrawn breath of surprise and focused on the woman before him. It wasn't hard. He hadn't been able to look away from her since she entered the room. "It's not a brand. I didn't burn you. You should be honoured."

Hel was literally shaking with rage, the thick cotton of the towel trembling where it hung partway down her thighs. "Remove it. Now."

Bast felt his own anger rising and strangling off his unformed words. His body was still raw from the effects of placing that mark on her ungrateful back. He'd gifted her the closest thing to immortality a human could achieve and she was throwing it back in his face? His nails dug into his palms as fists formed at his sides. A strong hand fell on his shoulder before he could step forward into Hel's space.

"Let's all just take a breath," Ra said, keeping a tight grip on Bast. "Sweetheart, this was part of the contract you signed. It's part of pretending to be his lover. If you really don't want it, we can talk about that once the time's up. But that mark comes with power. It makes you a little more than human. Just see how you go."

Bast fumed at the soft, reasonable tone Ra was taking with her. It was so like him to be the one to smooth things over. He was all about the messaging.

"I don't want to be more than human," Hel muttered.

"Would a tea help?" Ra offered.

Bast watched as Hel looked down at herself and finally seemed to realise she was standing in front of two men she barely knew wearing nothing but a towel. He waited to see if she would blush, but all she did was bite her lip as if she was forcing herself not to say what she was thinking. The heat of his anger sunk lower in his body as he watched the red of her lips caught between her white teeth and he almost hissed in frustration. What was with his reaction to this woman?

"I'm going to go get dressed. You're removing the brand the second we find the Archivist," she snapped.

Ra pulled Bast around to face him as the woman left the room and searched his eyes for something. "That's quite a mark you left on her. Do you know what you're doing? I didn't think you'd go there with someone you don't trust. Especially not with her."

Bast shrugged, refusing to answer the question in his voice. The wings he'd marked Ra with were not much more than a cuff around his left bicep, nothing like the intricate feathered design that covered half of Hel's torso. Part of him wished he'd never succumbed to the temptation because if he concentrated, he could now sense Hel's heartbeat through his skin and feel the echo of her breaths in his lungs. But another part of him wished he could cover every inch of her in his power so no one else would ever dare to touch her.

"You need to get your shit together. She's not going to do what you need if you keep acting this way and you can't show that kind of weakness to the council. Right now, I can't tell if you want to fuck her or kill her."

"Maybe both?"

Ra rolled his eyes and wrapped an arm around him, hugging him close. "How about you go with neither? I don't know why she hates you quite as much as she seems to, but you need to stop letting it hurt you or you're not going to be able to pull this off."

Bast let his forehead rest against his best friend's shoulder, breathing in the comforting scent of home. "Even if she didn't hate me for everything else, I took her choices away."

"To be fair, she was making the wrong ones," Ra said.

"That's not really an excuse."

"No. It's not. So, show her there's more to you than that sexy domineering alpha shit," Ra smirked.

It was Bast's turn to roll his eyes at that and he pulled away from the comfort of Ra's playful teasing. Movement caught his eye, and he turned to see Hel standing in the entrance to the living room, looking confused as her gaze flicked between him and Ra. She was wearing the same clothes she'd arrived in rather than the new ones he'd given her. He frowned.

"Are you two...?" she asked in disbelief.

Of course. How inconceivable that a human would hug a death mage as a friend. She was probably homophobic and a separatist on top of the rest of her judgmental everything. No wonder Ryker had taken the route he had with her. She was impossible. Bast stormed past her toward his home office before he could snap at her again as Ra's melodic laugh filled the room. He could just make out his friend's reply as he left.

"Sadly, I had to bro-zone him. He's family," Ra said.

Bast rolled his eyes at his friend and resisted the urge to look back and see how Hel took that comment. Instead, he used his bitter thoughts to reinforce the mental distance between him and the infuriating woman, not quite sure how it kept eroding in the first place.

CHAPTER 7
HEL

Hel stared at Ra and raised a scornful eyebrow as Bastion's black wings swept down the hallway behind her. Ra thought of an elemental as family? He was an idiot. The devil's advocate part of her brain played back the image of the two imposing men leaning against each other, the way Bastion's eyes were half-closed as he took a moment to just exist and accept the affection he'd been offered. A treacherous part of her whispered she was jealous. There had never been room for affection or family in her life as a fugitive from a father who wanted to sacrifice her.

As if he'd followed her thoughts, Ra slung a casual arm around her shoulder like it was normal to hug people you barely knew. "Bast tells me you're quite the fighter. Fancy a sparring session to work off that angst?"

Hel twisted her head to look up at him and searched his face suspiciously. What was his end-game here? Was he testing her? "Sure," she said, twisting out of his grip.

As they made their way back to the outdoor courtyard,

Hel took a moment to focus on her subconscious search for the Archivist. The sooner she found them again, the sooner she could get out of there. Her senses were still stretched as far as she could across the city and the fatigue from using the unfamiliar 'muscles' was not helping her grumpiness, nor were the niggling pings from the sickening contagion in the old Civic Square. At least Bastion's creepy death magic was good for something. She shuddered to think what would've happened to the city if the contagion was left loose. Frustratingly, there was still no sign of the Archivist's distinctive portal signature that had felt like liquid shadow when she'd sensed it the other day.

She froze in the doorway to the balcony courtyard as her power brushed up against an echo of another of her father's portals on the edge of her range. He'd probably sent someone to investigate the death of his hound. There should be nothing to draw the hounds to her, she reminded herself as panic threatened. At least she wasn't out running the streets as a courier like she normally would be. They couldn't stumble upon her as long as she stayed in the tower. She hated that she'd missed sensing the portal forming the previous night. Bastion must have done something to knock her out. She would never usually have slept through someone in her room like that. Fear radiated out from her spine like ice at how vulnerable she'd been without knowing it, or was that sensation coming from the death magic thrumming through the marks Bastion had left on her skin? She scowled at the thought. Bastard.

"Everything okay, sweetheart?" Ra asked. "Did you sense something?"

The empathy in his voice only stoked her anger. "No. And the two of you don't have to ask me constantly. Like I told Bastion, I want out and the sooner I find the Archivist, the sooner that'll happen. I'm on it!" she snapped.

He grinned and beckoned her forward, seemingly uncowed by her temper. "You'll feel better after you slap me round a bit."

Hel shook herself out of her thoughts and joined him in the centre of the deck. He was dressed like the day before in black jeans and a collared shirt, this one a silvery grey colour that brought out the colour of his eyes. He'd rolled the sleeves most of the way up his muscled forearms. She raised her hands into a casual guard position and scanned between his face and trim shoulders as she searched for a tell that would give away his first move. His feet were silent as he shifted slightly to her left, probably assuming she was weaker on that side. She wasn't. Amira would never have let her get away with shirking like that. She pivoted a little to keep him firmly in view.

"How much do you know about the ruling families?" he asked as he continued to circle.

So, that was his game. He was distracting her to make the tuition for her role in Bastion's stupid contract easier. "Enough."

Ra lunged forward with a jab/kick combination, testing her. Rather than give up any ground in the confined area, she stepped into him, avoiding the kick and grabbing his wrist as she twisted to redirect his punch and pull him off balance. He broke her hold and retreated before she had a chance to throw him to the ground, but she could see a new wariness in the way he watched her. She smirked. He'd thought she was all about keeping her distance and beating people off with a stick. He hadn't expected her to get close with the grappling move.

"You need to understand the power dynamics at play so you don't make trouble for Bast."

"I'm not really worried about whether or not I make trouble for Bastion," Hel said, feinting for his head to distract him as she tried to sweep his feet out from under him.

Ra grinned appreciatively as he stepped clear again. He was fast for a human. She didn't know everything she'd inherited from her parentage, but she'd always had an edge on any human opponent. She wasn't sure that held with Ra. Her head tilted sideways as she considered him. *A little more than human*, he'd said earlier. Bastion's mark on her back had been tingling against her skin since their sparring session started, or earlier, if you included the response to her father's portal. Did it respond to threats and give them an extra edge? That would explain Ra's speed. It felt a little like tendrils of icy power were rustling the stylised feathers on her back. "You bear his brand as well?" she asked.

Ra's eyes widened in surprise and he stopped moving. "You're very observant," he said, finally. He searched her face with suspicion as if he was wondering how well they really had her under their control.

Her stomach chose that moment to growl loudly. She hadn't eaten anything since the sandwich Ana had made her the day before.

The sound sent Ra's smiling smokescreen of an expression back onto his face. "We can play later. Let's get you some breakfast. You must be starving."

He shepherded her back inside, all hint of his more threatening edge disappearing as he settled her at the breakfast bar and made her a plate piled high with scrambled eggs as he launched into an Elemental Council 101 lecture. She tuned out most of it, deciding not to tell him she knew all about them already. Her education had not been lacking in that department. Her guardian had made sure she knew every intricacy of their relationships, every possible weakness, everything she might need if she found herself in a situation where they were her only hope of staying hidden. Much like now. She winced at the thought and shoved another mouthful of perfectly seasoned eggs into her mouth.

Her eyes became particularly glazed when Ra started reciting territory lines. The courts had always roughly split their domains by continent and the divide hadn't shifted at all since she was a girl when they'd tweaked the boundaries to match human longitudes for ease of mapping. The Lady of Water claimed everything from 150° East to 120° West, appropriately missing most of the world's landmasses other than what would've been eastern Russia and the western edge of the North American continent. In practice, she was happy to leave those areas to the nearest land-based courts to manage. Although, by rights, she should at least have challenged Lord Tyson for his continued incursions into the City of Souls, which was firmly bounded on all sides by her territory. In contrast, the Air Court encompassed the rest of North and South America, the Fire Court claimed Africa and Europe, and the Earth Court covered Asia and Australia. There were probably a few more pockets of independence around, but the only unaffiliated areas Hel was familiar with were the free cities of Aotearoa and the inhospitable poles.

"Are you even listening to me? We don't have long to prepare you. The council starts next week, but they could turn up any time if they decide to scope out why Bast is so keen to host them," Ra said, sounding annoyed.

Hel looked up and finished chewing before she

summarised the key political points of his lecture back to him, although not quite how he would've put it. "Everyone hates Bastion because his power is evil and he killed his father. Aliya's a narcissistic bitch who would watch the world die if she thought she'd get something out of it. Nerida doesn't care about anything but her patch of water. Tyson wants him dead no matter what. Mica's desperate enough to be a potential ally, or at least a neutral party, so long as Bastion can deliver the Archivist. Most of them probably can't even agree the world should be saved. Did I miss anything?"

Ra blinked in surprise. "Umm ... that's about it, yeah."

"Why is Bastion so keen to host them, anyway?"

Ra's expression became more guarded. That was interesting. There was something more going on there.

"They need the answers from the Archivist, and Bast, well, *you* really, but they won't know that, is the only one who's been able to find them," Ra said. "He's used that leverage to get them here. He needs to start building alliances with them to get a voice on the council. Otherwise, the city will always be under threat."

"And what else? What is it you aren't telling me?"

"You're too observant for your own good," Ra muttered instead of answering her.

Hel parked that question. "It sounds like they've not even agreed the contagion needs to be stopped, so why are they all so desperate to get the answers from the Archivist? Why did they agree to come?"

Ra sighed and ran a hand over his face as if the whole topic made him exhausted. "Honestly, I don't even know. I suspect Tyson wants the chance to shove a knife between Bast's ribs in person and Aliya is messed up enough that she may be coming along just to watch. It would take all four of them to force the Archivist to give them access to the other dimension, so in theory one of them could just not show up and the whole thing would be pointless, but none of them want to risk the chance the others get access to information they don't have. Plus, they can't afford to miss a council meeting in case there's a vote that affects their territory. So, here we are."

Hel sat back in her chair and listened to the eerie sound of the City of Soul's wind sweeping against the twisted metal that protected the windows. "And we have to play nice with them for two whole weeks?"

Ra nodded and opened his mouth as if to say something before looking down at the bench and taking a sip of tea instead.

"What?" she asked when the silence continued to stretch.

He tilted his head as if deciding how much to say. "Bast isn't the bad guy here, Hel. His past ... it didn't play out the way the elementals spin it. Like all the rulers, a lot of his reputation is smoke and mirrors. The safety of everyone in this city depends on his ability to earn the respect of the council. If they see you don't respect him, that's never going to happen. But if you're convincing enough that they think you love him, or at least want him, they might just start to see a man they can work with instead of a monster."

"You'll forgive me if I don't just take your word for his character. You're not exactly a neutral party. So, that's the real reason behind this stupid contract then? It's all about marketing? Selling the image? How very elemental."

Ra smiled a sad smile. "We all know reality is in the eye of the believer, now more than ever. You need to sell this

96

reality. Our city is depending on it. The world might depend on it. Do you want to look little Kaia in the eye and tell her you let the world burn because you couldn't be nice to her Uncle Basti for a few weeks?"

Hel rolled her eyes at the blatant emotional blackmail. "Fuck off."

"No, thanks. I'm pretty sure Bast called dibs." Ra's smile had turned wicked.

Hel raised her middle finger at him and retreated to her room. His words wouldn't stop replaying in her head, though. No. As much as she hated everything about this situation, she couldn't look that sweet little girl in the eye and tell her she wasn't going to help. She couldn't let down the humans in the city who depended on Bastion for their safety either. And, as infuriating as it was, the couriers had kept her safe all these years. She owed them more than just the debt Bastion had reclaimed from them. Fuck. She was really going to do this.

SOMEHOW, even in the confines of an apartment, Hel managed to avoid Bastion almost completely for the next two days. Although, it was more likely the other way round, given he knew exactly where to find her. The only time she saw him was overhearing a tense conversation he was having with someone on the phone early the second morning. She thought it might have been Ryker, but he'd cut off his words as soon as he realised she was nearby before quickly leaving for wherever he'd been spending his time. All she'd caught was a terse "What were you thinking? That's my name you were dragging—". She thought she'd been quiet, but he could probably sense her presence with his damn brand on her back. What had they been discussing? She couldn't shake the feeling it had been something about her, but she couldn't imagine what Bastion could be angry at Ryker about. He'd basically shoved Hel into Bastion's lap.

When the Lord of Souls wasn't around, she could almost make herself forget she was essentially a prisoner in the Tower. Or at least she could have if Ra and Ana weren't so focused on preparing her for the rulers of the four courts to arrive. She spent hours curled up on the couch chatting elemental politics with Ra and found herself falling for his charm despite herself. She'd never met someone so willing to put themselves out there and it was impossible to reject his constant annoyingly endearing casual embraces, although she gave it a good shot. If she hadn't known he was doing it all for Bastion, she would've pushed him away harder. She couldn't afford to have friends. Ana, in her typical ruthless fashion, recruited Kaia into pestering her into trying on the clothes and make-up in her room until everything had been altered, arranged, and practised so she could make herself presentable for any situation within minutes.

When she wasn't with one of them, she was exploring the public spaces of the Tower courtesy of the access card she'd been given. It was just as impressive as it had always seemed from the outside. Floors of hydroponic food supplies were interspersed with offices filled with advanced tech she couldn't begin to identify. And then there were the council chambers and ballroom stunningly decorated in a style of modern minimalism that echoed the black and silver of Bastion's wings and magic.

She steered clear of The Crypt, not willing to face the throngs of people, but explored down to the basement pools and the gym higher up to let off the ever-present steam of rage Bastion's tingling mark on her skin provoked in her. She tried not to be impressed by the competence and respect of the human and elemental staff she came across, but it was impossible. That was probably all Ana's doing anyway. *Lord* Bastion and his creepy magic would be above dealing with the masses.

Bastion probably hadn't envisaged she would use the access card to catalogue every balcony, exit, and hiding place in her memory. But he'd only told her not to leave the Tower. He hadn't said anything about what she could do within it. Thanks to her efforts, she knew exactly how long it would take her to get out of the building, what the guard schedules were, and the blind spots of the internal security cameras in relation to her exit routes. It made her feel a little better that she knew how to leave, even if she couldn't.

"What are you working on?" she asked Ra when he hurriedly shut his computer as she returned to the kitchen after her latest fashion session, with Kaia clinging to her back. The eleven-year-old elemental had yet to grow into her oversized wings and the soft feathers tickled Hel's arms where they wrapped around her alongside the girl's arms and legs. She wondered what colour the inner cream-coloured feathers would settle into as an adult when the electric blue of her outer wings was so striking already. She must be due to be tested for magic in the next year or two. Any children with power were shipped off to one of the courts to train where they gained the distinctive colouring of the families they served. She hoped the girl wasn't that powerful. She knew first-hand how hard it was to travel to another court to live with strangers as a young teen. She could only imagine how much worse it would be as a half-human elemental coming from the city of a pariah. She didn't want to see Kaia's beautifully unique wings replaced with the same-old colouring of the courts. And she definitely didn't want to see what that would do to the joy the girl exuded in everything she did. Not for the first time, she reminded herself she needed to keep her distance from these people. She wasn't sticking around. And when she got close to people they died. It was just the nature of her fugitive existence. Her father's hounds didn't care who got in their way.

Ra shifted in his seat as Hel waited for his answer and she raised an eyebrow, wondering what she'd caught him at.

"I'm just updating our social media," he said.

Hel let the girl slip to the floor and leaned against the breakfast bar. "Kaia, does that look like the face of someone doing something innocent?"

"Nope, Aunty. He looks like me when someone narks to mum that I've been flying in the dead zone."

Hel winced at being called Aunty, but let it slide. Kaia was even more stubborn than she was and the girl was taking this pretending she was Bastion's actual lover thing very seriously.

Ra mock-glared at Kaia. "Thanks for nothing, scamp. It's nice to know years of loyalty can be tossed aside in a few days. Go make trouble for your mum instead of me."

Kaia grinned and skipped off towards the door with a wave as Hel continued to wait for Ra to explain. "Well?"

"We need to make sure everyone here knows you and Bast are an item before the Elemental Council arrive, so that when they start asking questions everyone will back us up. We've been dropping hints and sightings with various news sites."

Hel felt ill as adrenaline shot through her system urging her to run far and fast. "What the fuck, Ra? The only reason I'm doing this is to avoid having my face put all over the news! Show me."

"Relax. There're no pictures or names. It's just anonymous tip-offs that a woman has moved into the penthouse with Bast and that he's marked you."

Hel looked over his shoulder at the now-open screen and winced at the headlines Ra had been checking: *Has the playboy ruler of the City of Souls finally found his soulmate?* Or even worse, *Mystery woman brings necromancer's heart back to life.*

"Ugh. Don't these people have anything better to do?"

"Nope. I know you don't want any photos, but we need some people to at least see the two of you together in person so they can corroborate the stories. Bast is going to take you to The Crypt tonight. And, before you complain, security will make sure they don't let in any cameras and Bast has spelled the tower to ruin any images taken. I'll have searches running to shut down any photos, just in case. You'll be totally safe."

Hel frowned at the thought of going anywhere public when she knew one of her father's hounds was out searching, but it wasn't like anyone was going to let a slavering starhound into the tower. She let out a frustrated breath. There wasn't a lot she could do about the situation. "Nice of Bastion to invite me himself," she said, focusing on the minor irritation instead of the big scary threat to her safety.

Ra sighed and rubbed his eyes. "He's got a lot on, alright? And it's not like you make it very easy for him to talk to you."

"Are you coming tonight?"

"No. I'm part of his party-boy image. We don't want you

looking like another casual hook-up. He needs to look enraptured with you and if I'm there you'd both use me to avoid each other. Not that I'd mind playing go-between on the dance floor," he teased.

Hel swallowed the lump in her throat. She really could've used the distraction of his presence. She didn't trust herself around Bastion.

KAIA AND ANA joined Hel for dinner late that night, but there was still no sign of her dark-winged antagonist.

"I'm not getting all dressed up for him when he can't even be bothered talking to me beforehand," Hel said as she reached for the salad that had been grown twenty floors below her. If she wasn't concentrating so hard on being mad, she'd be impressed again with how self-sufficient the tower was.

"He said he'll be here at ten to pick you up," Ana said, her voice gently chiding as if Hel was another daughter.

"He didn't say it to me," Hel muttered.

"Can I help you get dressed, Aunty?" Kaia's wings had flared out behind her, sending a draft of air across the table that blew their napkins to the ground. She was practically bouncing in her seat with excitement.

Hel couldn't help but smile. "How about I dress you up and you go instead?"

"It's already past your bedtime, Kaia. Go and get your pyjamas on," Ana cut in, shaking her head at Hel.

Hel sighed and finished her meal. She spent a pleasant ten minutes quietly working alongside Ana to clear the table and wash up before the older woman bundled her down the hallway and into her en-suite for a quick shower. As hot water beat down on her, she used the time alone to reinforce the barrier of anger she'd built around her thoughts in the hopes she could avoid falling prey to her body's traitorous reaction to Bastion again. After she dried off, she took a few minutes to put on as little make-up as she thought Ana would let her get away with, just smoky eyes and a pop of deep red colour on her lips.

"Oh, hell no," she said when she entered her bedroom and saw the short backless dress draped across her bed.

Ana pursed her lips. "Don't be a prude. The whole point is to show off that stunning work of art on your back."

"Art had nothing to do with it. Where the fuck do I carry a weapon in this?"

"You don't. You're with Bast in the nightclub he runs, which is in the building he owns, which is in the city he rules," Ana said tartly. "You don't need it."

"Bullshit. I'm not wearing this. I'd kill myself in those heels anyway."

"It's not like you're going to be running anywhere. You'll be fine."

"I always assume I'll be running somewhere. If I sense that Archivist anywhere we won't be staying put."

"If you sense the Archivist, Bast will fly you wherever you need to go so you won't need shoes anyway."

Hel ignored the irritating thrill of her racing pulse at the thought of flying and focused on the more important issue, negotiating a compromise with a woman who took no prisoners. "I'll need them when I get there. I'll wear the dress if I can wear it with my boots and still carry my baton."

Ana eyed up the dress and then inspected Hel from head

to foot. "I think we can work with that. It has a split up the left thigh so it won't ruin the line of the dress."

Hel's mouth dropped open. "It's hardly more than a scrap of cloth in the first place and they put *extra* slits in it?"

Ana smirked. "Stop stalling and get dressed."

The woman refused to leave while she changed, but she was that combination of motherly bossiness and sisterly teasing that made it impossible to kick her out without seeming plain rude. It was the work of seconds to slip into the dress, but it took longer for Ana to arrange Hel's thigh holster to her satisfaction. Hel twisted to examine herself in the mirror when everything was in place. In the reflection, she could see Ana's eyes lighting up with success behind her as she took her in.

The silky black fabric clung to her curves in a way she knew was going to draw attention she didn't want. Although, the attention was probably inevitable with the company she'd be keeping. The halter neck and low back that skirted the edge of scandalous left the infuriating sweeping wings of Bastion's mark on full display where they draped down her shoulder blades to her waist.

Despite herself, a tiny part of Hel could appreciate the way the black mark that spoke of protection backed by violence complemented her thigh holster and boots. It would've been a totally badass tattoo if it hadn't been a direct assault on her bodily autonomy. As it was, she could admit she looked more warrior than possession, which was just as well or she wouldn't have shown her face outside the penthouse in the ridiculous outfit.

"I'll leave you to it. You look stunning. Time to go, Aunty Hel," Ana said.

As she opened the door to the bedroom to leave, Ra's

laughter drifted from the living room in response to some inaudible comment from Bastion. Hel glared at Ana's back as the woman headed straight out toward the lift, abandoning her to face the men alone. Not that she needed any help putting Bastion in his place, she reminded herself. With that thought, she squared her shoulders and forced herself to ignore how exposed she felt in the dress as she strode out of the room.

Bastion and Ra were sipping amber liquor by the windows, staring out at the panoramic view of the twinkling city lights, when she entered the living room. They didn't notice her immediately and she had a moment to take in their twinned elegance. Bastion's sweeping black wings drew the light from the room, absorbing it, in the same way his presence drew her eyes. She wet her lips and glanced away in annoyance at herself as the action made her focus on the softness of his mouth in profile. She wished she could figure out why she was drawn so strongly to him so she could stop it. He wasn't the only attractive elemental around. Surely, she could convince her traitorous libido to look elsewhere. Preferably, somewhere that wasn't responsible for forcing her to live in debt and then blackmailing her into this sham that could expose her to her father's hounds and certain death.

Ra was the first to catch sight of her. "Hellcat. You look delicious. Maybe I will come after all."

"What a delightful nickname," Hel responded drily.

Bastion had turned around at his friend's words and Hel resisted the urge to shift in place as his gaze slowly travelled down her body and back up again, missing nothing. Now he was turned toward her, she could see his trademark fitted collared shirt pulling tight across defined chest muscles that held his wings carefully controlled behind him. She started a litany in her mind to drown out the inappropriate images his look had sparked: *murderer, blackmailer, asshole*. When that still wasn't enough, she spun on the balls of her feet and went to grab the whiskey off the breakfast bar. She was going to need it. As soon as her back was turned, Bastion's low groan sounded from behind her, quickly followed by Ra snickering.

"What?" she snapped, glaring over her shoulder at the two men.

Bastion turned back to the window rather than respond and Ra's laughter grew louder.

"Give him a moment to adjust to that masterpiece of his on your back that stakes his claim being all out on display," Ra smirked.

Bastion growled a threat back at him that was too low for Hel to make out, but his subtle adjustment of his pants didn't escape her notice. At least she wasn't the only one who was struggling to ignore their unwelcome attraction. In fact, now she was thinking about it, she could feel a tingling thrum of sexual tension in the threads of magical connection between them. That was *not* helping.

"Whatever," she said, knocking back the entire glass of whiskey she'd poured in one hit and relishing the burn down her throat that matched the embarrassing burn in her cheeks. The sooner that particular conversation was shut down the better. "Let's get this over with."

"I couldn't agree more," Bastion shot back, finishing his drink and gesturing for her to precede him out to the elevator.

Hel could feel the heat of his eyes on her as she walked ahead of him. She ignored it like she was ignoring almost everything else about him. It was safer that way. They stepped into the elevator together in silence.

"I don't suppose we could get out early and take the stairs. The elevator entrance is so exposed," Hel said. The elevator was reserved for elementals descending from the public balcony entrance a few floors down from the penthouse. It was the equivalent of the red carpet to the club, lit in a way that would ensure everyone there would mark their entrance and overlooked by the shadowy VIP balcony that would be the perfect spot for a sniper. She much preferred the human entrance from the stairs she usually took.

"No. That's the whole point. We want everyone to notice."

Hel watched the floor numbers tick down next to the elevator door as they descended. When they were two floors above the club, Bastion stretched his wings to fill the space, sending shivers through her as his soft feathers brushed her shoulders. His hand rested on her lower back, the skimpy dress meaning she could feel every callous of his fingers. Her cheeks flushed red again and she took a slow breath to avoid growling at him.

Bastion's lips brushed against her ear as he leaned toward her. "Showtime, Hellcat," he whispered as the elevator doors opened on The Crypt.

CHAPTER 8
BAST

Bast nodded to the guards as they exited the lift and gently propelled Hel around the curved outer passageway toward the double doors that led to the main bar and dancefloor. Above the doors hung a neo-classical bronze plaque from the days when the site the Tower stood on had first held a small human cabaret theatre over 100 years earlier. Designed in human Florence, a city in his brother's territory of the Fire Court, it depicted the god Apollo introducing the new art of cinema to the arts of dance, drama, and music. It was a piece of human history in the now very elemental tower, a reminder of the link between the Fire Court and the City of Souls, and a record of the evolution of the space.

At least half the crowd turned to stare as they entered the packed club, enough people that the tell-tale rustle of elemental wings was audible over the thumping bass of the music. Bast's eyes scanned the space for threats, pulling Hel flush with his body to hide the reluctance in her now dragging steps from their onlookers.

Catching himself stroking his fingers along the swirling black lines on the temptingly bare skin of her back, he almost stopped before reminding himself she'd agreed to this charade, however reluctantly. It helped that he could sense her emotions through their connection. As much as she hated him, she wasn't as averse to this as she made out. He smirked as he felt her shiver in response to his touch, quickly followed by her whole body stiffening in annoyance. That made two of them. He really needed whatever this compulsion was between them to stop. She was a selfish pain in his ass and he didn't have time for her drama.

"Relax. We're in love, remember?" he whispered in her ear, resisting the urge to nibble on the sensitive flesh pressed against his lips. The combination of the need to convince the people watching and the mixed signals he was getting from Hel were playing havoc with his self-control. He couldn't resist the urge to curl his wing tighter around her when Hel turned into his body to respond, though. Her breath against his neck sent tingles down his spine to straight below his belt.

"Just keep those hands above the waist, necromancer, or you can be the one to figure out how to explain my baton slamming into your pretty face."

Bast dug his fingers into her back too hard, fighting to hide the surge of anger at the disdain in her voice as she called him necromancer, even after he'd explained the term had been co-opted as a slur. It could've come straight from his brother's mouth. Despite Ra's best marketing efforts, the term soulweaver was hardly used outside his inner circle. He'd heard that same tone a hundred times as a child, always followed by feet that tripped him and hands that shoved him into the dirt. He responded in the only way he could in the crowded bar, conveniently also in the way that would most annoy her, by kissing her temple as if she'd been flirting with him. "Awww. You think I'm pretty. Drink?"

"Sure. I'm definitely far too sober for this."

Bast's teeth ached from how tightly his jaw was clenched as they made their way across the dancefloor. The distraction of greeting the people they passed was almost enough to take his mind off the spiteful woman beside him. Not that he could blame her for the attitude, given the circumstances. He kind of admired it when he wasn't wishing he could just kick her out of the Tower like they both wanted. How had so much ended up riding on the one woman in the city who wouldn't jump at the chance to be seen with him?

By the time they reached the bar, the bartender already had two crystal tumblers of whiskey waiting for them.

"Good thing I don't have any preferences of my own," Hel snarked, in a falsely cheerful voice.

"You mean, good thing we're so well-matched, sweet-heart. I'm happy to drink both if you don't want one," Bast corrected, gripping her waist harder in warning. Panic had descended on the poor bartender's face at the thinly veiled criticism. Bast reached out and clasped the man's hand in greeting to reassure him. "Good to see you, Dee."

He'd subconsciously flared a wing to replace his hand at Hel's back when he reached forward and his annoyance threatened to boil over when she flinched away from the embrace. This was never going to work if she didn't start playing along. "Don't make me start tallying up contract breaches, Hellcat. This is what you signed up for," he growled in her ear, his frustration all the more acute because he was *not* interested in forcing an unwilling woman. He wished she would make this a little easier so they could just get through it. He didn't even want her. Well, his brain didn't. His body was screaming something very different incessantly, but he was determined not to listen. This whole debt and contract thing had gotten out of hand, but he couldn't see any other way to keep her around and the stakes were too high to let her go. He took his responsibility to his people seriously and he was not going to risk the contagion levelling the city just for the sake of Hel not wanting an arm around her. "You have to at least pretend you can stand my touch. The wings are usually part of the appeal."

Hel stopped pulling away at the threat but made no move to lean closer. Bast wrapped a hand around his drink and forced himself to think calming thoughts. It was hard. As soon as he got his temper under control, he started noticing her smooth skin against the sensitive inner surface of his wings and something else threatened to get hard, too. His power, always bizarrely temperamental around her, flared in reaction to his inexplicable desire, casting a soft silver glow that made her look haloed in starlight.

Sparks of his silver soul-magic jumped between them at each point of contact in a sensory feedback loop that was going to drive him touch-crazy. Hel didn't seem immune, either, her pupils dilating as she glared up at him. When she used the excuse of leaning forward to grab her drink to extricate herself from his arms and put some distance between them, he watched in fascination as his power continued to dance across the bare skin of her back along the lines of his mark. It would've been almost invisible during the daytime, but in the dimly lit club, the drifting lights on her body were drawing every eye around them.

"What?" she asked.

Bast rubbed the back of his neck and winced a little in

anticipation of her reaction. "Don't over-react, but you might be glowing a bit. Sparking really."

Hel opened her mouth to reply, but he cut over the top of her in a harsh whisper, the words tumbling out before he could stop them. "If I think you're going to say something that'll give us away, I *will* shut you up by kissing you. This is important."

"For you, maybe," Hel muttered, but she pressed her lips together and kept whatever come-back she'd been planning to herself. "How long do we need to stay here?"

"Not too long. Just enough to be seen. It'll only help our story if everyone assumes we've gone upstairs to fuck if we disappear anyway, so no need to stick around."

Bast looked away as soon as he said the words he knew would only piss her off, scanning the club for threats again. He was surprised to feel Hel's forehead drop onto his chest while he wasn't watching her. She tried to jerk away as soon as he felt the first touch, but couldn't help himself as he tangled his fingers gently in her hair and tilted her face up to him so he could raise a quizzical eyebrow in question.

"I was trying to be good and hide my disgust from the room. It's not my fault you were standing so damn close," she muttered, but the delightful pink colour rising in her cheeks and the hitch in her breath said she wasn't telling the whole truth. He clearly wasn't the only one affected by this insane, and unwelcome, attraction between them.

Bast liked watching her so flustered. It was much more preferable to her usual setting of pissed-off aggression that made Ra's nickname for her so fitting. She was tall enough that, with her face angled up toward him like this, all it would take was a small bend of his head to bring their lips together. Recklessness shot through him as her enticing scent filled his every breath. She'd placed her hands on his chest, but she wasn't pushing him away. He wrapped his free arm around her, loose enough that she could easily pull free and careful to heed her warning to keep his hand at her waist. A distant logical part of his brain was sending up warning signals to pull back but he couldn't, and he didn't think she could either.

"At least three spies and my off-duty guard captain are watching us. We should give them a convincing show. Are you going to bite me if I kiss you?" he murmured in her ear, using her soft hair to screen his words from anyone watching.

Hel licked her lips and her nails dug into his pecs sending a shot of pleasure-pain through him. "I can play nice. This time at least."

Bast cocked his head to the side, watching her. The sight of her pink tongue darting out had just about undone him and he had a moment of regret for the foundation of lies and threats between them. Despite what he'd told her, despite how infuriating she was, he wasn't going to force her into anything. "Do you *want* to play, though?"

"Does it matter? You trapped me in this stupid contract," she hissed.

"It matters. I can hide us with my wings and just let people assume what we're up to. I'm giving you the power here, Hellcat. No repercussions." Bast traced a finger down her cheek and let his thumb rest on her plump lower lip. Adrenaline surged through him as she smirked and drew it into her mouth, biting down slightly too hard to be comfortable. He stifled a groan and forced himself to stay still. "I thought you said you could play nice."

"Just kiss me already, necromancer."

He lost his remaining control as she gripped his hair tight

enough to sting and pulled him to her, crushing her lips to his as a week of sexual frustration boiled over. Power surged between them through their connection along with a rush of shared sensation. He could feel the same tension he was suffering, the same unwelcome lust, mirrored in her essence. Even so, he wasn't expecting her tongue to slip past his teeth to battle with his, nor was he expecting the strength of her grip behind his neck as she crushed him just as close as he did her. The sharp tip of her concealed knife piercing the top layer of skin on his inner thigh in warning was less of a surprise given her violent nature. The pain did nothing to distract him from the growing ache of need in his cock. He could feel her self-satisfied smile against his lips as the blade broke through and he felt a single drop of blood drip down his leg. And all the time their tongues kept compulsively stroking against each and his power twined tight around her, ratcheting up their arousal and foiling any earlier desire to extricate themselves from the situation.

When Hel pressed the blade a little harder, he finally regained some presence of mind and released his hold so she could step away. She still didn't break their kiss. He groaned again as her teeth scraped down his lower lip, adding another delicious thrill of pain to their pleasure. She was a hellcat in truth, spiteful and violent and as contrary as any feline. He had no idea where she would take this if he didn't end it, whether pleasure or pain would win out. He needed to stop letting the ambrosia of her taste distract him before she slipped that knife a little higher or they ended up sleeping together. Either was likely to end in disaster.

Gathering the shreds of his control, he sent a jolt of power into her, just enough to make her feel like the tattoo on her back was trying to crawl off. Hel cursed and palmed the blade to hide it from view as she pulled away, finally allowing them to disentangle.

"Shall we go dance?" she said before he could get a word in.

Bast was slow to respond, victim to the whiplash of her reactions before he realised what she was doing. Grabbing her trailing hand, he shifted up next to her as she strode through the seething bodies around them. No way was he letting her take the lead in their sham relationship. There was only one boss in this arrangement, and it was him. When they were in the middle of the dancefloor, surrounded by people who'd ensure word of their relationship spread, Bast pulled Hel to a stop. He swallowed hard as she turned into him and threw her hands in the air like the other night when he'd watched her from above. Only this time, he could see every place the thin fabric of her dress pulled tight and he could feel the racing pulse of her arousal brushing against his awareness through the connection of his power.

As he reached out to place his hands on her hips, the music shifted to match the beat of the magic thrumming through him to Hel's heartbeat and the first lines of a remixed 'Wicked Game' drifted out across the dance floor. He glanced over to the DJ booth and saw a smirking Ra watching him. The cheeky bastard would've felt the echo of the effect Hel was having on his power through their much tamer connection to each other and he'd tweaked the tempo of the music to match. He'd always been a show-off that way.

Bast shook his head at his friend and returned his focus to the woman in his arms who seemed to have momentarily forgotten everything else in the world as she lost herself in the music and the haunting breathy tones of the female vocalist. Hel pivoted as her hips swayed and Bast stepped into her body until her back was pressed against his chest, the two of them moving in perfect synchronicity. He closed his eyes, sinking into the sensations. It was a mystery to him how their bodies could fit together so well when every spoken interaction between them was laced with spite, but there was no denying it. He'd never felt so compelled to touch someone.

Indulging himself, he dipped his mouth to her neck, brushing his lips across her skin and down across her exposed shoulder. Hel tipped her head sideways to give him better access and he could tell from the liquid rhythm of her movements that it wasn't calculated this time. His hellcat was just as drunk on their connection as he was, which was lucky because there was no hiding the way he was reacting with her body pressed against him.

Years of being hunted by his brother's assassins meant he could never totally turn off the part of himself that was constantly aware of the people around them. He could sense their unguarded curiosity now. He was known as a playboy, but the crowd would have to be blind to miss the fact that this was different. The clubgoers were used to him and Ra dancing with a crowd of women and men, loud ribbing flowing between them as they showered drinks and flirtation around like it was some kind of competition. They would never dance so single-mindedly as he was with Hel. As if she was the only one in the club. Which she may as well have been as far as his cock was concerned. Despite the point of this little expedition being to show off their fake PDA, he was struck by a surge of all too real possessiveness and he curled his wings around Hel's body that was beauty in motion, screening her completely from their audience with the soft darkness of his feathers.

His breath caught in his throat as he waited to see if she would keep dancing in the cocoon he'd created around them, but before he'd managed a single inhalation, his phone vibrated in his pocket. Hel startled against him at the intrusion as if she was waking from a trance, spinning to face him and pushing back to create a barrier of distance between their bodies. Bast bit his tongue to keep his curse to himself, unsure if he was relieved or disappointed by the interruption, and released her from the embrace of his wings to answer the call. He knew she'd only make a scene if he tried to keep her contained with him.

"This better be an emergency," he growled into the phone, shifting away from the speakers toward the quieter entryway.

"There's an orange glow on the horizon, my lord. The satellite imagery is picking up a line of fire across the ocean heading straight for the entrance to the harbour," one of Morrigan's scouts said.

"Fucking Tyson. He'd better not be calling up lava from below the seabed."

"I think you'd better meet him clear of the city, Sir."

"I'll be right up."

Bast was already striding toward the elevators. To Hel's credit, she didn't distract him with questions. She just flanked him as if they really were the partners they were pretending to be. Ra met them near the exit, waiting until they were inside the lifts before speaking.

"What's up?"

"Tyson's coming in on a line of fire, the prick. I need to head him off before he takes out any vital infrastructure. He's right over the underwater cables."

"They do like to make an entrance," Ra sighed.

"Is there any sign of the others yet?"

"I was waiting for you two to finish cosying up before I gave you an update. Mica messaged an hour ago to say he'll arrive tomorrow and the scouts spotted a school of water dragons approaching from off-shore that we think is Nerida's escort. She should arrive sometime in the middle of the night."

Bast groaned. "I knew this was a bad idea. What are the chances her escort plays nicely with the nesting griffins on Matiu? They've got fledglings at the moment and they dive-bomb first and ask questions later."

Ra winced at the thought, but his voice was gently chiding. "We knew what we were in for. It's too late to back out now. You're stuck on this ride to the end. Ana will sort out the logistics."

"What about Aliya?" Bast asked.

"A small piece of her stronghold is en route over the Cook Islands, so the whole gang should be here within twenty-four hours," Ra said.

"Where the fuck are we going to park a floating mansion? Surely, she doesn't think I'm going to let her anchor it over the city. It'd be an ambush waiting to happen."

Hel was still following behind him as he exited the lift and headed toward the patio to take flight.

"Okay. I'll go sort out Tyson. Could you let Ana know our guests are early and then sit down with Morrigan and sort out the least risky place to let Aliya park her house and what we need to do to the scout rotations to cover the extra predators?" Bast asked his friend and brother.

"Of course," Ra said.

"What about me?" Hel asked.

Bast felt his face stretch in a manic grin, taking perverse

pleasure in the thought of inflicting his Hellcat on his murderous brother. "Fancy a field trip to play the welcoming hostess for our guest?"

"How are you going to defend yourself if you're carrying me?" she asked.

"It doesn't make any difference to my power. If anything, having access to the small amount that's running through your body will only help. And I suspect Tyson will reign himself in a little with you there as an unknown quantity. He'll wonder what's so special about you that I put you in the line of fire."

"Gee, thanks. Feeling like my life is super valued right now," Hel grumbled.

"Bast's right," Ra said. "If he goes out alone, Tyson won't be able to resist taking a shot at him. With you there to bear witness, he'll have to rethink the risk."

"Awesome. I don't suppose I could put on something a little warmer before we go?"

Bast stalked over to her and pulled her into his arms with her back to him just like they had been minutes earlier. They didn't have time to delay or Tyson would take out the city's infrastructure just to show he could. "Only if you want to risk losing your fresh water and electricity," he said. Before she could reply, he launched them upward using a touch of his power to supplement the strong beats of his wings and get them airborne. He was already stretching his mind out to the network of souls across the city as they rose, explaining the incoming threat and, more importantly, why they couldn't kill it.

Whispering voices filled his mind as the leaders of the dead from the various soul-sectors across the city checked in. *Are you sure we can't kill him a little bit?*

Not even a little bit. I need you to focus on keeping the infrastructure stable and watching for hidden threats. He'll be assuming the city is a young version of their sentient strongholds that he can either disable by sending into shock with his fire or seduce away from me with his power.

He could feel the outrage of the thousands of dead whispering against his senses. *We are many, not one. And we are not children to be lured with magic like candy or run screaming from his threat.*

Bast smirked. He'd known they'd react to the perceived slight. The trick to managing the power of the dead was respect. And the trick to managing Tyson and his fellow rulers was leaving them guessing how his power and his city functioned. They didn't need to know that some aspects of his power, the parts that kept the city stable, were entirely dependent on a relationship, a negotiation, between him and the dead.

"What are you doing? I can feel your damn marks like ice," Hel said. Her voice held a slight tremor from the cold as the wind carried the sound back to his ears. He probably should have let her put some clothes on. The dress she was wearing was plastered against her, kept decent only by his body behind her stopping the fabric from flying up. She was the perfect distraction like this, though. He frowned as a part of him rebelled at the thought of Tyson, or anyone, looking at her exposed skin.

"Preparing our defences."

We like her. She's strong and she has honour. You chose her well, the voices of the dead said into his mind. Bast was glad Hel couldn't see his shock. What on the earths were they on about? He'd expected the souls to hate her, given her willingness to leave their family to succumb to the contagion

120

rather than help. He had yet to see any sign of that honour they were talking about. Usually he'd say the dead could see a person's nature with more clarity than the living. But in this case, surely they were wrong.

The arching mouth of the harbour passing far below them dragged him back to the present. He didn't have time for distractions. In the darkness, Tyson's orange-red glow on the western horizon had grown to a wall of magma heading straight toward them. As they drew closer, he could just make out his brother's winged form flying relatively low to the water so the molten fiery trail he was leaving behind him kicked up like water behind a jet ski stretching two storeys into the sky. The reflection of its heat and light made the sea around him look as if it had turned to fire.

His brother was such a fucking show-off.

Bast put on a burst of speed to cut him off and met him mere wingbeats away from the magma threatening to damage essential pipework. They both pulled up to a hover facing each other. Bast spoke quickly before Tyson could gain the upper hand in their exchange.

"Nau mai, haere mai ki Te Whanganui-a-Tara. Welcome on behalf of the realities that co-exist in the City of Souls. Now, turn your fucking fire sprinkler off." Names had always had power. He had made sure to acknowledge the Māori tangata whenua, the original inhabitants of the human reality here, ever since Ana's short and tragic marriage to Kaia's father had formed a bridge between their peoples in the earliest days after the Melding. Using both Te Whanganui-a-Tara and City of Souls showed their joint stewardship of this place. Something Ty would almost certainly fail to understand.

His brother's face was frozen in anger, his body impossibly stationary as he relied entirely on his power to suspend him above the water while his deep orange wings, pulsing with light that matched the oozing molten trail he'd created, spread wide behind him. Bast watched Tyson inspecting the woman he held wrapped in both his arms and the silver of his power. The souls that had hitched a ride on his wings gathered close to him, making the air around him glow like it was star-lit despite the grey clouds stretching above them. Halfway between the two brothers, that soft silver glow pushed against Tyson's harsh orange-red light, holding it in place. Bast had left his own invisible trail behind him, one that was settling into place around every pipe and cable as he waited. If Tyson kept his crap going, the souls would prevent any damage by holding the image of the functioning infrastructure in their minds. It wouldn't have worked if they hadn't travelled out here anchored to him. And it definitely wouldn't work in a crowded city where so many other people's minds would've interfered.

He needed to shut down his brother before he got any closer. He should probably want to kill him, too. But he didn't. He wasn't sure why when Tyson's last assassin had struck only days before. He tried to tell himself it was just because the courts would join forces to rain down retribution on the city if he succeeded in taking his brother's life. But deep down he knew it was also that last lingering thread of family between them. The only blood family Bast had.

Tyson finally broke the silence. "Found a human slut who doesn't care that you're a patricidal necro, brother dear? How nice for you. She can cry over your grave when I finally kill you."

Bast felt Hel stiffen in his arms. Her voice was edged in the same ice as his power when she spoke before he could reply. "Claiming hospitality and then insulting your host from the safety of sitting just outside his territory. The bravery of the Fire Court is truly a thing to behold. Your people must be so proud."

Bast fought to conceal his surprise at Hel springing to his defence with such perfect backhanded courtier language. His brother's face had lost its impassive façade and was twisting with anger at her sarcastic delivery. Tyson would not appreciate being put in his place by a *mere* human. This was more perfect than he could have predicted.

"Get your human under control, Bastion."

"She seems to have everything under control already, *brother*. Would you care to repeat your insult inside my territory? I'm sure the council would love to have its time wasted with a breach of guest law."

"Well, if you insist."

Bast cursed and twisted aside as Tyson surged forward, still trailing a fountain of lava. Anticipating such a move, Bast had already encased their bodies in a shield of power that prevented any damage, but the wave of heat that beat down on them was still enough to leave him sweating. He felt Hel reach for her baton at her thigh and placed a hand over hers.

"No. He hasn't attacked yet and he's crossed the boundary now. We can't throw the first punch," he whispered in her ear.

"He charged at you with fucking magma spraying behind him," she hissed.

"But he didn't spray it *at* me."

In his peripheral vision, Bast could see his brother turning back toward them to inspect the damage. If Bast hadn't laid the groundwork of souls behind him, that stunt would've severed their main electricity supply. Instead, reality clung to their own image and the attack was wholly ineffective. Tyson would've expected a direct defence, power against power, not the silent and all-but-invisible work of the dead holding stable. The frustrated confusion on his face was a gift, and Bast took a moment to dip his head and brush a kiss down Hel's throat as if he had nothing more pressing to do while he waited for his brother to finish having his tantrum. The acceleration of her pulse beneath his lips called to him, but he didn't let himself get distracted. Tyson probably wouldn't try to kill him this openly, but you never knew. He wasn't exactly stable.

"How did you do that?" Tyson spat at him, but he'd abandoned the insults. Now he was inside the city's territory, the kind of language he'd thrown out before would be just cause for attack in the eyes of the other rulers.

"If you're quite finished, shall we get you settled in a guest suite?" Bast replied.

Tyson spun and banked toward the city without saying another word, the trail of fire he'd been dragging behind him sinking into the ocean in billows of steam as he released the power holding it. Bast quickly caught up and overtook him to lead the way. In the distance, he could see the griffins that had been circling over Matiu Island drop to the relative safety of their nests. They could sense the more dangerous predators in the air and were retreating to defend their young. Meanwhile, Bast was leading the damn predator right into his own nest.

CHAPTER 9
HEL

I f Hel had been human, she would've been shivering from the cold by the time they finally made it back to the rooftop terrace of Soul Tower with Bast's homicidal brother. As it was, her body's resistance in combination with the heat radiating from Bast pressed against her back was enough to keep her comfortable, despite the skimpy dress. She tried not to think about just how comfortable. Or why she'd jumped in to defend him to his brother. Or why she'd suddenly started thinking of him as Bast instead of Bastion. She'd signed a contract. She was just doing her job. The fact she leaned into the warm muscles pressed against her for a breath longer than was necessary when her feet hit the tiles was irrelevant. And the less said about that kiss in the club the better.

She told herself it was that brief moment of taking control she'd relished, but the part of herself she ignored knew it was more than that. Her whole life had been spent avoiding any kinds of relationship. Alone. Her first and only friend had been murdered by her father's hunters alongside her guardian because of her. Over the last week, she'd had no choice but to make friendly with Ana and Ra, to indulge little Kaia's teasing, and now to let Bast's hands drift to her hips as they stood poised between the lights of the city and the cloud-strewn sky. She was only doing what she needed to survive, but it was the first time that damaged part inside her had ever been protected and included, even if it was all fake.

It would come to an end soon enough. An ache formed in her chest at the thought and she kicked herself for her weakness. Watching Tyson launch his vitriol at Bast had thrown her off her game. The Fire Lord looked like a more clean-cut but bitter version of his half-brother—the same strong jaw, lightly tanned skin, and pitch-black hair trimmed short instead hanging to his shoulders like Bast's. The resemblance was clear. She didn't want to think about how Bast's own family had hunted him down like prey, just like her father hunted her, and she didn't want to think about how he'd leaped to protect the city like that conscience he was pretending to have wasn't just for show. No. He wasn't anything like her and she needed to remember that. She'd been hunted just for being born. He'd been hunted for murdering his father.

They'd landed on the large public terrace of the tower rather than Bast's personal enclosed courtyard. The space was designed so winged visitors didn't have to enter through the ground-floor entrance with the humans. It lacked any kind of balustrade to prevent falls over the edge of the building and the patterned tiles directed guests towards large doors that led to the elevators. Tyson had already turned his back on them to stride toward the entrance and Hel could feel Bast's body stiffen behind her at the insult.

"You head home. I've got this," he said, too low for Tyson to hear.

Hel turned in his arms to peer up at him but decided to stay silent on the whole 'home' thing. Home was the feel of her weapon in her hands, not his damn penthouse. "Why didn't you tell me the real reason you contracted me like this?"

Tyson snarled from the other side of the terrace as he discovered the doors to the tower were locked, but she ignored him and focused on the frown lines forming on Bast's face.

"And what would that be?"

"To soften your rep. Humanise the monster. Run interference with that dick of a brother of yours."

Bast's expression was unreadable but she'd felt the tension in his body when she said the word monster. His hand stroked up her spine and then threaded through her hair until he pulled just enough to send infuriating sparks of need through her traitorous body. They both ignored the fuming silence of Tyson glaring at them from the other side of the terrace. "I am enjoying your interactions with my brother. I don't need to soften my rep, though. I just need to keep the families off balance while I get what I need from them."

"And what exactly is it that you need from them?"

"That's above your paygrade, Hellcat," he said, before kissing her cheek and propelling her gently to the side exit near them that would take her up to the penthouse.

Hel resisted the urge to glare at him as she stalked away, conscious they still had an audience, but she still looked back over her shoulder. Years of running wouldn't let her leave two threats behind her unobserved. She almost laughed out loud when she saw the rage on Tyson's face had been briefly replaced with dumb-founded shock, his jaw dropping open as he stared at the sweeping marks across her back. That expression alone was *almost* worth putting up with the tattoo for a few weeks. It only lasted a second before he jerked his eyes up to her face and snapped his mouth closed. Hel stared right back at him, cocking an eyebrow in challenge before letting herself into the tower.

As soon as the door closed behind her and she was out of sight, she sagged back against the cold metal. How was she going to survive weeks of this façade? The mark on her back was clearly a bigger deal than she'd thought, drawing even more attention she didn't need, and she could still feel the exact spot on her cheek where Bast's lips had touched. She groaned and took a second to let the coolness of the door seep into her and drive back the heat raging through her body. Then she shoved herself away from the support and took the stairs back up to the penthouse two at a time.

Ra was working in darkness in the lounge when she entered, the strong angles of his face lit by the glow from his screen. He looked up as soon as she stepped into view, despite the fact she hadn't made a sound. "How'd it go? Anyone lose a limb? Or a head?"

Hel sighed and threw herself down on the couch next to him. "No amputations or decapitations this time, sadly. At least, not while I was still with them. Bast is showing him to his room."

Ra whistled in surprise. "You must have a calming influence on him, love. I didn't expect him to play host so nicely."

Hel shrugged. "Personally, I would've just stabbed the prick and moved on. He's an asshole."

Ra chuckled softly. "You talking about Bast or Tyson?"

"Both," Hel snapped, and then she sighed again. "But I would have stabbed Tyson harder. Bast welcomed him as a guest and he still tried to start something. Typical elemental, throwing his power around and not caring if he puts thousands of people at risk. Plus, he was just plain rude."

"If I didn't know better I'd swear I hear a little protectiveness in that tone, sweetheart. Maybe I'm right and he's not so bad after all?" Ra teased, and then his tone dropped to something more serious. "I'm glad you were there to keep Bast's hands busy. You may well have prevented a war."

Hel grabbed his glass off the coffee table and took a swig of his drink, ignoring both comments. She had no good reply. She had felt protective, and not just of the city. Ugh. The object of their conversation arrived as she was putting the empty glass back on the table.

"Didn't stay to tuck your baby brother into bed?" Ra asked.

Bast scoffed and shook his head at his friend as he poured himself a drink before collapsing onto one of the backless chairs across from them. Hel toyed with the bottom of her dress and watched him in her peripheral vision. Wings must be a pain when you wanted to relax. She'd kicked off her boots shortly after she sat down and her bare feet were pulled up beside her where she'd curled into the plush cushions, but Bast was limited to chucking his cufflinks on the table to roll his sleeves up and leaning his elbows forward on muscled thighs. He'd let go of his control over his wings somewhat as well. When he was inside with other people, they were usually held tightly to his back and off the ground to avoid brushing against anything. In his current position leaning forward, he'd allowed them to drape around his body like a silken blanket. Hel wondered what they would feel like draping across her and then quickly shoved away the thought.

"How long until Nerida arrives?" Bast asked, and Hel could hear the fatigue in his voice.

She stretched and headed to the kitchen with the empty glass as Ra answered—"She'll be at the harbour entrance in an hour."

Bast groaned in complaint and Hel glanced back to see he was rubbing his temples with his eyes closed. As she watched, Ra shifted to stand behind him and started kneading his shoulder muscles.

"Need me to come with again?" Hel asked.

"No. There's no point in both of us missing out on sleep. And the rest of them shouldn't be as difficult as Ty," Bast said.

Good. That meant she could make herself a hot drink and retreat to her bedroom to spend some time focusing on her mental search for the Archivist and any more of her father's portals. Noticing the same signs of fatigue on Ra's face as those that lined Bast's, she grabbed an extra couple of mugs.

They both looked up in surprise when she placed two teas in front of them.

"Don't expect it every day," she muttered.

Bast grabbed her hand as she turned away and she jerked it out of his grip but paused to see what he wanted.

"Thank you," he said.

She shrugged and took her tea to the safety of her room. Honestly, she had no idea what was wrong with her. She wasn't trying to make friends with them. If anything, she should be doing the opposite. She should make them so sick of dealing with her that they let her go.

Her bed called to her as she slipped out of the wind-tousled dress, and she rolled her eyes at how soft she was getting. Bast might have earned the right to be tired, protecting the city, but all she'd done was go along for the ride. Not that being pressed up against Bast for so long had been relaxing—or spending the entire flight back braced for an attack from Tyson. And she'd been running on nothing but tension and anger for days. Sculling back her tea, she slipped into the clean, soft sheets, relishing the feel against her mostly bare skin. There would be time for searching tomorrow. She needed sleep. She couldn't afford to let fatigue dull her edge. Who knew what the courts' rulers were going to throw at them?

THE SUN on her face woke her the next morning. She'd forgotten to pull her curtains and being so high above the rest of the city meant there was no shade to protect her once it penetrated into her room. She shielded her eyes as she stumbled to the bathroom for a shower. Even the hot pounding water pressure wasn't enough to give her the energy she needed to face the day. Which was why she stood blinking in confusion at the window for slightly longer than should've been necessary as she tried to process what she was seeing on her way back to her dresser. In the distance, hovering over what was once the Basin Reserve cricket ground past the southern edge of the city, was a floating island.

From this high up, she could see straight across the island's surface. The sun reflected off ethereal architecture that swept in curving bridges and turrets. Her brain finally catching up, Hel realised either the Lady of Air had arrived earlier than expected, or she'd slept in longer than she thought. Possibly both.

The reminder that the rulers were converging on the city made her take a little more care than usual with her outfit. She was sure Ana would have put her in another dress, but she picked out tight black pants she could almost pretend were her familiar jeans and a white shirt that seemed the most conservative option on offer. It was crisp linen on the front and see-through fine mesh on the back. Almost everything in her wardrobe was designed to show off that damn mark. Although, after Tyson's reaction last night, she could see the strategy was probably valid. It clearly made people believe she meant something to Bast. And that shouldn't make her feel warm inside, dammit. Unless the warmth was anger at him. Which it absolutely was.

It wasn't until she pulled on the shirt that she realised Bast's mark wasn't all it showed off. The fabric split straight down the middle from her collarbone to just below her sternum, the narrow gap just enough to tease without being tasteless. She rolled her eyes and swore under her breath. Objectified much? If that was how he was going to dress her, she fully intended to use it to torture him. Every weakness could be turned into a strength and she could use this ridiculous connection between them to keep Bast just as off balance as she was until she found a way out of this mess.

By the time she'd strapped on her weapons, she felt a little less exposed and a little more ready to face the world. Another cup of tea and she might even be able to make polite conversation when she met the rest of the rulers. Hel groaned in appreciation as she took a sip of burning hot liquid energy.

"Now that's a sound I could get used to hearing in the

morning," Ra teased as he appeared from down the hall. He dropped a kiss on the top of her head as he moved past her and Hel reminded herself, again, that she was getting soft. Why hadn't she moved out of the way? He wasn't her friend.

"Who's arrived?" she asked.

"The whole happy gang! Aliya and Nerida turned up at almost the same time last night. Mica arrived at sunrise. Ana has them all settled and fed. We need to get you down there in time for the opening meeting so Bast can make sure to piss them off right from the start." Ra was grinning as he said that last part.

Hel couldn't help but smile at the perpetually playful man. She paused long enough to shove some honey and bread in her mouth and then pulled on the boots someone had tidied away neatly by the front door after she left them under the coffee table the night before.

"Lead the way, pretty boy," she said when she was ready.

Ra laughed and headed towards the lifts.

"Where to?" Hel asked as she followed him.

"Bast is in a briefing with the rest of the crew. We'll head there and then the two of you can head to the council meeting after looking like you've been together all morning." Ra pressed the button for the floor Hel had met Bast on the first day.

"Who's the crew?"

"The partnership of the city's leaders. The captain of the scouts—Morrigan, the human spokesperson, Niko, the head magical engineer, Zahra, but everyone calls them Zee, your old boss Ryker representing the couriers, and Ana. I'd usually be there but I volunteered to come and find your lazy ass."

Hel rolled her eyes at the insult, but Ra was hard to get

angry at. He grinned and nudged her shoulder with his own. "Do we trust them all?" she asked. She couldn't help being a little curious about the partnership of the city's leaders. It was rare to have such an even mix of humans and elementals on a governing body, and after watching the way Ra and Ana operated over the last week, she was starting to realise Bast's 'court' was maybe not as hierarchical as she'd expect from an elemental.

"Yes, but the fewer people who know about your arrangement the better, which means you need to walk in there and make yourself comfortable on his lap like a good little employee."

The elevator doors opening cut off any chance Hel had to tell him to stick his suggestion somewhere uncomfortable. Instead, she squared her shoulders and stepped out of the lift like the fighter she was, perfectly balanced, silent, and ready for anything Bast's inner circle might throw at her. She didn't wait for Ra to open the door to Bast's study and she didn't knock. As long as she was stuck pretending to be Bast's lover, she might as well pretend she owned the place. It was another way she could use the position he'd put her in to torment him.

Six sets of eyes flew toward her as she entered the room. She smiled at Ana and gave Ryker an up-nod in greeting. She wasn't sure what Ryker was going to make of their act. He knew her well enough to question what was really going on. Bast was behind his desk and the rest of 'the crew' were sitting fairly casually in various seats around the room. Bast's eyes dropped to the slit in her shirt as she sauntered into the space, letting her hips swing more than she usually would as she committed to turning this ridiculous outfit into a way to outplay the irritating necromancer. She was aware of the others glancing at him to gauge his reaction as she made her way around them. He must have noticed too because he sent her a sexy smirk to play up their 'relationship' despite the confused surprise she could feel from him at the turnaround of her behaviour. She wanted to punch it off his face.

"Found her!" Ra called cheerfully from behind her.

"You're late, sweetheart. What am I going to do with you?" Bast said.

The urge to punch him only grew stronger as he managed to turn the relatively innocent words into something dirtier. He was trying to call her bluff. She circled his desk and perched on the edge closest to him with her back to the rest of the room. May as well show off the stupid mark as long as she was wearing this stupid shirt. She would've glared at Bast but she was worried her expression might show in the reflection of the glass behind him, so she settled for giving him a solid warning kick in the shin with her boot. He retaliated by leaning forward and pulling her into his lap so she was straddling him.

"Morning," he smiled, pressing a chaste kiss to her lips.

"Behave," she said, and she almost managed to make it sound playful as she pushed herself off him and stood to lean against the window behind him where it was safer. Despite how fast she moved, he still managed to stand and extend a wing behind her so when she leaned back she was encased in his feathers instead. She resisted the urge to flip him off and gave him a saccharine smile. Ra made a noise suspiciously like a snort of disbelief from the other side of the room, or maybe that was Ryker choking on his own tongue. He could keep choking as far as she was concerned. He'd sold her out. Maybe he'd ask an awkward question and Ra could laugh at Bast squirming for a response instead of at her for once.

"Don't let me interrupt you," Hel said, slipping an arm around Bast's waist and under his shirt so she could dig her nails into his skin if he tried anything. That was a totally normal non-sexual defensive manoeuvre, right? Adrenaline tingled along their connection and she got the distinct impression they'd inadvertently started some sort of one-upmanship competition with each other. Bast's wing curled tighter around her shoulders as her fingers brushed tight muscles and she could almost taste the challenge in the move as he pulled her closer into his body.

A copper-winged elemental with a septum piercing and bright purple pixie cut spoke up as they settled. Hel assumed they were Zee because they were the only elemental she didn't recognise. The metallic sheen of their wings was broken up by veins of blue-green feathers as if they really were metal and had oxidised in streaks. "As I was saying, I've finished reinforcing the foundations on the buildings the wyrms were targeting. They won't be getting back in. The new bridge between the adjacent buildings here will be fully grown within the next day. It'll be ready well in time for the ball. One of the hapū down south has asked for some help with defences against an influx of pygmy dragons they've been dealing with. They need to enclose their causeways. I'll be gone probably three days dealing with that."

"But we need you and your magic here in case things go wrong with the council," Bast replied, his concern momentarily distracting him from the tortuous circles he'd been softly tracing on Hel's back as the tension between them grew from their silent game of PDA chicken.

Zee stared back at Bast unblinking. "I wasn't asking permission. It's better if Mica can pretend I don't exist anyway. Then he won't have to admit he lost me. I'll be back soon enough. Don't break the city while I'm gone."

Hel turned her face into Bast's neck to hide her smile at the exchange. Zee seemed like someone she might actually like. Conscious of the distracting sense of smugness emanating from the man at her seeming compliance, she took the opportunity to nip at his skin, biting down on the sensitive flesh above his collar. She was rewarded with a hiss of breath and a surge of satisfying annoyance from him that gave Ryker time to jump in as peacemaker.

"I'll have the couriers with magic-sense out and about to reinforce the scouts. We can make do," her old boss said.

Bast's eyes narrowed but he nodded and moved on, shifting Hel's body so she was encased in his arms with her back to his chest, safely out of biting reach. "What's the feel among our human citizens, Niko?"

Hel blinked in surprise that humans rated enough for Bast to check in on, given everything else that was going on. Niko was the Chair of the local human caucus and a trustee for the local iwi. She hadn't had that much to do with him but she knew by reputation that he was good people. The caucus took care of most of the day-to-day running of the city that didn't involve elementals, magic, or defence—ground-based transport, food distribution, housing allocation, human law enforcement. Everything that made the City of Souls somewhere it was not just safe to bring up a family, but also relatively pleasant.

The rich tenor of the older man's voice broke through her thoughts. "They're proud to host our illustrious guests."

Ra laughed. "Good to see our PR campaign is working. I hope it isn't making them complacent, though. Everyone the courts bring will be a spy on our streets."

Niko smiled back at Ra. "They're aware of the dangers and, like the couriers, our people will report back anything suspicious and take some of the load off the scouts. We've also got eyes on the separatist leadership in case they try to pull something while the council is here. Usually, I'd say we have a good relationship with them and they won't make trouble but the temptation of having all four rulers here might be too much."

An elemental with intricately braided hair and dappled azure and deep grey wings Hel recognised as Morrigan, the Captain of the Scouts, inclined her head in thanks to the human. "Kia ora, e hoa. Thank you. We need all the help we can get. With the extra guards on that contagion in the old Civic Square and the influx of predators we've had lately, I'm down a half dozen scouts from my usual rounds."

"We need to wrap this up, Bast. You're going to be late if you don't get going. All the preparations in the tower are in place, including the extra guards," Ana said.

"You heard the boss," Hel said, smiling sweetly up at Bast as she rubbed in the fact the leader of the city was being bossed around by his human tower manager.

"And here I was thinking you were the boss, sweetheart," Bast said in reply. Then he cupped her jaw and kissed her in front of everyone before letting his hand trace down the bare skin of her sternum in a way that sent infuriating sparks of excitement through her.

Two could play at that. She wasn't going to let him win whatever this weird game was. She deepened the kiss, sweeping her tongue into his mouth and smirking as Bast let out a soft moan and tightened his grip.

Ryker really did choke at that and Hel couldn't help but smile against Bast's lips at what had probably given her old boss and wannabe father-figure a heart attack. Her no tongue, no groping rule was well and truly broken and it was her own fault. Whatever. She could hate the man for blackmailing her and still enjoy winning this battle of wills. Not that she'd admit that to him. If she knew anything, it was that life was short and you had to hold on tight to small pleasures because they would always be ripped away. The pleasure being getting back at Bast by using his directives against him to ruin his composure, she reminded herself. *Not* the pleasure of surrounding herself with his touch and scent.

"After you," Bast said as he finally drew away and swept his arm towards the door, still slightly breathless. She couldn't say who had won that particular exchange.

"Have fun!" Ra called after them as they headed out to meet the council.

It was finally starting. All she had to do now was not draw any attention to herself while simultaneously distracting everyone with her presence and resisting the urge to kill Bast. Or to fuck him. Easy.

CHAPTER 10
BAST

Bast couldn't help but stare at Hel's form as she sauntered to the lifts ahead of him. He'd asked Ana to make sure his mark would be on display, but fuck, if he'd realised it would distract him more than anyone else, he might've had her dressed in polo necks instead. The mesh of her shirt was so fine he could see every sweeping line of the wings on her skin, and her pants were almost as bad, perfectly hugging her curves so nothing was left to the imagination. When he'd unthinkingly brushed his hand over her bare sternum in the meeting, it was all he could do not to order everyone from the room and beg to take her over the desk. Not that she would've let him. No doubt he would have ended up bruised and possibly broken. He wished that aggression didn't turn him on even more. It would be a liability in the meeting with the council, though. Any hint he was weak enough for someone to undermine him in public would have the courts' rulers going in for the kill, literally in his brother's case. And that would leave the city vulnerable to them.

"We'll welcome everyone together, but I'll have to play it by ear to see if they'll agree to let you stay. Don't give me any shit in there. I wasn't joking about the penalties in the contract," he warned. "Refuse an order or disrespect me and you'll be staying far longer than you want to."

Hel glanced over her shoulder at him and narrowed her eyes. "I'm already staying far longer than I want to. Don't worry, *my lord*, I know what I'm here for."

She sounded confident but she was biting her lower lip in a show of nerves. The image sparked another deluge of unwanted fantasies. He suspected they were both relieved when the lift doors opened at that moment and saved them from the building tension. It was safer all round if they kept their focus on pretending to be attracted to each other. If only his body would get the memo about the pretending bit. At least he wasn't alone in that. The thrill of excitement he could sense on the edge of their connection said Hel was in exactly the same place, her breathing a little too fast, her eyes trailing across his body in the same way his heated gaze was trained on her.

Bast placed a hand on the small of her back but kept his wings tightly furled as they exited the elevator into the receiving room that led to the council chamber he'd repurposed for the following weeks. He wasn't going to flare them in some alpha display and flaunt the strange darkness that had transformed his wing colour during the Melding or the lights of his soul magic on their inner surface. He already had an uphill battle to change the Council's view of him from monster and freak to equal. Plus, with his wings out of the way, everyone would get an eyeful of Hel's back sooner so there would be no doubt she was his. The thought filled him with satisfaction he immediately suppressed.

For a moment, when he looked on, the rulers of the four courts lounging before him, he was overcome with thirty years of hurt and rage. Ty had hunted him down like a dog for a crime he didn't commit and the rest of them had stood by all too happy to watch. Not one of them had said a word in his defence and at least one of them had been the one to kill his father. He *would* find out who it was.

Mica was the first to approach him from the gathering of elementals over by the curving panoramic windows. "Bastion, it's good to see you again. Thank you for hosting."

"Oh, please Mica. Give it up. We all know he blackmailed us here by promising us Tir. What a surprise the Archivist doesn't appear to even be here," Tyson's voice twisted with scornful petulance.

A chiming laugh rang out from Lady Aliya. Even here, away from human eyes, she had positioned her white-gold wings so they seemed to glow, backlit by the windows. She'd probably wasted some power making sure that glow was there. Always the 'angel'. Bast smirked as he noticed the shadows cast by the latticework of metal that covered the building spoiled the effect, making her glow appear riddled with a darker taint. How very apt.

"Don't hold it against Mikey, Ty. You know he's got a thing about everyone getting along," Lady Aliya said, her voice husky with seduction as her eyes traced down the Fire Lord's body. That was interesting. Bast knew she'd had a thing with his father before he died, as well. He wondered what her angle was.

Lady Nerida ignored them all, staring out at the harbour. Unlike Aliya's, her translucent blue-green feathers shone effortlessly, leaving patterns on the floor around her like sunlight

BAST

filtered through ocean waters. Her long deep red hair was pulled
up high into an intricate arrangement that showed off the wave
patterns in her undercut. The neckline of her dress revealed a
hint of the colourful tattoos decorating her light tawny skin that
spoke to a heritage from the East Asian islands of her territory.

Bast reined in his annoyance at the rulers and took
charge before they could side-line him completely. Like with
Ty the night before, he would acknowledge the human
reality here in his greeting, despite the fact the rulers
wouldn't let a human other than his supposed lover near
them during their sessions. They were the worst kind of
blind and arrogant. The human world was not without
power and it stemmed from the connection of its people to
the land. It might not be as flashy as the raging torrents of the
ley lines the elemental magic wielders used to build and
nourish their sentient cities or send flaming lava into the air,
but it was no less potent.

"Tēnā koutou. Nau mai, haere mai ki Te Whanganui-a-
Tara, City of Souls. Welcome. May I introduce my partner,
Helaine, to those who haven't met her already. Our home is
your home. I'm afraid the rules of guesthood apply even
though I'm a soulweaver, so you'll have to restrain from
trying to kill me while you're staying under my roof. Many
apologies for the inconvenience. Shall we adjourn to the
council chambers?"

"What are you playing at?" Tyson snarled, no doubt
pissed off at Bast taking charge even though he was the
fucking host.

Bast was surprised when Hel spoke up from beside him,
her voice calm and inflectionless as if she was a teacher in
the classroom. "He welcomed you with respect, *Lord* Tyson.

I'm not familiar with elemental courtesies but generally the guests would respond in kind."

"Given he's a—" Ty began, but Mica clasped a firm hand on his shoulder and cut him off. "Thank you for the welcome, Bastion. We have a lot to discuss and the contagion is spreading every day. Please, lead the way."

It didn't escape Bast's notice that even Mica hadn't given him the title Lord during the formal greetings. The title might be nothing more than a subterfuge to wrest independence from the courts, but the fact the council were here was an acknowledgment of his status, which they would've made explicit if he were any other elemental. Bast resisted the urge to call them on their rudeness and drew Hel along with him as he made his way towards the council chamber. He'd barely turned his back on the gathered rulers before Aliya's husky voice spoke up again.

"Goodness, Bastion. I love a human as much as the next person, but you don't gift them a mark like that. They make enough trouble with a normal lifespan. I hope you're not planning on letting her attend."

Bast felt Hel stiffen next to him and he pulled her closer to his body instinctively, pressing every part of them he could together. He wasn't sure if he was using the movement to remind her or himself to ignore them.

"I can't disagree with you on the trouble they cause Aliya, but even you must realise how xenophobic you sound. Does your little cult know you feel that way about them?" Nerida's soft voice came in response.

Bast looked up at the quietest of the rulers in surprise. Nerida hated the polluted mess the humans had made of the oceans in this reality. He hadn't expected her to defend Hel like that, although it wasn't surprising she was taking a dig at

Aliya. The two women couldn't be more different. Nerida lived in relative isolation like some sequestered eco earth goddess, whereas Aliya revelled in the worship of those she'd tricked into believing her an angel.

"My followers know and feel exactly what I want them to and nothing more," Aliya shot back.

"Lady Aliya's right, though. You can't expect your whore to sit with us in session," Tyson sneered.

Bast had spun to lunge at Tyson before he finished speaking and no one was more surprised than him that it was Hel who held him back. Her body shifted until they stood chest-to-chest, her hands gently but firmly grasping the edge of his wings to keep them from flaring out in a show of aggression. The shock of her touch there was enough to return him to his senses and focus every part of his attention on her.

When he stopped pressing forward to try and reach Ty, she released her grip on his wings and snaked her hand around the back of his neck to pull his face down toward her. Soft lips brushed his own and for once there was no challenge in the move. No anger. At least, not at him. He didn't push it any further, resting his forehead against hers when she finally pulled away. Ty was already calling her a whore. By rights, he could be challenging him with a blade, but that was exactly what he wanted. Better to treat him like the pre-schooler he behaved like and ignore the bad behaviour while modelling the respect they should be showing Hel.

"I wouldn't want to upset your baby brother. I've got things I need to get done, anyway. I'll come and find you later," Hel said, loudly enough for everyone else to hear.

Bast smirked at the way she managed to blatantly and outrageously insult Tyson in a way he couldn't call out. If the implication he was acting childishly wasn't bad enough, he would be livid at the reminder they were related. In his peripheral vision, he watched Aliya take Tyson by the arm and guide him over to a circle of couches, Nerida trailing along behind them. Bast couldn't hide the way he watched Hel's body as she walked away. She was a study in contradictions.

"She's quite something, isn't she?" Mica said, coming to stand next to him.

"Don't even think about trying anything," Bast growled.

Mica burst into laughter. "I wouldn't dream of it. She's good for you."

Bast finally turned to face him, searching the older elemental's face for hidden meaning in his statement. All he could see there was polite camaraderie. The moment alone with the Earth Lord reminded him of the real reason he'd wanted them all here—to divide and question. Could he have been the one to kill his father and frame him for his death? Mica had been fucking Aliya at the time and it had come out shortly after the murder that she'd been cheating on him with the now deceased Lord of Fire. Or perhaps she'd been cheating on his father with Mica. It was hard to say after the fact. He doubted either of the men had been aware before the murder. By the way she was leaning into Tyson just then, it looked like she might be planning a repeat performance with the new Fire Lord. Aliya had always used her body to get what she wanted.

If Mica had found his lover in bed with the Lord of Fire, would he have gone into a jealous rage and killed him? The rulers were ruthless and quick to defend their honour, but Bast couldn't imagine it of the ever-composed Earth Lord. Although, he couldn't imagine how he'd ended up sleeping with Aliya in the first place either. He'd have thought they were as poor a match as Nerida and Aliya would be.

Bast sighed and let the questions go for now. He needed to focus. He could question Mica later about the night his father died. "Let's go sort out this contagion," he said, heading toward the couches where the split in Aliya's white dress was now revealing most of one of her perfectly toned pale golden legs as it pressed up against Tyson. Nerida had settled on the couch next to them but was otherwise ignoring the show.

Bast sat opposite his brother, as far away as the seating allowed, and Mica settled nearby. One of his staff had already left coffee for them and he poured them each a cup, using the time to get his head back in the game.

"So, where are you hiding the Archivist then? The sooner you magic them up, the sooner we can all get the fuck out of here," Tyson said.

Bast breathed deep and ignored his brother's tone. "One of my people managed to cuff them, but Tir severed their own arm to get away. It's just a matter of time before we locate them again. Then it's up to all of you to contain them."

It was an unfortunate irony that containing the Archivist specifically required four powerful magic-wielders working together to stop them gating to their pocket dimension. Then they would still have to bargain with the frustrating creature to let them into the Archives. Why the council thought it was a good idea to store their vast treasure of knowledge with such precarious access he had no idea. Although, it had never been a problem until the Melding changed reality's rules, breaking the long-standing portal to the Archives and leaving enough confusion for Tir to evade them.

"And then what?" Nerida asked softly.

"Then we'd better hope we find something in the Archives that will cure this contagion," Mica said.

"We should search the Archives for a way to re-separate the realities and be done with it. We never had a problem with the contagion before. It must be an Earth thing. Leave the humans to it," Tyson said.

Aliya leaned her breast into Tyson's arm and stroked a hand down his front. "Don't be in such a hurry to write them off. They're not all bad. I don't even know that the contagion is worth all this effort anyway. Our magic can keep people clear."

"Only someone living three hundred feet off the ground could suggest we don't need to cure the contagion. Do you honestly think it won't find you? It will reach your citadel one day and, when it does, you'll wish you'd acted now," Mica growled. "Even if we keep people clear, I've lost 30 percent of the farmland around my stronghold in the last year alone and every outbreak is slowly growing. It's only blind luck that means we haven't lost more than animal lives. And there's no reason to think it wouldn't remain if we found a way to re-separate the Earths."

"Perhaps you're hoping to keep milking the whole 'end of days' thing a while longer, Aliya?" Nerida asked.

"I might be able to help with the slowly growing bit. My power can keep it contained at least," Bast cut in, enjoying the shocked silence that followed his words.

"Like any of us would trust a *necromancer*," Ty spat.

"Don't be so hasty, Tyson," Mica said.

"Even if Bastion can shield all the outbreaks, it doesn't solve the problem. We don't know where it's coming from, so we can't stop the source. More will come. And who knows how long his power will hold it. He is only one man," Nerida added.

Bast inclined his head in agreement and left them to their argument as his phone buzzed in his pocket. Knowledge was power and he wasn't willing to offer any more insight into how his worked, so there was no point in wading into this debate. They wouldn't be here if they didn't want access to the Archives and, once they got that far, he could search for a solution himself. He was more interested in using the time to question them. Hopefully Hel wouldn't find the Archivist too soon. He leaned back in his seat and pulled out his vibrating phone, leaving the others to their bickering.

Ra: *Took your girl to the gym to burn off some of that steam. Sure you don't want to join us? She's flexible as fuck.*

Bast almost groaned at the photo of Hel attached to the message. She'd changed into tight leggings and a tank, and was mid-way through smashing out a kick higher than her head into the bag. A thin layer of sweat glistened on her exposed skin. The power she'd put behind the strike was clearly visible in the angle of the bag as it rocked away from her. He shifted in his seat and willed his body to calm down as his brain tried to fill with images of what all that strength would feel like in bed.

Bast: *That's really not helping.*

Ra: *Would you prefer I keep this view all to myself?*

A surge of jealousy choked him and he changed tack. Two could play at this game. Ra had a long-standing crush on the Earth Lord although Bast had never figured out what attraction the staid elemental had to his playful adventurous friend. Or maybe that was the appeal, the ability to mess up the too-formal lord.

Bast: *Mica's wearing that bowtie that drove you nuts last time and he's trimmed his beard. He looks very Lucifer.*

Bast hid his grin as he watched the ellipses on his phone pulse as Ra presumably typed and deleted multiple messages.

Ra: *No fair. I sent you a pic. Where's mine?*

Bast: *Come see for yourself at lunch.*

Ra: *For a guy with wings, you're a terrible wingman.*

Bast: *At least I'm not getting sweaty with him at the gym.*

Ra: *Ugh. That image is not helping.*

Bast: *And now we're even.*

By the time lunch rolled around, everyone was ready to call it a day. The first session hadn't been much more than posturing and agenda-setting. The ball had been set down for a week's time and the business of the council proper wouldn't start until the next day.

Ra and Hel came to join them for the meal of savoury waffles along with the limited staff who had followed the rulers to the city. Each one was allowed no more than three attendants, although Aliya managed to skirt that rule by having her usual household staff on call on the fucking floating island of a castle she'd parked nearby.

Bast cheered himself up from the frustrations of the morning by tormenting Hel, pulling her into his lap and feeding her bites of his lunch. He could feel her vibrating with annoyance while she kept a polite mask on her face. It was almost as entertaining as watching Ra flirt shamelessly with Mica while Tyson glared at them all.

"Is your suite okay? If you need *anything* at all, let me know," Ra was saying, his playful voice lowered in suggestion.

Bast turned to watch Mica's response and raised his

eyebrows. Was that a hint of red in his cheeks? He wouldn't have thought the centuries-old Elemental would be at all susceptible to Ra's, admittedly significant, charms. He watched Mica shift a napkin onto his lap and wondered if it was hiding what he thought it was. He didn't catch Mica's response, but whatever it was had Ra looking like a predator whose prey had just run into the open. He frowned at the thought. He needed to eliminate Mica from his investigation before Ra got too enamoured. He was 70 percent certain Mica wasn't the type to kill the old Fire Lord just for banging his lover, but he needed to make sure. Especially given Ra's approach to relationships. Not that he ever hid what, or who, he was doing from any of his partners.

"Jealous?" Hel murmured in his ear as she watched his expression.

Bast let out a genuine laugh at that, ignoring the way it made people turn towards him in surprise. "Just protective of my people, sweetheart."

His phone started ringing before Hel could respond and Bast grinned as she jumped in his lap at the vibration from his pocket before making her escape as he took the call.

"What's up?" he asked Morrigan, moving out of hearing of the group.

"One of the outposts has called in a predator incident over in the Wairarapa."

Bast frowned in confusion. The dry remote region beyond the range of hills just visible on the horizon was well beyond the area they could safely defend without stretching their resources too thin, and the few people who remained in the dilapidated settlements there were ruggedly self-suffi-cient. But Morrigan knew all that already. "You know we can't respond to that. And now is definitely not the time to play white knight while I have a tower full of people who want to kill me."

"I'm not an idiot, Bast. You need to see this. The report is of a screaming wyrm trapped by shadow."

Bast's mind spun as he worked through the permutations. It had to be the contagion, although what it was doing in such a remote area he wasn't sure. It had always seemed to appear just outside population centres. He could easily deal with the subterranean dragon himself, but this might be just the excuse he needed to get Mica alone and question him. The Earth Lord had offered to help with the contagion already, so it wasn't such a stretch. Bast had never in his life called on the courts for help and he didn't want to set a precedent, but he could argue this was a purely diplomatic move to build relationships while they were present for the council.

"The council session is finished. I'll head out there this afternoon," he said

"Do you need me to sort back-up?"

"No. I don't want the city weakened. I'll take Lord Mica with me."

"Are you sure that's a good idea?"

"Positive."

MICA HAD JUMPED at the opportunity to escape the bickering of the council, and it was only twenty minutes after Bast's conversation with Morrigan that the two men launched into flight over the city from the rooftop terrace.

Bast let his mind wander as they flew. Usually, he would have been focusing on keeping his pace down to the speed of his escort and watching out for predators but with another powerful magic user along for the trip whose wingspan was almost as large as his own, he could relax and let loose, pushing himself to fly faster and harder. The wind tore across his feathers as they headed toward the rolling hills to the north and he couldn't resist turning with the prevailing gusts to launch into a brief barrel-roll. Mica's laughter drifted on the air at his antics. The usually reserved Earth Lord seemed to have let his guard down a little. Bast flicked the other elemental a grin. He hoped Mica hadn't had anything to do with his father's death. He was one of the few elementals not from his city who treated him with respect.

"You look like a teenager on their first solo flight," Mica called, banking in toward him so they could hear each other.

"Better not join me, old man. Ra will have my balls if I wear you out before he's had a chance to play with you."

Bast grinned and put on a burst of speed as Mica sputtered behind him. It didn't take him long to recover, though. "Who are you calling old?" Mica cried as he swooped above him and then executed a vertical drop right in Bast's flight-path that forced him to barrel-roll again to avoid him. Bast flicked up his middle finger at the other man as they both snapped open their wings in perfect synchronicity to stop their descent, one high, one low. Mica's laugh rang out again.

Below them, the bush-clad Remutaka Ranges unfolded. Bast shivered as he looked down at the remains of a concrete bridge. Had it only been twenty-five years since he'd stood in that spot, exhausted and out of magic, facing down the phoenix his brother had sent to kill him and knowing he'd reached the end? He'd stood waiting for the beautiful creature's three draping tails of burning fire to consume him. And then the Melding that had taken so many lives had saved his. It had hit just as the phoenix charged him, destroying the secret resting spot of its egg in some distant land and killing the poor creature. If it hadn't died, he would have. He'd lain there, helpless and vulnerable, as the power of countless souls snuffed out in an instant by the Melding tore through his body. That power was what had left him with the shadow wings he now bore. His feathers had become the absence of light that had gripped the world as the two realities collided, the silver of his necromantic powers learning to dance across that absence.

It had taken him weeks to convince the mass of souls to contain themselves to his inner wing surface so he could at least hide the tell-tale light when he was standing with them furled. He'd drawn enough attention when he stabilised the crumbling high-rises of the city in a wave of power without looking like walking fairy lights all the time.

He could still hear the teasing tone of the soul of the kuia who'd spoken to him when they'd agreed to permanently shield his outer wing surface from whatever magnetic force attracted their power—*You ashamed of us, boy?* The question, and that tone that said she couldn't imagine why he would be, had left him momentarily speechless because he'd been told to be ashamed of his power his whole life, that it was unnatural, dirty, defiling the memory of the fallen. It had never occurred to him not to be ashamed.

That old woman had seen his pain, of course. There was no hiding from the dead. *You can take nothing that is not freely given, son. You hold my people safe and we'll be here for you. Always.* It was the first time since his foster parents died that he felt like he had a family. At least, he'd thought it was at the time. He hadn't yet realised that Ra was already family for him. Ra being Ra, his friend had adopted him the moment he'd seen the pain in his eyes and there was no way he was letting go. It was that moment with the old woman's soul that allowed Bast to let go of his shame and accept what his friend offered. That was the day he'd stopped hiding his power and forced the elemental courts to acknowledge his protection of the city.

The cool air gusting up from Lake Wairarapa as they passed the last of the foothills jolted him from his thoughts. Mica was flying just behind him to his right, leaving him to his introspection. The two men angled toward the coordinates Morrigan had sent him earlier, a limestone chasm to the east of them formed by some combination of water erosion or the mating habits of the local wyrms, depending on which reality you hailed from. Who knew which reality had taken precedence in such a remote area?

His eyes scanned the ground for the tell-tale corkscrew limestone formation that had given rise to one of the foundation stories of his people. The pitted pale rock looked like the twisting inside of a giant sea snail's shell had planted itself in the landscape, nestled into the grassy hillside. In his original reality, it was the site of a battleground fought by proxy where the fire dragons of the sky had been set against the wyrms, the earth dragons, who nested in the chasm. The writhing death throes of the wyrm as it spun itself upward in a final attack had scarred the earth forever. The singed black limestone where the punishing flames of the aerial predator had scorched the area was still visible all these centuries later. The stories said the battle had taken place in the days before the treaty and the courts when the distant islands here were sometimes used as a playground of war away from the young and vulnerable sentient strongholds of the other continents. The fire court still lorded 'their' win at Patuna

Chasm over the earth court even now. They loved a good marketing image like that.

Bast glanced over at Mica as they landed on the twisting pathway of rock and saw the Earth Lord was just as distracted by the sight as he was.

"It's been an age since I've been here. It has a beauty to it like home," the other man said, reaching out to touch the stone. "I keep expecting it to speak to me, though. The silence is unnerving. Do the dead speak to you here, Bastion?"

Bast watched Mica's introspection and tried to assess if there was anything malicious behind the question. There was nothing in his voice but curiosity, but even discussing soulweaving was punished in most courts. "I hear only silence like you. Not all souls linger. If they did, I could've asked my father who killed him."

That got Mica's attention. "You still maintain your innocence." It was a calm statement, not a question.

"And do you still maintain yours? Of everyone, you had the most motive."

Mica's laugh was bitter and strangled by the limestone nearby that deadened the sound as it absorbed it. "Aliya was not one of my brightest moments. I thought I could achieve in bed what I couldn't in the council chamber—temper her driving power-hunger, nudge her to be something more ... compassionate, for her own court at least if not our people as a whole. It might have taken me too long to see I was just another stepping stone for her ambition, but we were equally calculating in our 'relationship' with each other. I certainly didn't care enough about her to kill someone for sleeping with her, and even if I had, it would have been her I would kill. She was the one who betrayed me."

Their conversation was interrupted by a keening roar of pain in the distance.

"We have business to attend to," Bast said, launching himself out from their perch.

Mica flew so close their wings almost brushed. "Is this question the real reason you lured us all to your city?"

Bast ignored him and dropped down through a gap in the trees to fly between the limestone walls of the chasm proper. Mica was too intuitive for his own good, but he didn't think he would give the game away with the others. It was against the nature of the rulers to share information when it wasn't necessary.

"You really didn't do it, did you?" Mica asked from behind him. The wails of the wyrm ahead of them so loud now that Bast almost didn't hear him.

"No. I really didn't."

As they drew closer to where the wyrm was trapped, its brain-piercing cries were accompanied by waves of feeling so thick Bast was surprised it didn't weigh down his wingbeats. While the courts claimed their magic gave them control over particular predators that matched their branding, it was dominance, practice, and the creature's communication methods that really mattered. Even Bast with his magic that was so foreign compared to the rest of his people could do it, and right then the poor creature was trying to shove its tortured pain at whoever would listen. He blocked as much as he could, but the wyrm was old and powerful and the sensation still screeched against his nerves like fingernails down a blackboard.

The chasm was so narrow in places that his wing tips brushed each side as he angled his body to avoid the walls, startling the pigeons perched there into flight and sparking a muffled curse from Mica as they swooped past his face. Below them, so close he could almost touch it, the cool water of the stream ran in the opposite direction, sometimes blocked by the carcasses of bloated feral sheep that had fallen to their deaths and now fed the thriving native tuna— freshwater eels. If Mica ambushed him here, he wondered how long his body would bloat in the water before his army of souls brought him back. A heavy drop of water on his wing from the limestone above almost sent him careening downward to escape a non-existent attack from the elemental at his back. Fuck. He needed to get a hold of himself. He built an extra layer of shielding around his mind to push back the predator's fear that had been infiltrating his subconscious.

They found the wyrm writhing below cascading sheets of water that fell down the moss-covered stone wall of the chasm. Its eel-like body was easily as wide as the full breadth of Bast's own wingspan, and its eyes were blank with pain, oblivious to their presence as it gnashed teeth as long as his forearm and let off another anguished roar. The two men banked to a stop, ignoring the water seeping into their boots as they landed in the rocky streambed.

"Calm down, ancient one. We're here," Mica called, his calming tone laced with command.

Bast watched as the wyrm's body settled and its head slumped to the ground with a splash as if it had been waiting for them and no longer had the energy to keep fighting. The waterfall above them was splashing down right next to the creature's front claws, and the spray that drifted across its face was creating rainbows in the air. It made it look like a portal to the next world was opening for the poor animal and Bast felt deep sympathy for it.

"I need to get a look at whatever has trapped its tail," he said, careful to keep his voice low.

"I'll keep him calm," Mica said, stepping forward to stroke a hand down the creature's snout as if it couldn't swallow him whole with one short lunge.

Bast edged past the wyrm's body, forced to scrape his wings against the rock walls that surrounded them. The smell of decaying flesh was overpowering. How long had the poor thing been stuck there? He'd stretched his power out before him as soon as they entered the chasm, searching for the pool of darkness he'd hoped they wouldn't find. It was there though, that same dark absence that had emerged at the old Civic Square.

As he shifted alongside the wyrm, he could see what had happened. The creature had crested into the streambed from a tunnel that its lower half was still submerged in. When it had emerged from the earth, it must have done so exactly in the spot where the drop of contagion had seeded. Unfortunately, he doubted he would be able to extract an answer from the delirious wyrm itself about whether that was just pure awful luck or if it had sensed the threat and tried to attack it. Even as old as this one was, they only conversed in feelings and images, and its pain was overwhelming everything else.

He knew from his discussions with Mica that most creatures were oblivious to the contagion because it was a vacuum—no scent or light or sound to give it away. That's why birds flew through it even when their dead brethren littered the ground underneath. But the older predators from his reality had magic running through them. It was entirely possible the wyrm had sensed it. It was too late now though; the pinprick of darkness was consuming the wyrm's life force, the tiny stalagmite of contagion piercing the creature's torso and slowly drawing its organs into itself, dissolving them to nothing. The wyrm had enough power that it had managed to slow its growth, but that was only drawing out its suffering.

"I can put a shield around the contagion, but it will probably kill the wyrm. Be ready for its death-throes," Bast called to Mica.

As if it had understood him, the creature chose that moment to thrash wildly. Bast winced as its body smashed his into the rock wall. He was grateful for the layer of moss that protected his feathers from too much damage as his wings were crushed behind him. He bit off a curse as the unforgiving surface bruised his back.

A second later, the scaled weight shoved against his chest relaxed as Mica increased his influence over the wyrm. Before it had a chance to get worked up again, Bast reached out with his power and let the silver threads form an ever-thickening mist around the contagion, crushing it as tight as he could. His body shook with effort as he fought the darkness. Here, far from his wellspring of power in the city, he was limited only to what he had stored in his body, shining from his wings. He held firm. Crushing it smaller and smaller. By the time he felt his mind slipping with exhaustion, the contagion was encased in a sphere no larger than his fist. He anchored the power in the bones of the dying creature beside him before disconnecting the shield from his essence, barely feeling the final twitches of the wyrm's body against his own as the late afternoon light faded to darkness and stars filled his vision.

"I could do anything to you right now." Mica's voice sounded distant like he was speaking from the other end of the chasm and the noise had carried on the backs of the pigeons they'd disturbed.

"Yeah, but you need me to deal with the contagion."

"You'd gamble your life on that?"

Bast grinned, dragging his aching consciousness back to some semblance of presence. "Plus you want to bone my best friend. He'd be pissed if you killed me."

Through blurry double-vision, Bast still managed to catch Mica's pinched expression and was that *another* blush? Something suspiciously like a giggle tumbled out of his mouth.

"You used too much power. You're basically drunk. The hangover's going to be unpleasant." Mica sounded far too pleased at the prospect.

Power. Right. Bast forced himself to concentrate. "I need you to do your thing that makes everything avoid this spot. This area is too far from my territory for me to monitor."

Mica looked like he wanted to ask why Bast hadn't done that with his own power, but instead he just nodded and got on with it. Bast sighed with relief and let his eyelids slide closed. "I wouldn't say no if you wanted to lift this wyrm off my legs either. He's fucking heavy."

CHAPTER 11
HEL

"Uncle Basti's home!" Kaia cried when the click of the door from the terrace interrupted their game of cards.

Hel avoided looking over on principle, but almost rethought her strategy after seeing the shocked glances exchanged between Ra and Ana that they were slightly too slow to hide.

"What did you do to him, babe?" Ra joked, but there was a hint of steel in his voice.

Hel finally gave in and turned around just in time to catch a glimpse of Bast leaning heavily on Mica for support before the Earth Lord lowered the staggering man onto the couch next to her so close he may as well have been in her lap. Mica was still treating her like a relative stranger, which was a stroke of luck. She'd spent almost six years in his territory as a young child, but she'd never seen him up close back then and from his reaction it seemed there was little chance he recognised her as the stray itinerant girl who'd been travelling with her guardian.

"Honey, I'm home." Bast's voice sounded slurred and he slumped sideways until his head was resting on the far arm of the couch, throwing a forearm over his face as if the fading evening light was too much for his eyes.

"I didn't do anything. He just used too much power," Mica said, owning his space in the room as if he belonged in Bast's inner sanctuary.

Hel shifted to her feet, partly to make room for Bast to stretch out on the couch and partly because of the tension flying as Ra tried to figure out whether Mica was friend or foe. Not that she should care about either of those things. She wasn't being paid to run defence. In fact, wiping a debt that never should have existed didn't really count as being paid at all.

"How did you even fly back in that state?" Ra asked Bast, already grabbing a blanket to tuck around him as Ana went to make tea.

"You forget. I've had a lot of practice. I flew in this state more times than I can·count when Ty was sending his phoenix to assassinate me before the Melding. I'll be better in a minute. I just need to recharge," Bast said, still not removing his arm from his face.

Hel knew exactly what he meant. She was no stranger to running past exhaustion when you were being hunted. That ability to survive never left you. She reminded herself again that their situations were *not* the same. She hadn't killed anybody except in self-defence ... and defence of Bast, of course. She still didn't know why she hadn't just left him to Tyson's assassin. At least the Fire Lord didn't seem to realise she'd been the one to kill her. Not that he could admit to sending an assassin while he was supposed to be Bast's guest.

Hel could feel the mark on her back pulling inward, like

the power Bast had placed there was responding to his need. It was ticklish in the same way that someone running the tip of a dagger across your skin was ticklish, with an edge of danger. She could see Ana frowning as she rubbed the spot on her arm where her own mark sat. Kaia had perched herself on the floor next to the couch and was leaning on Bast's shoulder. Hel watched as a faint shimmer in the air like a heat haze gathered where they touched. By the time Ana was placing mugs for everyone on the table, the sensations from her back had shifted to an icy trickle and the pressure was slowly abating.

"That's a clever trick, child. Careful not to give him too much or you'll end up just as drained as him. You're still growing into your power," Mica said, addressing Kaia.

Panic flashed across Ana's face. She stepped between her daughter and Earth Lord, pulling Kaia to her feet. "You've got homework to be doing," she said, dragging the girl out the door with her while continuing to screen her from view.

Mica sighed and dropped onto a seat. "You know the few rebel magic-users you have here aren't going to be able to train her how she needs. Would you really put her at risk like that? You should be making arrangements for her to be fostered at a court, not hiding her."

Hel frowned, screening her reaction by taking a sip of her tea. She'd known Kaia was near the age where her power would either grow exponentially or flatline. She hated the idea of the friendly, trusting girl being forced to move alone to one of the courts to train. She'd heard stories of what happened to the untrained, though. It was more common for parents to try and make do out here on the edges of civilisation than it was in the four courts' territories. The free cities had formed from those who wanted to escape the rules and hierarchy of the courts, after all. With fewer ley lines crossing the land to tempt the young to play with their power and no sentient strongholds interfering, it could take a few years before they started getting into trouble. The lucky ones were shipped off after they had a big enough accident to draw attention. The unlucky ones dropped from the sky, consumed by power they hadn't learned to control. It happened about once a decade. Hel gripped her cup harder and tried not to imagine Kaia's body crumpled on the pavement.

Bast finally opened his eyes to look over at Mica and sighed. "I'm working on it. Ana already lost her husband. She isn't ready to lose her daughter as well."

"She can lose her for a few years to training or permanently if the girl dies when her power comes in. Her potential must be huge if she's already capable of feeding you magic like that. Her mother may be human, but she must have known the possibility if she married one of our kind."

"I said I'm working on it," Bast snapped, dragging himself upright.

Mica glanced over at Hel. "Maybe your partner can help. It might be easier to hear coming from another woman, another human."

Hel resisted the urge to shift in her seat. Mica was testing her, but she'd be damned if she'd tell a mother to send away her only child to one of the vipers' nests that were the elemental courts. She couldn't exactly say that and keep up the charade of her relationship with Bast, though. "Are you offering a solution or just criticisms?" she challenged.

Mica's mouth twitched up in amusement. "I might be able to help. Depending on how this month goes." Well, fuck. His message was clear. If Bast delivered the Archivist as promised then Mica would consider fostering Kaia. He was the best choice of a bad lot. The safest. There was another reason to help find that damn Archivist. Not just to save the world, but to save one specific little girl.

Now Bast was sitting upright again, Hel returned to her seat by his side, playing the game. He placed a hand on her thigh as she settled into the cushions, squeezing gently. She glanced up at him and caught a moment of unguarded expression on his face. "Thank you," he leaned in to whisper in her ear.

Hel glanced over at Mica and saw he was distracted by some story Ra was telling. "For what?" she murmured back.

"For opening up an option for Kaia. If I'd brought it up, he would have used it to leverage more than I have a right to give. His is the only court I could stomach sending her to and he knows it." He kissed her temple despite the fact Mica wasn't even looking.

"Yeah, well. She's a good kid," Hel mumbled.

"She is, but I didn't think you'd look past the fact she was one of my kind. You seem to hate us."

His words reminded her that he thought as little of her as she did him. As if she was nothing more than a petty brat who wouldn't even help a child. Hel stiffened where she sat and let her anger burn through the confusion his tender kiss had sparked. Her tension must've been obvious because Bast's fingers gripped tighter on her thigh in warning, almost enough to leave a bruise. Mica was watching them again, tilting his head as if he was trying to figure them out.

"Well. I hate to break up a good party, but we've got that meeting with the scouts to get to, my lord," Ra cut in. He must've sensed how close Hel was to exploding.

"Of course. I will leave you to it," Mica said, standing.

Hel used the excuse of walking Mica out with Ra to escape Bast's hold, leaving him to recuperate on the couch.

"Thank you for looking out for him," Ra said softly when they were out of earshot.

Mica turned toward them as they reached the door. "He was right. He is well practised at flying in that state. He didn't need me. I stayed below him the whole way back but he didn't so much as falter until we landed. Keep an eye on him tonight. He will feel it after ignoring his body that way."

Hel nodded and said her goodbyes, leaving the two men to a moment alone by the elevators. When she stalked back into the living room, Bast was hunting through the fridge for something to eat.

"Did you get any sense of the Archivist while I was out?" he asked.

Hel exhaled sharply in annoyance, her illogical anxiety for his health combining with her anger from his earlier words to leave her incapable of any veil of politeness. "I told you already, you'll be the first to fucking know," she growled.

"Are you even looking? It's been days," he snapped back.

"There are exactly four strong power signatures within walking distance of the city. One is just the left-over from the Archivist's last portal, and the other three aren't relevant. If I have to trust you not to expose me then the least you can do is trust me to do my damn job."

Ra had walked back into the room during her outburst and it wasn't until both men stayed staring at her that she realised she had given too much away with her rant. Shit.

"You seem to know an awful lot about using your magical senses for an untrained human," Bast said, stalking closer to her.

Hel shrugged, trying to step back and keep her distance

but just ending up trapped against Ra behind her. "I spent half my childhood with elemental couriers. Ryker purposefully recruits for magic-sense. It's a major advantage." She didn't mention she'd never been allowed within hearing distance of any of the couriers' training sessions on using it. What they didn't know couldn't hurt her.

"And how is it that you can sense these power signatures that none of my scouts have picked up on?" Bast asked, now so close she could feel his breath on her face.

"It's not my fault if your scouts can't do their job."

"How do you know the three others aren't relevant?" Ra asked from behind her.

Hel hid another wince. She'd never had trouble keeping herself or her power hidden before. What was it about these men that made her drop her guard so disastrously even while she was gunning for a fight? "I can feel the difference. They don't feel like the Archivist's portal. One of them is that darkness the scouts are guarding in the old Civic Square."

"What are the other two?"

"Why would I know?" Hel said, skirting the edge of lying again. There was no way she was going to admit they were the left-over signatures of her father's portals.

"You will take me to them," Bast growled.

"No, I won't. The deal was that I find you the Archivist. Whatever those signatures are, they're not what you're looking for."

"What if they're a threat to the city?"

"I'm sure you'll find a way to spin it so you're our saviour if they are."

Hel smirked as Bast spun away from her in disgust.

"Would it kill you to be on our side? Just for a little bit?

You know, the side trying to save people's lives," Ra said, as she shifted further away from him.

"Yup. Pretty sure I would drop dead on the spot. I'm going for a walk. I've had just about all the 'teamwork' I can deal with."

"Don't leave the tower," Bast snapped at her.

"Where the fuck am I supposed to walk if I don't leave the tower?"

Ra grabbed her elbow and gently moved her away from the still-fuming Bast. "Why don't you go wander around the hydroponics floors, Hellkitten? They're basically like a garden. Lots of green leaves."

"Hellkitten?" Hel asked as she let Ra direct her out of the penthouse.

"When you stop acting like a bratty child I'll upgrade you back to hellcat."

Hel punched him in the guts and left him doubled-over and wheezing in the doorway as she walked away. She could swear the weirdo was laughing.

RA WAS right about the hydroponics level. It was stacked from floor to ceiling with layers of edible plants. Whoever had designed the space had laid it out, not in sensible straight rows, but in sweeping curving paths that allowed visitors to wander through like a maze in an old English garden. There was even a tiled pond filled with rainbow trout like some sort of reflection pool.

Despite her scorn for elementals, she could admit they did some things well. They always valued form as well as function. It was just as important for the self-sufficiency of this tower for people to be able to submerge themselves in something approaching nature as it was to provide a ready supply of greens and protein. Somewhere lower down the building there was a floor with free-ranging chickens and fruit trees. Zee's skill at magical engineering had transformed the human structure into something more akin to an elemental stronghold. The constraints of concrete and steel were nothing when the elementals could use their power to grow just about any structure they could imagine from the trace elements that surrounded them.

On some flight of whimsy, Zee had formed the planters that lined this hydroponics floor from copper that matched the colour of their wings. The magic that shaped its cells avoided the inconvenient human challenges of heavy-metal poisoning and the result swept through the space in under-stated structural beauty. Hel had heard the magic-wielders often didn't even have a shape in mind when they grew spaces like this; they just sent intention and feeling into their work and let the minerals create their own artwork, their own reality. She could still remember wandering the gardens of the Earth Court's stronghold as a child where the sentience of the very walls around her had created not just a moment of static artistic beauty in her surroundings but constantly shifting fractals that matched the moods of the cave system that housed Mica's people.

The sound of the small fountain splashing into the trout pond slowly distracted her from the frustrations of the day and she tucked herself into a cosy niche screened by twisting columns of basil plants suspended by raw twine. The dim light and fragrant leaves drove away the last of her stress as she closed her eyes, letting the sensations of growing things and life hold her in a pocket of still calm.

When the first hint of a hissed whisper reached her ears, her eyes snapped open in annoyance. Was it too much to ask that she be left alone for five minutes? She froze when she realized who the speaker was. Lady Aliya's distinctive white hair and white-gold feathers flashed across the pool from her. It was her voice she'd heard. The human she was speaking to was so quiet she would likely not have even realised he was there if she hadn't opened her eyes. Aliya looked for all intents and purposes like she was on a tour, pausing to look at the water feature, but something about the situation struck Hel as suspicious.

From her position behind the plants, she only had a thin strip of visibility, which was what kept her unnoticed by the two people engaged in what could only be called a furtive discussion. No matter how hard she strained to hear, she couldn't make out what they were saying until they had almost finished their conversation and were walking back past the spot where she sat so tense her legs were aching with cramps. She still hadn't got a good look at the man past Aliya's silhouette.

"You're sure you have a way to contact them?" Aliya asked as she passed within two paces of where Hel was hidden.

"Yes. If you give me the signal, I can get the message out fast enough for them to evade any hunters," the man replied.

"Good enough. My watchers will contact you."

Hel sat on the cold tiles long after they left, wondering what kind of human would work with Lady Aliya. Had they been talking about the Archivist? She thought about telling Bast what she'd seen but immediately discarded the idea. It wasn't like it would come as a surprise that Aliya was working against him, and Hel didn't owe him shit, especially after how he'd treated her. She wasn't planning on making a loud-speaker announcement when she sensed the Archivist so if that was who they'd been talking about, she didn't see how the human would get wind of it in time anyway.

HEL HAD THOUGHT LIVING with a bunch of competitive elemental couriers was bad, but that had nothing on the endless machinations the rulers of the courts engaged in. Even on the outskirts of their meetings, she was about ready to pluck their irritatingly beautiful feathers from their wings after only a day. At least then their endless squawking would be justified. After two days, she'd taken to stroking her weapon like a cat for comfort, no matter how often Bast glared at her. None of the arrogant rulers around them seemed to care. What threat was a weak human to them? She wished she could show them how strong she really was.

After three days, even Bast's fingers were starting to edge toward where she knew he had a concealed blade. The group was sitting drinking the ridiculously expensive imported coffee and eating scones like they were in some pre-Melding salon, but if anything filling their mouths seemed to only sharpen their tongues.

"You've got a pet human, Bast. Why don't we just send her to deal with the separatists? Let their own kind waste their time with them," Aliya sniped, smirking at Hel over the top of her cup.

Hel's hand stilled where it rested on her weapon and she focused on the woman dressed all in white. The rulers had done an impressive job of ignoring her existence over the previous few days, but apparently that was about to change.

They'd been discussing the growing sabotage and vandalism incidents of the separatists in their courts and it hadn't escaped their notice that the City of Souls was almost unaffected. Hel thought back to Niko's comment at the city's leadership meeting and wondered just how close Bast and his partnership were to the separatists. It wouldn't be that surprising given the city had been a haven for rebels from the courts long before the Melding when it was known simply as the "Free City". She wouldn't put it past them to have even supported the separatists against the courts where it might benefit the city to do so. The humans who made up the guerrilla movement were trying to restore the balance of power long since lost to the magic of the elementals and their ability to control the deadly predators that now stalked the Earth.

Bast's muscled hand shifted to her leg, pressing down gently, probably to remind her to 'behave'. She didn't take her eyes off Aliya. "Are you not living up to your PR image, *Angel*? All out of miracles to deal with the pesky humans? Maybe you could try something new, like basic respect," Hel said, sweetly.

"Do you think your necromancer lover can protect you from me?" Aliya hissed, surging to her feet and flaring her white-gold wings out from her body.

Tyson's laugh sounded from over by the window he was staring out. "Please tell me you shacked up with a separatist, Bastion. That would be too perfect. Can I kill her now?" he asked, turning to the other rulers.

Hel remained leaning back in her chair, faking nonchalance mostly because Bast's hand was pinning her to the seat now, preventing her from facing off with the infuriating woman.

"She's not wrong though, is she? Touch her and I will

take it as a personal attack," Bast said, directing his low threat to no one and therefore everyone in the room.

Hel's breath hitched. She knew he had to pretend to care about her but this seemed like more. She'd been pushing it with the way she'd talked to Aliya and she knew it.

"No one is killing anyone while we are guests here," Mica said, even his long-suffering patience sounding like it had worn thin.

"It's not an insult if she's telling the truth, Aliya. You've spent as little time on diplomatic efforts with the separatists as you have on addressing the pollution on your coastlines. Just because your stronghold floats in the skies, doesn't mean you're above the work the rest of us do every day," Nerida added in her soft voice.

Hel couldn't keep the surprise off her face at that. Apparently they were all running out of patience. She was almost disappointed when she felt the first tingle against her senses, distracting her from the confrontation brewing in front of her. She froze as she recognised the phantom taste of liquid shadow—the Archivist was back. Bast must have sensed the change in her because he leaned closer while keeping his eyes trained on Tyson, who still hadn't shifted from the window.

"What's up?" he whispered.

"Time to go hunting," she whispered back.

Bast pulled her to her feet, wrapping an arm around her waist. "I'm calling an adjournment. We all need to calm down. The council chamber will be locked until tomorrow," he said, before striding out of the room without waiting for a response.

Hel could do nothing but trot alongside him as he pulled her along. The sounds of the rulers' annoyed protests followed them out. Bast had barely left the room before he was on the phone issuing orders to Ra about blocking any attempts they made to meet without him while they were away from the Tower.

"Where to?" Bast asked as they headed to the roof.

Hel closed her eyes and focused on the sensation tickling on the edge of her senses. "South-east. Why are we going alone? I thought you needed the other rulers to contain this creature."

"By the time I convinced them to come, the Archivist would be well gone. The creature can't portal away if they're unconscious. We'll do this the old-fashioned way and knock them out before they have a chance to run. Then we just need to keep them that way until we get them back to the Tower and the council."

The winds gusting across the roof of the Tower were fierce as they stepped outside. At least Hel was wearing more clothes than on their last flight. Her shirt was plastered to her body and she tied her hair up into a messy bun as they crossed the exposed space, but the cold blasts were more refreshing than anything else, sharpening her mind after the morning stuck inside dealing with the council. Bast held his arms out to her as they neared the edge of the roof terrace and she gritted her teeth to hold back a snarky comment as she stepped into his embrace. If this went well, she'd be free. She just needed to get the job done.

She'd wondered if flying in daylight would be scarier than their last late-night trip, but as she felt Bast's muscles tense to launch them outwards and they dropped away from the building, all she felt was an adrenaline rush that left her grinning despite herself. The harbour was glittering under the sun, cerulean waves capped with white peaks where the wind caught the water. The graveyard of the crumbled remains of buildings yet to be salvaged from where they'd been consumed by the ocean looked like the scattered toys of a child from this height.

Below them, the city itself was a patchwork of the buildings from their two realities—high-rises of the human world interspersed with the organic bridged constructs of the elemental free city. Even the human buildings showed the signs of elemental architecture now, though. Zee's work reinforcing them against predatory attack had come along with other improvements—green walls and terrace gardens abounded. The roof of every occupied building welcomed winged visitors and contributed to the city's food supply—some private and some sporting thriving bars and community spaces.

"Which way?" Bast asked, raising his voice to be heard over the wind rushing past their ears.

Hel pointed a little to the left of their current trajectory. "I think we're heading to the old bus tunnel. It's a good out-of-sight hunting spot like the Spiderhive."

"And another warded location that will help screen their presence," Bast added.

Bast's powerful wingbeats were carrying them quickly toward their destination. From her position, Hel could feel every flex of his chest muscles where her hands rested lightly against them and his strong arms wrapping tight around her were not helping the inappropriate thoughts their surging flight had sparked in her. She tensed slightly as she gave her libido a stern talking to. The sooner they wrapped this up the better. The idea of hate sex really shouldn't be so appealing, especially when they were mid-air. Her movement had drawn Bast's attention and he smirked as if he could read the direction her thoughts had taken. She scowled at him.

"Don't get any ideas."

Bast strengthened his wingbeats, simultaneously shooting them higher and grinding their bodies together harder with the momentum. "When you're excited like that I can feel it like champagne bubbles down our connection."

"That's your own damn fault for putting your mark on me."

"I wasn't complaining, Hellcat."

"I am."

"I know. It's part of your charm." Bast ran his nose up her neck and she felt him inhale her scent. She shivered as she finally isolated the sensation he was talking about from the physical sensations of him pressed against her along with the wind and gravity. He was right, their connection felt almost effervescent across the sensitive skin of her back and it was definitely contributing to the hint of giddiness that she'd put down to adrenaline from the flight. Was that her own excitement or his she was feeling? She pushed the thought away before she fell down that particular rabbit hole.

"Just focus on flying, necromancer," she snapped, and she told herself she didn't feel a sense of loss as he stiffened around her at the word thrown at him so often as an insult. The bubbles of sensation turned static and cold.

Aliya's floating home-away-from-home hovered to their right as Bast started his descent. She'd seen photos of the Air Court's stronghold that floated above the Americas. This was just a small shard of that sweeping city, but it still left her breathless as she stared over Bast's shoulder at the ethereal glistening structure made of crystal and glass so fine it almost looked made of air. She could see shadowy figures moving within, crossing gossamer-thin bridges as they went about their work. Something about the material it was made from hid them and the contents of the building from view beyond that hint of their shape, even while the structure itself seemed completely transparent other than the floating rock it rested on. She could make out every detail of the landscape in the distance superimposed behind the ghostlike outline of the manor house as she looked through it.

As they reached the closest they would come to that piece of Aliya's stronghold, Hel felt a brush against her senses. She'd spent much of her early childhood in or around the Earth stronghold, so she was familiar with the curiosity of the sentiences that resided in them. But where the Earth Court had felt calming, this shard of the air stronghold felt like its hackles were raised in warning. She shielded herself from its inspection by habit, making herself seem like any other oblivious human. The ruling families cultivated the loyalty of their homes obsessively and even this tiny satellite of awareness could expose her if it decided to alert Aliya there was something different about her compared to the normally oblivious and non-magical humans.

"What did you just do? I can still feel you, but the resonance changed like you've been dropped into a soundproof room," Bast said as they dropped below the floating rock toward the tunnel.

Hel cursed silently. This damn connection was definitely a problem. It was becoming harder and harder to keep her true nature concealed. Bast was too smart not to realise there was something more to her ability than she was letting on. It was probably only the fact he didn't directly have any experience drawing on power from the ley lines that meant he hadn't already challenged her on it.

"Aliya's flying status symbol was getting interested in me. I didn't think we wanted to draw attention so I hid myself from it."

Bast's arms clenched tighter around her as if her explanation bothered him, but he didn't pursue it. They landed on the cracked asphalt of the long-disused road near the bus tunnel. There was no need to hide just yet because the entrance was boarded up as well as magically warded. Nothing inside could see them. "We're overdue for a conversation about how you're using that power of yours, but now is not the time," Bast muttered, his eyes searching the vacant boarded-up houses around them for any sign of threat as he moved silently toward the tunnel.

Hel's stomach churned at the thought of exposing any part of how her power worked to him. Then she shook her head and followed behind, focusing on their target. If they delivered the Archivist to the council that afternoon, she could avoid that conversation altogether.

The way the looming overgrown concrete walls narrowed as they approached the arched entry made it feel like they were being drawn into a funnel-web spider nest. Hel shivered at the memory of her last arachdryn interaction and she could feel her fight or flight response kicking in. The old bus tunnel was riddled with holes from various juvenile wyrms in the area and a raft of magical predators used the warren to travel out of sight from the dragons and griffins that would otherwise hunt them. In addition to the wyrm nursery, she knew the tunnel was home to outlier nests of arachdryn and who knew what else. The fact the Archivist voluntarily entered the nests of monsters suggested they were the most intimidating of all.

A wash of tingling sensation across her back told her Bast was gathering his power as they approached. It was followed by the magical equivalent of her ears popping as he breached the shield over the tunnel entrance. Much like the Spider-hive, it was impossible to permanently remove all the creatures from the location, but, by blocking all the entrances that faced the city with these kinds of shields, they encouraged them to hunt outside its bounds instead.

The liquid shadow of their target flared again in her mind and Hel launched into a run.

"They're about to use a portal," she hissed, pushing past Bast to kick open the small trapdoor in the entrance. There was no point going for stealth when the Archivist was making a run for it.

She charged into the dark narrow space just in time to see the after-image of the Archivist's tentacled form fading from view as the light of their portal disappeared.

"Fuck."

Bast's low growl sounded from behind her and she spun to face him. He was looking up at the dank wall where another dim light was fading. Scrawled in whatever power the Archivist had was a message: *You'll have to be faster than that.*

CHAPTER 12
BAST

How the fuck had Tir known they were coming? They must've done to have the time to leave a taunting message. Bast glanced over at Hel suspiciously as he drew on the power he needed to re-seal the tunnel and stop any of the predators from getting loose on this road that led straight down into the city proper. Was she working against him? It seemed unlikely given how effective his threat of exposing her had been.

If he hadn't been actively channelling his power at that moment, he might've missed the resonance that set the skin on the back of his neck prickling. Something was nearby that shouldn't be. Something dangerous. He drew his power around him and took the two strides needed to reach Hel and drag her to his side, telling himself it was because he needed her to find the Archivist and had nothing to do with the surge of protectiveness that arose every time she was threatened. She started to protest, but she must've sensed something as well because her head snapped to the hillside to their left before any sound left her mouth and he felt her body tense against his, ready for a fight.

Bast reached to the souls in this quadrant of the city, asking for their help. Their ethereal awareness wasn't great at spying on everyday activities but was perfect for spotting a stray threat in an otherwise deserted location. Their voices were silent today, as if they too were distracted by the instinctive need to scan the horizon. He was shocked when Hel twitched and tucked herself further into his wings, wrapping herself in his feathers like a cloak.

"Kill it. Quickly," she whispered, so quietly he could barely make out the words.

Her keen eyes had spotted what he couldn't until the souls he'd connected to saturated his vision in power, turning the daylight around him into a world of light and shadow. Lurking in the bush was a huge black hound like the one his scouts had found the other day. Only this one was still alive and staring at him with eyes that glowed with blood-red flame.

The monstrous creature realised it had been spotted. Its lips drew back to expose huge fangs curving down below its jaw and it poised to lunge. It had the high ground and, as big as it was, that was going to be a problem. The souls around him screamed a warning like a banshee choir, shunting more power to him until he and Hel were bathed in silver light. His instinctive response to hide the woman burrowing into him for safety had him forming the shield around them to be opaque. When the beast finally lunged, the impact of the shadowy hound against his shield sent him staggering back a step as the hunter's wheezing whine filled the air. The fact it was still alive after such a forceful impact with the burning screen of his power was alarming. He'd no sooner thought that than silence fell around them. But without transparent shielding, he couldn't tell what the hound was doing.

"It's gone through another portal. We should go before it returns," Hel whispered.

"Was that thing the cause of the other power signatures you felt?" he asked.

Hel shrugged.

"What was it?"

Hel shrugged again.

"Is it the reason you're so determined to hide?"

Hel looked up at him and for a moment he didn't see the raging, selfish, hellcat he'd grown used to; he saw only a woman, tired and vulnerable. He left the shield around them, blocking out the outside world, and waited for an answer.

"Its Master is," she finally whispered.

"Has he found you then?"

Hel shrugged a third time. "The hounds don't know what I look or smell like. They would've followed the portal signature like we did. The Archivist's scent was still on the wind. It might not have realised who I was."

"Then why did it attack?"

"Because it's not supposed to be seen."

"Did you duck before it got a good look at you?"

"Perhaps. I guess we'll find out."

"I can protect you," he said, half serious and half trying to spark the kind of scornful, defensive reaction from her he'd come to expect. Anything was better than this antipathy.

Hel pulled away from his embrace and looked up at him. "Perhaps," she said again.

Her short, dejected answers made him want to tear this

hound's 'Master' apart. She seemed defeated. He missed her fire. He even missed her snarky comments. This woman who cowered beneath his wing was not the fighter he knew. As he gathered her up into his arms, it was a measure of how flat she'd become that she didn't complain when he hooked an arm under her legs to carry her like someone would carry their partner over the threshold of their new home. He kept a screen of his power around them for the entire short flight back to the tower, cradling her against his chest even as he pushed open the door to his penthouse and made his way down the hallway to her room. When he deposited her in her bed, she rolled over to her side and curled away from him as soon as she hit the sheets. Who was the Master of these hounds that he could inspire such a reaction when the combined presence of him and the four elemental rulers had seemed to make no impact on her at all?

He drew the curtains to screen her face from the afternoon light before closing the door quietly behind himself on the way out.

BAST HAD BARELY LEFT the room when he was rocked by the screams for help of the souls watching the sector they'd just returned from. Images of death flashed in his mind from their thoughts—bodies severed by a creeping darkness where everything the contagion touched became nothing, extinguished in an instant, leaving the partial remains of corpses to collapse to the floor of a building, organs exposed to the air. The deaths weren't accompanied by the rush of power he would usually have felt feeding his magic, the contagion somehow stealing the life-force that should have returned to the world.

Yanking his sat phone from his pocket, he called Morrigan as he strode back out to the balcony. "Contagion. Sector six, on the eastern edge of the safe zone. We've got casualties," he said as soon as she picked up.

"I have eyes on it. It's growing far faster than the last one. It's hit that isolated low-rise past the Embassy Theatre. The one with the crèche in the bottom that takes the children into the greenbelt. Looks like the darkness is just outside the only entrance, blocking it. It's growing thicker by the minute."

Bast swore and used his full power to accelerate his flight as he took off back the way he'd just come. "We told them that area was too dangerous to occupy. Are the kids in the building?"

"I don't know."

Bast's phone flashed in his hand with an incoming call and he added Ryker to the conversation. "You have information?" he asked the head of the couriers as he spied Morrigan's azure and grey wings ahead and lifted his hand in greeting. He banked his flight into a hover as he waited for the man's response, taking a moment to observe the situation.

"The upper floors are hired out for events. We were running deliveries there this morning for a conference. There're at least 200 people inside. Mostly human."

Bast watched as a violet-haired woman smashed out a window on the ground floor on the far side from the contagion and placed a blanket over the ragged glass before climbing out and turning to take a crying toddler from someone still inside. Three storeys up, an elemental did the same, smashing out a window and launching himself out into the safety of the air before turning back to grab a human, wings faltering under the weight as he coasted further down the street to place them clear of danger before heading back.

"I need every available courier and scout here evacuating humans from the south side of the building. I'm landing so I can contain the outbreak," Bast said. He didn't wait for Ryker or Morrigan's replies before hanging up. There wasn't any time to waste.

He set down in a green space facing the building's entrance that was landscaped with boulders brought from who-knew-where and the twisted trunks of pōhutakawa trees and native harakeke flax. A fountain splashed to his right filled with metal lotus flowers cradling tiny flames. He'd read the business case when it was presented to the city's leaders. It was supposed to "celebrate the elements and forge a gateway to the nature preserve of the greenbelt so the citizens of the city could reclaim its surrounds". What it was, was a giant headache. They should never have allowed it to be used. Even if the owners had argued it would only be occupied at specified times and with adequate protections in place. Bast's shoulder blades itched with the feeling of being watched and he glanced over his shoulder. If one of those hounds was still around it could be hiding anywhere. This was the perfect place to slink in shadows unnoticed among the visual stimulus of the over-engineered setting. He didn't have time to worry about someone sneaking up behind him though.

Turning back to the building's entrance, he saw the contagion had formed an eerily smooth twisting vine of absence ahead of him. Whatever the darkness was felt like absence to his power, but given the way it had speared inward and up through two storeys of the building, he suspected this outbreak was a little like an invasive ivy chasing the sunlight of intelligent life. The faster growth rate certainly suggested the power of the deaths the souls had screamed of was acting as a catalyst. The building was starting to crumble as the contagion ate away at its existence.

He could feel the souls around him trying to retrieve the power of the recently dead from the absence of that darkness as they channelled magic for him to form into another containment sphere. This one was far more complex than the ones he'd made at the old Civic Square or Patuna Chasm because it couldn't be a condensed shape. He was forced to throw a broad net of power, hoping the reverse polarity effect would shepherd the contagion away from the people inside and into something more manageable.

He hadn't achieved more than halting its growth when the thump of feet landing nearby broke his concentration. His head snapped up and he almost lost his tenuous control as he saw Ryker's familiar burgundy wings furling to his back as he landed and released the all-too-familiar woman in his arms.

"Why the fuck would you bring Hel here?" he growled.

Hel barely spared him a glance as she ran for the crumbling wall to the left of the contagion and started hauling broken concrete blocks out of the way to reach what he now recognised as the muffled high-pitched voices of panicked children. She was going to get herself killed.

"You said every available courier," Ryker snapped, running to help Hel as he wove his limited magic into something that might stabilise the building long enough to keep it from collapsing on top of them.

The contagion must have sensed the influx of life nearby because it started fighting his power, drawn to the promise of the beating hearts Hel was scrabbling to reach. Bast froze with cold dread at the thought of that absence claiming the woman so full of life. He flooded more power into his net, heedless of the drain on his resources as he forced the darkness into a smaller and smaller space, crushing it with the force of his rage at the thought of any harm coming to Hel.

He was distantly aware of the continuing efforts around him as he held firm against the encroaching contagion. The shield would continue to drain him until he found somewhere to anchor it. Given the state of things, that something was going to be the crumbled remains of this building, which at this point was only being held together by the combined stubborn efforts of the twenty low-powered elementals flitting back and forth from its windows as they ferried people to safety.

Just as his vision started turning dark, Hel's voice filtered into his awareness, her hand leaving a trail of light down his spine as she reached out to him. "It's done."

Bast let the dregs of his power carry his voice to those whose magic streamed around him. "Release the building."

He shoved at the structure with his mind as it collapsed, ensuring the twisting concrete, metal, and glass coalesced into a tightly knit mound of materials that nothing would permeate. Then he anchored the containment sphere in its depths and finally snapped its connection to him.

Slumping down into a crouch where he'd been standing, he collapsed back against a friendly tree trunk. "Any idea why it formed here?" he asked Hel. He had his own theory. The timing with the hound finding them was too convenient a correlation.

Hel tipped her head to the side and watched him. "There was a power signature here around the same time. The hound's portal. It could be related," she finally said.

At least she wasn't trying to hide it. "Whatever is hunting you is a threat to the city."

She shrugged and looked away. "I'm ready to go home."

Bast suppressed another wave of frustration at her refusal to offer any information. She *wasn't* as uncaring as she seemed. He'd just watched her ferry twenty children to safety from a building while risking death from its collapse or worse than death from the dark power only a stone's throw away. She knew more than she was letting on. So, why wasn't she telling him what he needed to know to keep the city safe?

Somehow, their guests had missed the drama of the contagion outbreak, although he was sure it was just a matter of time before their spies reported it to them. Hel disappeared back to her room as soon as they returned and he managed a quick nap and some food before a message came through from Ra.

Ra: *Nerida's alone in the pools. I've cleared the floor.*

Finally, some good news. Maybe he could extract some information on his father's killer even if he couldn't extract any information from Hel.

Bast: *I'm on my way now.*

Ra: *I forgot to ask in all the chaos, any luck with Tir?*

Bast: *Someone tipped them off.*

Ra: *Well, fuck. I'll check the camera footage here.*

The pools were down in a basement level and had some function in maintaining the heating and humidity of the building, which Zee had explained to him at length but he'd never quite had the patience to absorb. Something about the interaction of the water and the ley lines in the area with the aspects of the building that were grown through magic. Whatever the reason, they were a welcome addition. The pools were spacious, taking up most of the footprint of the building and allowing groups of elementals to mingle with enough room to submerge their large wingspans.

It was unusual for the pools to be unoccupied, but Ra had done his job well. His friend knew he needed time alone with each of the rulers to question them. When he reached the softly lit space, there was a tray of tea waiting for him to take inside and the entire area was empty but for Nerida, who was reclining in one of the smaller circular pools that couldn't fit more than two or three elementals comfortably.

Her semi-transparent aquamarine wings were wrapped around her body so she looked cocooned in ocean light and her eyes tracked his movement as soon as he entered. No one in their position stayed alive for long if they weren't aware of their surroundings.

"May I join you?" he asked.

"It's your pool."

"And you're my guest. Your comfort is my priority."

Nerida laughed softly and the sound trickled around him like the water her court was named for. The rulers loved pulling tricks like that with touches of their power. "And I would be rude to refuse you. Especially after you've gone to all the trouble to speak to me alone. Pour me some tea then, young Bastion."

Bast set the tray down and poured her the steaming kawakawa tea before slipping off his pants and shirt to step into the water that was almost as hot. It had been too long since he'd soaked the strain from his wing muscles and he relaxed despite himself as he sank into the water. They sat in silence for a while, Bast contemplating how to approach discussing the death of his father with the Lady of Water and Nerida seemingly content to wait him out. Centuries of life and her tendency to avoid company had left her with a wealth of patience.

Movement from the doorway caught his eye before he'd formed his purpose into words. The guards had been ordered to turn everyone away. He almost frowned before he caught himself. He couldn't afford to imply any weakness to Nerida. As the figure moved closer, he bit back a curse. He should've given Hel orders to stay put, but she hadn't seemed like she was going to move. The guards didn't know she wasn't what she seemed so they had no reason to stop her. This whole pretending to everyone she was his lover thing was becoming an annoyance.

"Sweetheart. I thought you were taking a nap," he said when she'd skirted the bigger pools to approach them.

"I thought a soak might do me more good. Don't you think?" Hel asked.

He could see the calculation behind her eyes as she tried to figure out what he was doing there alone with the Water Lady. He was tempted to point out there was more than one pool, but he couldn't risk giving the game away.

"Of course, dear. Come join us. I hear you've had a busy afternoon," Nerida replied, and something about the smirk on her face told him she knew he hadn't wanted Hel around. Apparently, it hadn't taken long for news of the contagion to spread to the rulers. At least it might distract everyone from noticing their earlier failed field trip hunting the Archivist.

Bast glared at Hel as Nerida laid her head back on the side of the pool and closed her eyes, but the infuriating woman just raised an eyebrow and proceeded to slip off her boots and then her shirt, revealing the defined muscles of her abdomen and skin so smooth it was begging to be stroked. He looked away as she kept undressing, but it didn't help. By the time she was shimmying out of her jeans, he was hard. He couldn't resist reaching up to brush a hand up her calf as she stepped into the steaming water. The damn hellcat retaliated by settling on his lap, shifting back into him until there was no way she hadn't noticed the effect she was having on him. What was she playing at?

"Jealous of me with another woman?" he whispered in her ear, shifting her a little away from the part of his anatomy that wasn't paying any attention to his efforts at control.

The moment of hesitation from Hel as if he'd accidentally struck a nerve caught him by surprise. Then she snorted softly and leaned back against his chest. "Just keeping an eye on you."

The move left her breasts half clear of the water and it took all his self-control for Bast to force his attention away from the body that was brushing against him in too many places and return it to the Lady of Water who was now watching them.

"I guess you weren't trying to seduce me by clearing the room, then," Nerida said, although the way she spoke said she knew the suggestion would enrage the woman on his lap.

"I wouldn't disturb the balance of power like that. We all know what happens when the rulers start forging relationships with each other," Bast said, seizing the opening to direct the conversation where he needed it to go—his father's death. Lady Nerida wouldn't be above killing someone to restore order if she thought it necessary and she would've been threatened by the voting block Aliya had been forming by sleeping with both Mica and his father. The old Lord of

Fire would have been a prime target for Nerida after the debacle not long before his death when he'd set her seas aflame. The Water Lady took her stewardship of her territory seriously. She had just as much motive as any of the others, despite being the only one of the rulers from that time who wasn't caught up in the awkward love triangle.

"You can't help but disturb the balance of power by your very presence, Bastion. The council is at a stalemate on so many matters of import. No one is interested in letting a tie-breaker wildcard join the ranks," Nerida replied, ignoring his fishing expedition in favour of cutting him off at the knees.

"You would rather be ineffective than admit a fellow ruler to your council?" Hel asked, not bothering to hide the scorn in her voice.

Bast kissed her bare shoulder that was resting against his chest before he could think better of it. That was the second time she'd jumped in to defend him and he had to admit he found it endearing. Her advocacy didn't mesh at all with the front she portrayed of not caring for the city. Only time would tell which version of her was the truth. He needed to get this conversation back on track, though. This might be his only chance to question Nerida.

"An impasse is sometimes preferable to the risk of failure. Although I suspect young Bastion and I might align together more often than we clash. We share some causes in common," Nerida replied.

"Indeed. Just like we shared a dislike of my father," Bast said.

"Your dislike was somewhat more personal than mine."

"And yet yours was noticeably more homicidal. You threatened war with him mere weeks before he died."

The water swirled as Nerida sat upright, her wings

creating eddies around her as they flared. "Interesting," she said after the silence had stretched too long to be comfortable. Then she was standing to leave, water flying from her body and catching in the light through her wings until she looked like she was showering drops of blue-green tourmaline crystals.

Bast searched her face for any clue of her thoughts, but she was impossible to read. Subtlety hadn't worked. It was time for a more direct approach. "Did you do it?" he asked, as she grabbed a towel nearby.

Nerida glanced over her shoulder at him. "I think you know the answer to that already."

She didn't wait for a reply before leaving. What the fuck had she meant? Did she still think he murdered his father or was she just saying she was above accusation?

Hel shifted off his lap and settled on the bench next to him. "Well. I don't think she bought what you were selling. I certainly wouldn't."

Bast growled. "I wasn't selling anything. I didn't kill the fucker."

Hel shrugged. "Says no one but you. Don't take your daddy issues out on me. I've got enough of my own to deal with."

Bast growled again and surged to his feet. Somehow despite all the antagonism between them, it was this one comment that tipped him over the edge. After how they'd worked together to save those children, after all she could sense through their connection, how could she still think he was capable of murdering his own father? "Your presence is a hindrance with the council. The ball is in four days. You can stay in the penthouse until then," he snapped out.

"You're grounding me? What about the Archivist?"

"Act like a child and I'll treat you like one. If you sense Tir again, I'll come fetch you. Not that it will make any difference if we can't figure out who tipped them off."

He left her sitting in the pool with her mouth dropped open in outrage. On the way out the door, he messaged Ana to ask her to make up the spare suite next door to his office so he wouldn't have to exist in the same space as Hel's petty bullshit. He might have to pretend they were together in public, but that didn't mean he needed his meals and down-time ruined.

His house manager must have passed on the message to Ra because his friend texted him an hour later.

Ra: *If you're sleeping elsewhere, does that mean she's fair game?*

Bast: *Fuck off.*

Ra: *lol. That's what I thought. She's sunbathing on the patio if you want to re-think your position.*

Bast ran his hand through his hair and tried not to picture that image. It didn't work. He swore under his breath. This woman would be the death of him. He was more determined than ever to avoid her as long as he could. Of course, if Ra was going to keep up the running commentary of everything she was doing for four days that might be more difficult than it sounded. The man could make doing the dishes sound like a dirty wet dream.

Bast: *Could you quit with the match-making?*

Ra: *Just do her already. You're perfect for each other.*

Bast: *She hates me.*

Ra: *And you hate her. See? Perfect.*

CHAPTER 13
HEL

Hel wasn't sure why she'd tracked down Bast to the pools after the disastrous hunt for the mysterious Tir and the chaos of dealing with the contagion other than that she couldn't leave things where they'd been. The shock of coming face to face with one of the hounds she'd spent a lifetime running from had brought back too many unwelcome memories and she needed to take back some power after the combination of that and Bast's annoyance at her inability to tell him anything about how the contagion was spreading. She hadn't realised it had anything to do with her father's portals before, but she had a sinking feeling the answers they were seeking might be intrinsically linked with her past. Of all the shitty luck.

She'd lingered in the pools long after he left, knowing she wouldn't be permitted anywhere but the penthouse once she emerged. The discussion with Nerida had left her recalculating what she knew about Bast. The questions he'd asked about his father seemed like the hidden motivation she'd sensed behind this sham, but could he really be innocent of the crime he was infamous for having committed? Elementals were experts in manipulating public opinion and he'd certainly played on his reputation to keep the city in line and their enemies at bay. That told her nothing about whether the stories about him were true or not, though.

If Ryker were around, she knew he'd be telling her to stop insulting the man who held her future and safety in his hands. She couldn't help herself though and she, once again, shoved down the guilt she felt at the way Bast reacted to the words she threw at him. Better that than have that ever-present connection between them deepen even further. Their breaths and heartbeats had harmonised on the flight back to the tower and the black marks of his power on her skin had felt like they'd sunk a little further into her, as if they were extending roots into her essence. She couldn't risk entwining their lives together any further than they already were. Those hounds today had only reinforced that. She needed to be able to run. And a connection to her never worked out well for the other person involved; her past was proof enough of that. Bast had enough people trying to kill him without bringing her father into the mix.

She'd barely processed the thought when she wanted to slap herself. The man had bought her like property and then threatened her into this sham. He didn't deserve either her pity or her protection. It had to be the weirdly intense attraction between them that was messing with her head. There was no reason she should've felt compelled to jump to his defence with the other rulers when all she wanted was to fade into the background. He didn't even need her help with them. He just needed her ability to track Tir, and wasn't that working out just great? Frustrated at her spiralling thoughts and aware the popular pools wouldn't stay vacant for much longer, she rose to her feet and stepped out of the water. She wasn't going to solve anything by sitting there. Bast seemed determined to avoid her until the ball and the best thing she could do was reinforce the walls he and his family had been crumbling while she waited.

Her resolution was tested the second she set foot in the penthouse to find Ana and Kaia tossing pizza bases between them as they prepped dinner, the girl giggling as her wings became dusted with flour and the dough stretched into weird amoebic shapes from their play. A flash of movement was all the warning she got as Ana launched the next one straight at her face. She did her best to catch it on her fists to avoid puncturing it and just managed to keep it from dropping to the floor.

"Nice one, Auntie Hellkitten!" Kaia called.

"I'm going to fucking kill Ra for that nickname," Hel muttered.

"Watch your language," Ana snapped, but she was smiling as Hel passed the dough back to the woman.

She couldn't afford to let these people in, she reminded herself. They were supporting Bast and, by extension, her indenture. And the last thing she needed was to draw the hounds' attention to little Kaia. Determined to get some emotional distance, Hel retreated from the kitchen to finish drying herself under the sun on the patio. There had to be some advantages to being stuck in the Tower and private sunbathing with a good glass of whiskey was definitely one of them.

I<small>F SHE</small>'<small>D THOUGHT</small> Ana and Ra were going to let her get away with being a loner for four days, she was sorely mistaken. Bast's enigmatic right-hand man seemed to constantly have an excuse to be in the penthouse, pestering her to play chess or spar on the deck. Ana was in full-on mother hen mode measuring her for last-minute adjustments to the ball gown she had yet to see and guilt-tripping her into 'babysitting' Kaia when she tried to growl the two adults into leaving her be.

For her part, the girl was impossible not to love and by the second day of looking after her, Kaia had already conned her into exchanging hand-to-hand combat lessons in return for a tutorial on making friendship bracelets. What the fuck was she going to do with a friendship bracelet? Her wrist now sported four bands of Kaia's creation, a mixture of brightly coloured embroidery thread and woven black and brown leather. "One for each of our family," the girl had explained brightly. Hel didn't have the heart to remind her she was just pretending to belong to the weird little family unit Bast, Ra, and Ana had made for the girl. The black leather was definitely for Bast and she guessed the plaited shades of blue and cream embroidery thread represented Kaia. That left the brown leather for Ra, much like the contrast shoes he liked to sport, and the final threaded bracelet for Ana. That one was a collection of blue, black, brown, and a deep green not dissimilar to the colour of Hel's eyes. When she asked the girl about it later, she said it was because Ana held them all together.

Through all of that, Bast kept his word and didn't show his face in the penthouse. Hel told herself she wasn't disappointed, that the heavy feeling in her stomach was entirely because she felt trapped and not even slightly because she missed him. Ra only hassled her the once about the way she carefully didn't look up whenever the door to the apartment opened. That was probably because she'd thrown a knife that narrowly missed his face and left a hole in the wall. Ana wasn't impressed.

ON THE AFTERNOON of the ball, Ana hustled her into her room to prepare with an expression that was positively gleeful. By the time she'd spent two hours in a chair having her hair twisted and styled and her face painted with who knew what, she was itching to start throwing knives again. It didn't help that she was wearing nothing but a short silky robe.

"Perfect," Ana said, finally stepping back.

"I should hope so after taking that long," Hel shot back.

Ana just laughed. "You can't rush art, my dear. Now let's get you into that dress before Bast gets impatient waiting."

"He's actually here?"

"If he's not, he'll be getting a stern talking to from me. He can't hide from you forever and the guests will be arriving within an hour."

"Who's coming?" Hel asked, realising she should probably have asked more about this event earlier.

"Every elemental in the city with any kind of status, plus the council and their entourage. Usually they'd have had more of their court join them for the night, but they're all wary when it comes to Bast and the City of Souls. That's fine, though. It'll be more fun with the local crew anyway. Ra's teed up some of The Crypt's music acts to perform."

"And will Ra be joining us?"

"Last I heard, Bast had decided he would bring whoever

he pleased, human or not. So, yes. Don't expect him to run interference for you, though. Ra's more likely to shove you into Bast's arms. If he's not too busy chasing after Mica."

Hel sighed. "Yeah, I know."

While they spoke, Ana had fetched the garment bag that had been delivered to the room partway through her primping session after whatever adjustments had been made to it. She hung it up in the doorway to the en-suite and beckoned Hel forward. "Come do the honours."

Hel stepped closer and unzipped the bag, carefully pulling the covering away from the delicate fabric beneath. It was another halter-neck design that would leave her back exposed. No surprises there. It was the fabric that caused her breath to catch. "What is this?" she whispered, fingering the exquisite cloth.

"Zee reached out to one of the rebel elemental fabricators up north. It's pure elemental magic woven into matter," Ana explained.

The dress was an exact match for the silver that danced on Bast's inner wing surface when he drew on his power, right down to the way it almost sparked under the light. When she draped it over her hand, she could barely feel the fabric. She could already tell she would feel naked wearing it. Despite its incredible appearance, it was barely substantial and she wondered what the chances were that some stray power surge would make it disappear entirely.

"Well. Try it on then," Ana urged.

Hel sighed and abandoned her robe before Ana carefully slipped the dress over her head. She jerked in surprise when the fabric moved of its own accord, wrapping around her back to drape itself around her body. Her immediate reaction was to grasp at the silver moving across her like it was a living threat. The fabric was stronger than it looked. She had no sense that she might pierce the gossamer threads with her nails. Ana slapped her hand lightly and she released her hold. When the gown had settled into place, every thread perfectly positioned, she felt like she was wearing liquid starlight.

Ana pushed her wordlessly toward the full-size mirror and she looked at her reflection. Her hair was piled high on her head to avoid obscuring Bast's mark on her back, but the tendrils of her pitch-black hair that had been left to drift down her face provided the same contrast with the dress as Bast's shadowy wings did to his power. The neckline draped down to a point near her solar plexus, the dress cinching in just below to show off her waistline before cascading down to the floor. The fabric, which still seemed to have a mind of its own, didn't gape or bunch, no matter how she moved. There was no chance she would flash more skin than was intended, although whoever designed it had intended a fair amount to be on display. Even she could see it worked, though. The skirt was split almost up to her hips on both sides, but a second layer of semi-sheer black fabric underneath kept it tasteful with a mere shadow of her silhouette visible.

"The fabrication power works a little like how Zee grows architecture. That's how Bast can look so put together when his shirt and suit jackets need to fit around his wings. The garment shapes itself to fit the body until you want to take it off," Ana said, answering her unspoken questions—how and why?

Hel just nodded, still inspecting the effects of Ana's hard work. Her make-up was relatively subtle despite how long it had taken, eyes lined in black and skin dusted with something that made her look like her eyelids and high cheek-bones had been sprinkled with diamond dust when it caught the light. The most striking aspect were her lips, which were a solid sparkling silver.

"No weapons or combat boots this time," Ana said sternly, holding out a pair of stiletto heels. "But I think you could use these to stab someone in a pinch," she added.

Hel took the heels without comment and slipped them on. "I guess I'm ready then," she said.

"Not quite," Bast's deep voice sounded from the door-way. He was holding a small box in his hand, which she only belatedly noticed because for a long moment all she could do was drink in the incredible image he made in his black-on-black formal attire. It was perfectly tailored, hinting at every muscle that lay beneath. Although how it managed to do that in monochrome was a small miracle. As he came closer, she noticed the magic fabrication Ana had mentioned because there was no dye in existence that should have been able to come close to mimicking the absence of light that was his feathers. Whoever the genius tailor was had managed it somehow, and the way it made the light bend around each seam was what was emphasising his physique so clearly.

"You look exquisite," he murmured when he was within arm's reach.

"You're alright, too," she replied, before glancing around to notice that Ana had snuck out of the room while she was distracted. Ugh. She needed to pay more attention. That was how people got caught.

Bast passed her the velvet box in his hands and his fingers brushed against hers as she took it. The connection between them seemed to flare at the contact as if making up for the days apart. A shiver of energy that felt like pure sex shot across her back and down her arm to where they touched. Bast groaned and jerked his hand away. "I really should've thought through that connection better."

"Yes. You should have."

Another gasp left her as she opened the box and saw it contained earrings that would hang like post-modern sculptures of light from her ears. They were made of thin bars of criss-crossing rhodium that had been spelled to release sparks of silver that matched the dress. When she slipped them into her ears, the delicate structure hung down most of the length of her neck, the sparks jumping in random patterns from there to touch the line of the halter-neck grown.

"Beautiful," Bast said.

When she dragged her eyes away from her reflection to look at him, she saw he was tracing his eyes down every inch of her.

"Eyes up, necromancer."

Bast visibly stiffened beside her like he did every time she insisted on using the disrespectful term he'd asked her not to and then his face turned thoughtful and he smirked at her. "You know that word starts to take on a whole different meaning if you only use it every time you're thinking about kissing me."

Hel's jaw dropped. "I'm not ... oh for fucks sake. I don't have to justify myself to you," she said, ignoring the zing of energy that shot through her as she brushed past him on the way to the door. "Let's get this over with."

Bast caught up to her as she left the penthouse and she felt his arm wrap around her waist at the same time as his wing draped around her shoulders. His hand had slid beneath the edge of her gown to sit snug and warm against her skin.

"No one's watching here. You could wait until we get downstairs," she growled.

"All you have to do is ask me to stop and I will. Scared you might like it too much?"

Hel snorted and twisted to look up at him. "Why? Are you?" The words slipped out before she thought them through and she hated that she hung waiting for an answer as the doors shut them into the elevator. She was all too aware she hadn't asked him to shift his hand. She wasn't going to think about why.

"More like pissed off," he growled, and the low rough tone sent a shiver through her she struggled to hide.

"That makes two of us," she snapped back.

"Good. Then we don't have to worry anything will happen."

"Exactly," Hel agreed, and she tried not to shiver *again* at the challenge in his voice. This was ridiculous. It was like they were hard-wired to each other, their sensory feedback loop kicking back in now they were nestled so close together.

"And if anything did happen tonight, it would mean nothing," he continued, and she didn't miss the hidden proposal in his voice or the way his breath brushed over her bare shoulder.

"Nothing at all," Hel agreed, before giving herself a stern talking-to. The man thought he *owned* her. That was not sexy. At all. But somehow this draw between them overshadowed even that. She should not be entertaining whatever his addictive voice was suggesting, especially when he was telling her it wouldn't change a thing about the situation he'd entrapped her in. "—because nothing is going to happen," she added, belatedly.

"We'll see," Bast murmured in her ear, and his teeth closed on the sensitive lobe before he straightened as the lift doors opened.

As hosts of the ball, they had to be on hand to greet the important guests, which meant a fair amount of standing around making polite small-talk with various civic leaders while they waited for the powerful and influential to arrive. Hel circulated at Bast's side, not paying much attention to who was who or what joke she was laughing at. His fingers continuously stroked across her back, reinforcing the connection his power had imbued between them until she was intoxicated by sensation. She wasn't sure whether he was following up on his murmured dare or if the movement was subconscious. Despite the constant brush of his fingers, he kept his hand frustratingly north of where she wished she didn't want it. Unbidden, an image of him lifting her skirt and discovering the nothing she was wearing underneath flashed into her mind. Perhaps in one of the curtained alcoves around the room that had been set aside for private political manoeuvring and not-so-clandestine liaisons.

She looked up at him as that unwelcome thought crossed her mind and saw his nostrils flare as he met her gaze. "What's going through that beautiful head of yours, Hellkitten? Our connection just sent me a shot of energy that was not at all G-rated." He'd twisted into her as he spoke, encasing them in his wings as he pulled her toward his body.

Hel fought to keep her breathing steady as her breasts brushed up against him. Cocooned against the inner surface of his wings, the silver glow of his power was even more pronounced than usual as it ricocheted against her dress and whatever Ana had painted her face with. She closed her eyes as magic rushed through her body like adrenaline, pushing herself more firmly against Bast's muscled thigh and wrapping both arms around his neck. All logic fled her mind as his mouth dropped to kiss her neck and her hand was cupping his face to tilt him closer so their lips could meet when a loud throat clearing sounded from just behind her. The reality of where they were came crashing back at the noise and she tried to jerk away but Bast held her tight for another second before letting her pull free.

"How are my two favourite lovebirds doing?" Ra's cheerful voice asked.

Hel smoothed the front of her dress even though the intelligent fabric didn't need it. It had re-settled into its perfect lines as soon as she'd stopped rucking it up against Bast's leg. She spun to glare at Ra, not sure whether she was more annoyed or grateful for the interruption. Shit. Grateful. She was definitely grateful. She really needed to keep a safe distance from Bast. As if he'd heard that thought, Bast wound his arm back around her.

"We *were* doing just great," Bast growled to his friend.

Ra stepped close enough to keep their discussion unheard by any guests. "You know I'm team Hel-ion all the way. But you didn't even notice Ryker and Morrigan enter the room. Mica is on his way down. You need to focus," he whispered, barely moving his lips.

Hel blinked in surprise and glanced around. The man who'd watched over her throughout her teenage years raised a glass to her in salute from the bar nearby.

"Keep an eye on her," Bast growled, before stalking away toward the new arrivals.

Hel felt an almost physical tug of separation as their

connection stretched. Cool air met her skin where before it had been encased in the heat he emanated and she couldn't help but rub her shoulders where his mark peeked over from her back.

"The connection doesn't usually work that way," Ra said, still keeping his voice low.

"What way?" Hel asked, dragging her eyes away from Bast's retreating form.

"I only get a sense of him if I concentrate hard and even then all I get is a hint of his heartbeat and whether or not he's in trouble. It's the same for his sense of me. The two of you ... anyone watching can tell there is power weaving between you, through you. And anyone who knows him well can see the effect it's having."

"It's so visceral. It's like a part of him's inside me. And not the part it might be fun to have inside me," Hel said absently, still fighting to pull her mind all the way back to reality.

She winced as soon as she realised what she'd said and Ra threw back his head and roared with laughter, drawing the attention of the groups around them.

"If I didn't know it was impossible, I'd say you were succumbing to a mating bond. What's so different about you?" he asked once he'd stopped laughing and the people nearby had returned to their conversations.

The question chilled Hel's blood and anchored her scattered thoughts instantly. Ra was far too observant. Was the fact she wasn't human exacerbating this intense reaction between them? What effect would it have if their connection continued to grow? Conventional wisdom was that a mating bond shouldn't be possible between species, but maybe that was just because most humans lacked the necessary magic to make it stick. She definitely wasn't lacking in magic. A mating bond was the integration of two elementals' powers in a way that intrinsically linked their essences and it was pretty uncommon because it was so invasive. On rare occasions, she'd heard it could happen without the express decision of the elementals involved, but what if her biology was messing it up somehow? Fuck. She needed to lock down whatever this was. And now her secret was at risk from Ra trying to get to the bottom of what was going on.

"Blame the victim why don't you. Why does it have to be something I did? Bast's the one that branded a mark the size of a small child across my back."

She could see Ra wasn't fooled by her response. "This isn't the time or place to discuss this," he said, finally.

Hel shrugged and pivoted to head toward the bar and what she hoped was enough hard spirits to get her through this train wreck. She could feel the eyes of everyone around her locked on the marks on her back. The combination of that with the fact she could barely feel the weight of the gown left her feeling indecently exposed. When the bartender distractedly put the whiskey bottle down next to her glass, she topped it up another three fingers.

"Settling in I see, Hel. You look quite the lady," Ryker said from her right.

She took a gulp of whiskey that sent burning fire down her throat despite its smoothness and turned to face him. Her old boss was inspecting her outfit, but he wasn't checking her out so much as openly incredulous she would wear something like that. He knew her too well. She swallowed the rude retort on the tip of her tongue when she saw Lord Mica standing by his side. A quick search of the room revealed Bast was deep in conversation with Lady Nerida, but he was watching her with a slight frown as if he was worried what she might say.

"You know me. Always up for free booze," she said, purposefully misunderstanding Ryker's comment.

"She's perfectly matched to him, don't you think?" Ra cut in.

"Bastion has always surrounded himself with beauty," Mica said, his eyes fixed on Ra.

Hel looked over at Ra and was amused to see a faint pink tinge to his cheeks. It was about time he was dished out some of his own medicine.

"Ra was just trying to talk me into some fresh air on the roof terraces that have been decorated next-door, but I don't think Bast can spare me," Hel said, ignoring the hidden kick Ra directed at her ankle. The rest of the city was having its own celebration on the public rooftops and the bridges between buildings Zee had grown, the masses carefully directed away from the danger of the contagion mere blocks away. She knew they'd picked this location for the ball because it was on one of the lower floors with an open balcony that allowed the elementals to launch out into the city and join the less formal revelry happening elsewhere.

"So keen to get away? The night has barely started," Mica said with a slight frown.

"It'd be too long a trip on foot anyway," Ra said, head cocked to see if Mica would take the bait.

Hel smirked at the obvious opening that went right over the oblivious Earth Lord's head. "I'm sure you could catch a ride if you wanted to go, Ra. Maybe one of those muscly commerce chamber types over there," she said, pointing to a small gathering of elementals.

Mica scowled at her and she gave him her best innocent

look. He cleared his throat. "I could use some fresh air myself. Perhaps I could accompany you."

"Have fun, kids!" she called, as Mica offered his arm to escort Ra to the balcony. The human looked like a cat who'd got the cream.

Ryker was struggling to contain his laughter when she returned her attention to him. "What?" she asked.

"Only you would dare something like that with an elemental lord," he chuckled.

"Something like what?" Bast asked, coming up behind her and wrapping both arms around her waist.

"Hel just manoeuvred Lord Mica into taking your side-kick on a date."

"To be fair, he didn't need all that much convincing," Hel said.

"And here I was thinking you didn't have a sweet bone in your body," Bast said, kissing her neck and sending those thought-destroying shivers through her body again.

Ryker laughed even louder at that. "Oh good. I was worried you had her under a compulsion or something to play so nicely. I'm glad to hear she's still the same old brat to you as well."

"I wouldn't dream of it. Besides, there's nothing like a woman holding a blade to your balls to spice things up," Bast said.

Hel rolled her eyes and threw an elbow back into his ribs hard enough to make him grunt.

"See?" he laughed.

Ryker grinned and shook his head. "You're a braver man than me."

"You two know I'm standing right here, right?" Hel snapped.

"Let an old man be happy for his charge, Helaine."

"You're immortal. Old isn't even a thing for you. And I was never your fucking charge, unless you mean that in the sense of charging extortionate interest."

Ryker sighed and the smile slipped from his face. "Believe what you like, sweetheart. I'm happy for you regardless. Now if you'll excuse me, I need to go corner someone about a breach of contract," he said, clasping Bast's hand briefly before he left.

Hel took another large sip of her whiskey and then yelped in complaint as Bast scooped her glass from her hand and finished it off.

"Hey! That's mine."

He grinned and pulled her toward the dancefloor. "You're edgy. Come and work off some of that angry energy."

"That's the last thing I want to do," Hel snapped.

"Liar," Bast said as he drew her into his arms and set them moving to the beat of the music. His wings were creeping further around her again and she could feel the throbbing of his power against hers mirrored in the throbbing of her need for him.

"Fine. One dance," she said, as her body relaxed into the rhythm despite herself.

One of her hands drifted down his chest, feeling the taut muscle beneath his shirt. She slipped it inside his jacket without thinking and then froze. It always seemed to happen this way with him. If she wasn't on constant guard, her body acted without any direction on her part to seek out what it wanted.

She felt his heartbeat accelerate through their connection as his hands tightened around her waist and one slipped down to her hip, pulling her pelvis closer. She buried her face in the side of his neck, avoiding making eye contact because she knew if she did that she'd kiss him for real and that was not part of the plan.

How the fuck was she going to stop anything happening between them? And did she even want to?

CHAPTER 14
BAST

Bast drew in a deep breath to try and calm the ragged edge to his breathing and was rewarded with a lungful of pure temptation. How could a woman smell so intoxicating? Her lips were pressed to his neck but they were still, unlike the rest of her body, which was undulating against him like pure sin to the music. He groaned as his fingers skimmed down her body and he realised she was wearing nothing underneath her dress.

Fuck this. He couldn't take it any longer. He needed to get this woman out of his system. Their movement had taken them near to one of the curtained alcoves. Hoisting her up into his arms, he felt a surge of satisfaction when she instinctively wrapped her legs around his waist as he strode the three paces to privacy and jerked the thick black velvet curtains closed behind them.

"What are you doing?" Hel gasped, belatedly trying to get back to her feet.

He kept his hands under her thighs, holding her up for now, and kept walking until her bare back was pressed against the curving cold glass of the floor-to-ceiling window. He'd barely thought about tipping her stubborn face up to kiss him when he felt the slightest draft at his back and dropped her to the ground to spin and face the threat.

"I hope I'm not interrupting," Tyson drawled, re-closing the curtains behind him. "Mica tells me I need to make nice, so here I am." He was carrying three glasses of red wine, which he put down on the small side table next to the only furniture in the small space, a chaise longue Bast had intended to lay Hel down on to see if she tasted as intoxicating as she smelled.

Bast drew his power around him, letting the tell-tale silver glow give him away as his wings spread wide to screen Hel from his half-brother's view. He used his magic to shift his sight until he could make out the thin veil of fire Ty was wearing like armour. A flash in the corner of his eye drew his attention back to the glasses and he noticed two of them glowing with a muddy mixture of silver and blood-red in his mind.

What is it? he asked the souls that fed his sight.

Blood of a dead phoenix, they replied and for a moment he was overwhelmed by their keening sadness as they mourned the creature's death.

Tyson probably hadn't given a second thought to the wisdom of trying to hide a substance taken from the dead from a soulweaver. The poisonous blood would have been undetectable to a normal elemental. His mind spun at the thought. Was that how his father had died? Cause of death had never been established because of the damage caused when his corpse went dancing in the street. It would make a lot of sense. It was the perfect crime. One Tyson was

215

uniquely placed to accomplish with the nests of phoenix near his volcano stronghold.

"Did you really need to try and poison us both, brother? What did Hel ever do to you?"

The woman in question was pushing around his wings as he spoke, of course. She had no sense of self-preservation. Nor did she understand the distraction she caused when she pressed against his sensitive wings, the gown he'd had made for her barely registering as a barrier between them. The fact that had even registered when his homicidal brother was standing right in front of him trying to kill him had him seriously concerned.

Ty's face showed his surprise for a moment before his mouth twisted in a sneer. "Trust you to sense a dead thing."

"I hope you didn't kill the poor creature on my account. That seems a bit heartless even for you. Is that how you killed our father?"

Tyson's face turned a shade of red that was deeper than any of the fires he conjured. "How dare you?" he hissed, and then he was lunging forward, the flash of a blade in his hand forcing Bast to shove Hel out of harm's way rather than defend himself.

The incision of the knife into his bicep barely registered as he changed his momentum to jerk himself free and send his other elbow crashing towards Ty's face. He grunted in pain as the invisible flames coating his brother seared a hole through his clothes and left the sickly sweet scent of his burnt skin on the air. The souls around him responded to his subconscious pull by coating him in a barrier of ice-cold death magic that protected him from any further damage. Ty must have expected the flames to make him back off because he hesitated as he recovered from the elbow strike. Bast took advantage of the reprieve by kicking Ty's knee out from under him and wrapping him into a choke-hold.

"Did you kill him? Is that why you sent all those assassins after me? So you wouldn't be found out? Were you that desperate to be lord?" he growled as he tightened his arm around Ty's neck and started to squeeze.

"If you're looking for a response I think you're gonna need to ease up there, love," Hel said, her tone saying she didn't care one way or the other if he did.

Bast growled and loosened his hold. The sound of Ty dragging air into his lungs grated against his need for revenge.

Ty's voice was strained and gravelly when he answered and he addressed his words to Hel. "Unlike my brother, I loved our father. If you're stupid enough to buy this act, you deserve everything you get for sleeping with a necromancer," he spat, the last word strangled as Bast tightened his hold again.

"I love a dead elemental ruler as much as the next girl, but I'm guessing this might not be your smartest move," Hel said softly.

Bast forced back the memories of years being chased down like a rabid dog by Ty's assassins and made himself meet her gaze. Her deep green eyes looked concerned instead of angry and that threw him enough for him to release his brother and shove him towards the curtain. Ty didn't even look back as he stormed out, pausing only just long enough to wave his hands at the glasses and burn their contents to vapour, destroying any evidence of his attempted crime. The heat made the crystal stemware shatter, sending shards of glass ricocheting like shrapnel across the room. Bast grabbed Hel and twisted to protect her with his body, which was still shielded by his power. The music from the DJ outside faded and the sounds of crystal tinkling as it fell to the floor filled the silence.

"You okay?" Bast asked.

"Yeah," Hel said, reaching up to brush a stray piece of glass from his arm. Her fingers came away red from his stab wound. "But you're not."

"I'll be fine as soon as I find someone to guard you while I go kill that fucker for trying to poison me in my own goddamn home," Bast growled.

"Why don't you call Ra? Get a second opinion on your best course of action," Hel said carefully.

"He was going to kill you!" Bast whisper-shouted in exasperation. She could have died! All that beautiful strength snuffed out in an instant before he'd even had a chance to explore what this relentless need was between them.

Hel's eyebrows raised in surprise. "Is that what's got you so mad?"

She reached up and pulled his mouth down to hers. He groaned as her tongue pushed into his mouth and he tasted her, all whiskey and sass. Any other thoughts were lost to the sensation of her body pressed against him, her lips against his, his fingers raising goose-bumps on her skin.

Too soon, she broke off and they stood forehead to forehead, both of them panting for breath. "I'm fine. Call Ra," she said.

"No one's watching here. You could have waited until we were back out there," Bast said, mirroring her comment from the start of the night.

"Scared you might like it?"

His response was interrupted by the curtains moving again. "What the fuck happened this time?" Ra asked from the entry. Then he took in the way they were standing together, heads just touching. "Oh, shit. You two are too cute."

"How was your date?" Hel shot back, breaking their physical connection.

Ra arched a playful eyebrow and backed out of the alcove laughing. Bast knew he wouldn't have hunted him down if it wasn't something important, though. He placed a hand on Hel's lower back and steered her back toward the noise and light of the ballroom, both of them staying silent on what had just passed between them.

Ra hadn't gone far. He was leaning on the wall of the next alcove over, still in the shadows away from the people dancing. As Bast approached, he could just make out a female moan from nearby. It was that time of the night when people started pairing off, or maybe he and Hel had started a trend.

"What's up?" Bast asked, ignoring the distraction.

"Aliya hasn't shown up. She's hosting a separate ball on the island we let her park here. The scouts spotted her people flying humans up there."

"She's trying to sow dissent. She and the council banned me from inviting humans here so it makes it look like she's rebelling against my 'prejudice'."

"She'll be recruiting to that fucked up cult of hers as well," Ra added.

"She's handed me the perfect excuse to get her alone and go on the attack then."

"To help those humans or so you can question her for your personal inquisition?" Hel's voice chipped in.

"Both," Bast snapped, annoyed they were back to this animosity so quickly. Every time he thought he was getting through to her, she seemed to panic and throw insults at him.

"Whatever. You pretend you're so selfless and saving the world but it's obvious what you're doing here and it's all about you," Hel said, and then she was striding away back to the bar.

Bast watched her go, her sleek body moving like the predator she was as that dress he was regretting making her wear showed every curve and exposed the flashing lines of his mark on her back to the room. Damn that woman.

"She's got you good," Ra said.

"She's a means to an end."

"Sure thing, bro. Whatever you say."

Bast glared at his friend. "I'm going to go deal with Aliya."

"Sure you don't want to take some back-up with you?"

"Our people are visiting her already. If they wouldn't lift a finger to save me then I don't deserve my position here."

"Don't be naïve. We might be on okay terms with the separatists, but we have our share of malcontents. You'll be outnumbered there."

"I'll be fine. I have an army of the dead behind me, remember?"

"There's only so much they can do. And we haven't allocated as many souls to that sector because there's so little left there. Make sure you're prepared."

"Love you too," Bast said, already making his way to the balcony to leave. But he did as Ra asked and strengthened his connection to the souls here who'd shielded him from Ty's flames.

The cold shock of the wind tugging at his feathers as he stepped outside cleared the last of Hel's warmth from his system. He'd felt her eyes watching him as he left, clinging to her judgements. It was past time he had it out properly with Ryker about her past. He launched himself out into the air and focused on powering up above the cityscape, forcing himself to clear his mind with each surging wingbeat.

Aliya's 'floating status symbol' as Hel called it, outshone any other lights nearby, looking like a white-hot burning meteorite had fallen to earth and paused just before it would have hit its surface and annihilated the city. It was entirely intentional. Aliya loved a good Armageddon story. That was why she wasn't all that worried about the contagion. Yet.

He pushed himself higher until he was hovering above the shard of Aliya's stronghold. Looking down from this angle, he could see into the central courtyard that was screened by the surrounding deceptively transparent crystal structures that acted like camouflage. Angling his wings upwards until they were almost vertical, he let gravity plummet him toward the floating island in a steep dive. The statement entrance was worth the ache along his muscles as he snapped his wings out at the last possible moment to slow his descent, a subtle use of his power helping to cushion his joints from the hard landing.

The local elementals from the city shifted nervously as he strode toward the receiving hall where he knew Aliya would be holding court as if she was the ruler here. He didn't take the time to glare at them but he smiled inwardly when, without any direction on his part, every single one of them took off in a flurry of wings, abandoning the gathering.

"Bastion. So nice of you to join us," Aliya called as he crossed the threshold into her airy domain.

The pillars of the hall were made of twisting caged cyclones and the floor beneath his feet was all but invisible, displaying the three-storey drop down to the building's rock foundations. He couldn't tell if he was walking on reinforced crystal or hardened air. It didn't really matter, either. With a sentient stronghold, Aliya could cajole the entity into disappearing the floor in an instant either way. One of his greatest weaknesses was his inability to sense and communicate with the strongholds the way even the least powerful elementals could. Growing up in the shadow of the Fire Court, it had been like missing an essential organ.

"You're in breach of the agreement you signed to park this glorified zeppelin here," he told the woman who was standing three steps higher than him across the room, wearing a long-tailed white jacket with nothing beneath it to hide the curve of her breasts and white pants that hugged her legs right down to her three-inch stiletto heels. "Everybody out!" he added. He didn't raise his voice to make the order, instead using the souls gathered around him to carry the message directly to the ears of everyone in the room. It would feel like someone had stomped over their grave and then used their connection to life like it was a string telephone. He kept walking through the room as a collective shiver ran through the gathered crowd and people ran for the exits.

"Was that really necessary?" Aliya asked, sauntering down the stairs with a sway to her hips he wasn't remotely interested in.

"No more necessary than killing my father," Bast replied when she was close enough that no one else would overhear.

Aliya's laugh rang out across the space, resonating against the crystal walls until it sounded like a chorus of tinkling diamonds had been poured onto the floor. Bast rolled his eyes at the pretence.

"Why would I kill your father, necromancer?" Aliya said

finally, stepping closer to stroke her palm down his chest. "Your family are so delightfully ... structured."

His skin crawled at the contact and he pushed her hand away. "Have you got a bingo card going or something? How many rulers are you aiming to seduce?"

Aliya's face twisted in anger at his rejection and she turned her back on him to grab a drink from the nearby table. "Bastion, dear. I didn't figure you for a slut-shamer."

"It's not the sex I have a problem with. It's the survival rate," Bast growled.

He could just make out the reflection of her face against the glass walls. A flash of expression crossed her face as she poured a glass of sparkling wine. Guilt? Disgust? It was too hard to pin down. He watched her carefully as she turned back towards him. Was it telling that she hadn't denied or been at all surprised by his accusation? It was impossible to say. The politics of the elemental courts were twisted and conversations seldom what they seemed.

"Have you talked to your father about this theory of yours?" Aliya asked, sipping her wine.

Ah. There it was. She wasn't certain what information he might have and she didn't want to commit to a line if he was better informed. Interesting. He wasn't going to admit he'd tried and failed to reach his father. "I want to hear it from you," he said.

Aliya smirked. "Never going to happen."

Bast could sense the answers he desperately needed slipping out of his grasp. "I'd be the first to tell you I understand the urge to kill the bastard. What happened? Did he hurt you?"

Aliya's chin dropped and her shoulders hunched

inwards. "He was a demanding man," she said, the slightest tremor in her voice.

Bast almost growled in frustration. He could believe their relationship might have been volatile, but there was no way Aliya wouldn't ever give as good as she got. No one with half a brain would buy her victim act. She was renowned for cold-hearted manipulation and a willingness to sacrifice anyone to win. "Nice try," he said.

She smirked again and shrugged, shaking off the momentary affectation. "It was worth a shot. Why are we really here, Bastion? Revenge? Even if I knew, I wouldn't tell you who killed your father. Losing a ruler to your quest for vengeance is the last thing we need in times like these."

"We're here to stop reality from succumbing to a death of a thousand cuts, or did you forget about the contagion while you were trying to lure my people into betraying me?"

Aliya took another sip of her drink and watched him thoughtfully. "Such a death takes time. There are opportunities in that delay. You understand the power humans can give us. You and I are the closest to them of any of the rulers. Together, we could shift the balance of power."

Bast hid his disgust behind a polite mask. "I'm curious. How do you deal with the cognitive dissonance of your prejudice against their weakness while simultaneously craving their power?"

"Human women have managed such feelings about male rulers for millennia."

"You are not human and they have not been rulers in decades. Would you shift the balance of power back to them?"

For the first time since they started talking, Aliya looked visibly shocked. "Are you insane?"

"No more insane than a woman who would watch the world burn to grab control of another territory or two. You're like a child chasing a butterfly only to hold it so tight that you crush it between your fingers. You berate me for wanting vengeance on the person who made me an outcast, but you'd abandon your people to die fighting the contagion alone when the only chance we have is standing together."

"It would serve them right for the way they treat me. You think you were the only one whose reputation was ruined that day? My sex life is the punchline to a joke for them. They know *nothing* about what I felt for him."

Bast's eyes widened in surprise. Maybe she was still acting, but the emotion in her voice, whatever it was, seemed genuine. This was his chance to push while she was off-centre and vulnerable. "Even if you cared for him, it doesn't mean you didn't kill him."

"Leave. Now."

Bast raised an eyebrow and his voice lowered in threat. "You breached our agreement. I expect your island to be out of sight from the city by sunrise. And I suggest you start being more of a team player or I might just tell the others what you offered me."

"You think they'll ever believe you over me? I may be a joke to them, but you're the monster. Your father should have killed you as a baby."

"Sunrise," Bast growled, before turning his back on the pathetic excuse for a ruler and heading to the cleansing darkness of the night sky as fast as he could without looking like he was running away.

Had she killed his father? Who knew. But judging by the expression on Aliya's face, she was now actively gunning for him. She could get in fucking line.

CHAPTER 15
HEL

The dancing looked like it would carry on until Soul Tower was bathed in the red light of the rising sun, but Hel wasn't going to wait for Bast to deign to return. Ryker cornered her as she made her way toward the lifts.

"Nothing to stick around for now your man's left?" he asked.

Hel scowled and wished she could point out that Bast wasn't her anything. "I've had enough of being stared at for the night," she said.

Ryker reached out and touched a gentle finger to her collarbone where the tip of Bast's mark curled over her shoulder. "I'm glad you've found a place to belong. You were always so determined to be alone despite everything we did."

"I wonder why," Hel said, her voice dripping sarcasm. "Stockholm syndrome was never really my thing."

Ryker looked genuinely distressed at the comment and she felt a moment of guilt that she quickly quashed. She didn't owe him anything. She was only a child when he'd purchased her debt in a move that was barely a wingbeat away from slavery.

"It was never what you thought, sweetheart," he said, reaching out to touch her again before dropping his hand to his side as he thought better of it. "I only bid on your indenture because otherwise Aliya's steward would have bought you. You looked so young and vulnerable in the holding cell and the rumours of what her court did with their humans were even worse back then when wars were still breaking out. We've always had more applicants than positions and, by all rights, a human child should've been a terrible investment. The fact you took to it so well was pure luck. I thought you might've figured this out by now."

Hel blinked in confusion. "But you kept adding to the debt."

"Only because I knew you'd run as soon as it was repaid and we could all see the way you flinched at shadows and trained night and day to defend yourself. We wanted to keep you close. To protect you. We would've set you free as soon as we thought you could be safe."

"You sold me back to Bast."

Ryker shook his head. "Bast was mad as hell when he heard the story we'd fed you. Indenture isn't permitted here. You know that. He's already wiped the official record of it. I assumed he would've told you..." The confusion on her face must have tipped him off that he'd said too much and his voice trailed off.

Hel's mind spun. Half the reason her debt had hurt so much was because she knew there was no one else in the city indentured like she was. The foundation of what she knew about her place in life was all a lie. Where did that leave her? It was too much to deal with on top of everything else. She pushed past Ryker and ignored his concerned calls after her. How and why would Bast simultaneously wipe her debt while threatening her into helping him? She already knew the answer, though. She'd seen it in the way he worked with the city's partnership and how he'd drained himself dry to save the people in that building. She could feel it in the nature of his essence through their connection. He'd do anything to protect the city and his people. He'd lied about the debt. Had his threats been empty as well? Could she leave whenever she wanted? She cursed as she realised she wouldn't be able to look herself in the mirror if she did. The final death toll of the latest outbreak had been twenty-seven, including three children.

Somehow, she made it back to the penthouse without realising and she was standing in the kitchen staring vacantly at the cupboards as her thoughts continued to spiral. She grabbed a bottle of whiskey and took a swig from it without bothering with a glass. The fiery burn of the alcohol did nothing to hide the ember of emotion Ryker's revelation had woken in her. He actually cared. He'd always cared. She hadn't ever been as alone as she'd felt.

The walls she'd built around herself were crumbling. Could she really blame Bast for saying what he needed to secure her help? She took another long swallow of whiskey. It didn't matter anyway. Maybe he wasn't the devil she'd made him out to be, but her father wouldn't hesitate to sacrifice him and his city in his pursuit of her. The image of her one and only childhood friend unrecognisable and bleeding out as she was dragged away by hounds flashed into her mind and morphed into a child with electric blue and cream wings crumpled in a pool of blood. She was poison to those around her. She needed to stay away from them. As soon as they found the Archivist, she'd put as much distance as possible between them.

She kept drinking from the bottle until the raw pain she didn't want to admit to became a dull throb and she could finally succumb to the retreat of unconsciousness in her bed.

THE NOISE of her curtains being yanked apart quickly followed by the stabbing pain of bright sunlight on her eyelids was what woke her at too-early-o'clock the next morning.

"Morning, Hel. Bast was called away last night to help Mica with a contagion outbreak in his stronghold. Even as powerful as they both are, it's still twelve hours flight each way and we're running out of time. He wants you scouting the city for the Archivist while he's gone," Ana said.

"Should he be leaving the city right now?" Hel asked, frowning.

"We're running interference with the other rulers so they don't realise and the souls shielding the Tower will keep us safe while he's gone. It's not ideal, but he needs to be on Mica's good side," Ana said, mouth tightening a little at the words. The woman wasn't naïve. She knew the reason Bast needed to endear himself to Mica would take her daughter away from her.

A quick mental calculation said even if Bast had left shortly after he'd abandoned the ball, he was probably still en route to the Earth Court. He wouldn't be back for another twenty hours or so at the earliest, and that's if he wasn't left too exhausted to fly by dealing with the contagion. Hel thought of the red eyes of her father's starhound from the other day and shuddered. Could she risk an outing when there might be more out there? Maybe she could stay undercover and travel by the causeways instead of the streets. Except she knew she couldn't. They were difficult to make a quick exit from if she sensed anything and being grown between human buildings from elemental magic they were like walking in an echo chamber for her magic sense that responded to the connections between worlds. It would be much harder to notice the early warning sensations of a portal from within a causeway.

"Fine. But I'm wearing my own damn clothes this time."

It only took twenty minutes to shower, change, and eat the bacon sandwich waiting for her on the bench. Throughout, she carefully avoided thinking about Ryker's revelations from the night before. She couldn't afford the distraction. The thoughts crept in despite herself as she stood waiting for the elevator, though. Ugh. She needed to focus. She could figure it out later.

For the first time since she'd agreed to stay, she headed to the ground floor exit to leave. As she made her way down the long-paralysed escalators, she caught a flash of movement from the interior bridge she was passing beneath. She glanced up as she descended and saw an unidentifiable form, half-obscured by shadow and the blooming bougainvillea vines that twisted through the space. Her footsteps faltered as she saw the figure's face light up in the dim glow of a sat phone and she felt an inexplicable chill of foreboding.

She shook off the feeling and forced herself to keep moving. There was no reason to think there was any threat from whoever it was enjoying the garden installation while they made a phone call and, even if there were, she could defend herself better than most. She kept reminding herself of that fact every time she checked over her shoulder as she walked away from Soul Tower and stepped out into the city.

Wariness took Hel the opposite direction from the bus tunnel where they'd run into the last hound, even though she knew there was no direction that would be safe. She doubted the Archivist would visit the same location twice, so, rather than return to the Spiderhive where she'd first spied them, she headed up the hill behind Soul Tower towards the university.

The multi-disciplinary experimental physics department at the university where elementals and humans worked together to mess with reality and trial new forms of magic had always played havoc with her senses. She usually avoided the campus for that reason. It tended to leave her with a sensation a little like motion sickness, complete with phantom movement of the ground beneath her feet if she stayed there too long. It was possible something underway there could've formed a black spot for her search for the Archivist. If she walked to the far edge of the campus and double-checked for any portals, she should be back to the tower in time for a late lunch and Bast couldn't claim she wasn't trying hard enough.

Ugh. Thinking about Bast brought back memories of the night before. The panic she hadn't wanted to admit she'd felt when she'd seen him bleeding. The instinctive urge to reassure him she was safe with the kiss she never should've initiated. In light of what she'd learned from Ryker, she thought she might actually believe he was innocent of killing his father. Where did that leave her feelings for him? It was entirely possible Bast had spent years being hunted for a crime he didn't commit, in much the same way her father had hunted her throughout her childhood when she'd done nothing to deserve it beyond being born. Shit. The last thing he needed was her lumping him with her baggage of family issues to paint a new target on his back.

She forced herself to focus on taking the steps up to The Terrace two at a time, pushing her speed and testing her body's tolerance for lack of oxygen by refusing to take a breath until she reached the top. By long-standing habit, her eyes scanned all around her as she ran—skimming the boarded-up houses, side-alleys, and the slice of blue sky that was visible as she searched for any hint of danger. As she reached the final step, she thought she caught a hint of feathers pulling back from a rooftop overhead. Had Bast sent someone to keep an eye on her? The figure in the atrium had her spooked. Tyson could be out for blood after the scene the night before. And who knew how Bast had left things with Lady Aliya.

The campus itself was fortress-like enough that she hoped the twitch she was developing from waiting for an attack that never came might abate once she reached it. It was the roads she'd have to take to get there that were the problem.

She drew her baton from its sheath as she walked, the weight in her hand comforting as she slipped through the narrow space between buildings that was an ambush waiting to happen. When she emerged on the other side without incident, she finally allowed herself to take a breath, although she still couldn't relax. This part of the city was a weird no man's land. Technically, the university came under Bast's protection, but the buildings were isolated from the interconnected causeways of the CBD that created safe passage. And the proximity to the arachdryn's feeding grounds in the botanical gardens meant the area was largely unpopulated. It wasn't a problem for the flying elementals, of course. But for those forced to travel on foot, it was a danger zone.

She stuck to the curving old human road as she continued upward, reluctant to use the riskier shortcut through the cemetery she usually would've taken without a second thought. An urgent vibration against her wrist drew her attention as she passed the cracked concrete tennis courts. She glanced down at the red flashing screen. Years ago, she'd snuck into Ryker's office and hacked the controls on her smartwatch so she'd be notified whenever anyone pinged the GPS on it. That was how she'd known Ryker had been ignoring her late-night practice sessions at the parking building. It had always mystified her why he hadn't pulled her up on it, although she guessed now she knew. This alert was different, though. Ryker had no need to trace her and Bast could find her far faster with the mark he'd left on her skin. So, who was using the watch to stalk her location?

She glanced around herself, moving faster toward the occupied buildings as she tried to seem casual while searching for whoever was following her. If she took off the watch, an alarm would go back to Bast's systems, or perhaps Ryker's if he hadn't swapped them over. She'd get in trouble for that. It was probably a breach of contract, but she was starting to think maybe Bast wouldn't enforce it like he'd said. The watch's alarm would also send someone out to investigate and she could really use the backup if Tyson or Aliya were coming for her. At least it would if the someone who'd hacked it didn't block the signal and if anyone was keeping an eye on it while Bast was out of the city. Her best hope was to ditch the tracking device so she could at least hide while she regrouped and waited to see if any help turned up. Decision made, she ducked into the cover of a nearby tree before untwisting her baton into its hidden double blades and using the tip of a knife to pry the watch from her wrist. The crawling sensation on her skin intensified as she kept her back to the road so her actions were screened by her body. After tucking the watch into a knot of the rough bark, she abandoned all pretence of casualness, spinning to face the invisible threat with both blades in her hands.

Two sets of glowing red eyes at the far end of the road between her and the city were all the motivation she needed to sprint in the opposite direction. Her father's hounds had scented her. They might not know for sure who she was yet, but there was no point sticking around for them to find out.

Her first thought was to head for the relative safety of the campus, but the sickening sensation of a portal forming on the road ahead had her swinging right toward the nearby abandoned park instead. The hunters were systematically herding her away from anyone who might help. She just had to hope someone noticed the alarm from her watch soon. As she skidded out onto the exposed knee-high grass far faster than any human could have run, she spotted a group of griffins resting in the morning sunshine, taking turns splashing in the circular fountain in the distance.

One last crazy dash of hope entered her as she dropped her speed to avoid startling the magnificent but deadly creatures ahead. As a teen, she'd briefly entered the parkour scene to learn how to use the city to her advantage. The bravado and competition between the young humans had resulted in the daring routes becoming more and more dangerous until even predators were used as part of their stunts. She'd only managed to catch a ride on a griffin once, and she'd lost her grip twenty feet in the air and barely been able to hide her injuries from Ryker. Hopefully, this time would go better.

Trapped between two very different threats, she turned her back on the griffins to face her more sinister pursuers, slowly backing closer to the winged cats and hoping the fact she wasn't making eye contact would keep them from taking flight before she reached them ... or deciding she'd make a tasty snack. Her shoulder blades itched where she imagined a sharp beak driving into her. The thought didn't last long, because on the edge of the bushes slinking out into the open were three of her father's starhounds, each one almost as large as the griffins towering behind her. As close as they were, she could see the venom dripping from their hinged fangs onto the grass.

Two of the hounds had circled outward so they were arranged in a semi-circle facing her. The world slowed as she watched their muscles bunch, poised to strike. She couldn't help but flinch back even as she held her blades steady before her. This was it. She could tell they'd realised she was their long-hunted prey. Given the tracking on her watch, someone had probably tipped off her father about her identity. After years of running, with her only advantage being that they didn't have her scent and had no idea even what gender she was, she was now fully exposed. Despair filled her as she realised there was nowhere she could be safe anymore. As the first one leaped toward her, she screamed an involuntary "No!" that echoed with the depths of her anguish. With her senses still stretched wide from her search for the Archivist, she felt the desperate word infuse with her power and she watched in shock as the hound dropped to the ground with a whine and all three froze in place.

As silence fell in the wake of her scream, she sensed another of her father's portals opening nearby—a response to whatever it was she'd done. If the hounds hadn't been sure she was a person of interest before she'd stopped them with a single word, they were now. Clicking her knives back together, she holstered her baton, trusting whatever unknown power of hers that held the hounds in stasis would last another breath. Then she turned to face the griffins who were now on high alert facing the threat of the hounds. Shit. On the plus side, they had no attention to spare for the seemingly defenceless human figure that happened to be in between.

Hunching her shoulders down, she slipped around the side of the family group until she was outside of their narrow range of vision. Right. She could do this. What was the worst that could happen? She pushed aside the image of her body being rent into pieces by griffin beaks as she fell hundreds of feet from the sky. Taking a breath, she took a silent running leap towards the closest copper-feathered form and wrapped her arms tight around its neck. The creature's eagle scream of outrage startled the whole group into flight. Hel's muscles screamed in sympathy with the griffin, straining to maintain purchase as the creature lurched into the air. Wrapping her legs tight around its torso, she took hold of two large handfuls of feathers she hoped weren't due to moult any time soon. At least she was taller than she'd been the last time she'd tried this. Maybe the longer reach of her arms and legs would be enough to keep her on this time.

She felt a moment of relief as the ground dropped away beneath them and the hounds became distant shadows. As the griffin executed a sharp turn, she thought she caught sight of a looming form joining them on the field, but the griffin veered away too quickly to be sure. The griffin's feline body bucked and twisted as it tried to throw her off, the city growing smaller and smaller beneath them. She clung on grimly. Thank the Earths it was griffins and not dragons she'd come across. The melding of eagle and cat was a less aerodynamic form and no matter how much she'd pissed off the poor animal, it was not going to be able to flip mid-air to shake her off, especially with her extra weight pulling it off balance.

Unfortunately, the griffin seemed to realise this too and began to head straight back to its home nest where it could land in safety to deal with her. Home being Matiu Island in the middle of the fucking harbour. She was so screwed. At least she hadn't fallen to her death. Yet.

The griffin's powerful wings were propelling them all too fast away from any hope of safety. The city streets below gave way to crumbled buildings half sunk in the ocean and then to white-capped waves. Her hands were aching from her grip on the golden feathers beneath her. Their altitude finally dropped as they approached the island where the griffins nested. Hel's eyes were watering from the combination of the cold gusts of wind and the surging wingbeats on either side of her that threatened to heave her off at any second. She blinked to clear them and watched the blue-green sea growing closer.

She calculated they were low enough for her to safely jump when they were still well clear of the island. The griffin was probably taking a lower approach to steer clear of the dragons that nested and circled on its peak. Up ahead were the rocky outcrops that rested by the old lighthouse, her only chance of finding a defensible position along the coastline. Hel took a deep breath and braced herself, before launching backward over the griffin's tail and arrowing head-first towards the water. A shape swooped towards her from her left and she tucked into a tight roll at the last minute to make herself a smaller target, one of the griffin's nest-mates attacking now they could reach her. White-hot pain spread across the side of her thigh as claws raked her just before she hit the water with an inelegant slap.

Thankful she didn't have to breathe as often as a human would, she dived as low as she dared, hoping no water predators would be drawn by her bleeding wound before she had a chance to get to shore. Her eyes stung from saltwater as she kept them open searching for threats and the gash on her leg throbbed with every stroke she took as she kicked in what she hoped was the right direction. She almost sobbed in relief when her fingers finally hit rough rock, but she could tell by the shifting shadows above her that she couldn't risk showing her head yet. Clinging grimly to the outcrop to fight the surging tide, she peered up at the distorted image of the sky, waiting for the predators to leave. Her lungs ached and spots filled her vision as she approached the end of even her impressive lung capacity. Or maybe the encroaching darkness was from blood loss. Just as she thought she'd left it too long, the shadows cleared and she let herself bob up out of the water, gasping for breath.

Her wrinkled, swollen fingers struggled to haul herself to shore and dizziness threatened to send her tumbling back into the ocean's depths with every crashing wave. She knew she couldn't waste any time once she was on dry land. As she hauled herself up onto the beach, step by staggering step, she watched in all directions for an attack. Bushes dragged against her skin as she staggered up the hill toward the over-grown lighthouse. She hissed and almost cried out when a thorned branch caught at the angry raw edges of the gashes on her leg.

Somehow, she made it to the door of the low white cylindrical building without anything trying to gut her, but that's where her luck ended. No matter how many times she charged her poor abused shoulder against the entrance, she couldn't get inside. Groaning softly, she peered up at the broken glass two storeys up. There was no other way in and she needed shelter desperately.

How the fuck was she going to get off this island? She had no watch and she'd lost her phone somewhere on the flight. No one had the slightest clue where she was. She shook her head at her weakness and squared her shoulders. She'd never relied on anyone to save her and this was no different. She'd figure it out. But first, she needed somewhere safe to rest and bind her wounds.

The ledge she needed to reach to pull herself up looked as high as Soul Tower as far as her exhausted body was concerned. The first jump as she launched herself high enough to catch the top window sill over the entrance was the worst. She had to rely on her damaged leg scrabbling for purchase as well as the remaining strength in her aching arms to haul herself up. Once she reached the peaked gable halfway up the building it was easier going. A screeching call from across the small inlet warned her she was running out of time. The griffins had spotted her.

Adrenaline flooded her system, giving her the boost she needed as she reached for the rounded ledge and pulled herself up to the top floor, rolling into the exposed upper beacon room of the lighthouse with a crunch of glass just as a sharp beak and claws snapped behind her. Fuck. Would it try to follow her inside? She scrambled further back into the relative safety of the building, shredding her hands on the glass shards in her urgency, before tumbling unceremoniously down the stairwell she hadn't noticed. She winced as her head bounced off something hard on the way down.

At least the griffin was out of sight.

She dragged herself to the driest and clearest part of the room to hunker down, shaking with cold and adrenaline. Carefully brushing the stray shards of glass from her hands, she took stock of her sodden freezing body. The wound on her leg was distracting but not life-threatening. She shrugged off her leather jacket and pulled off her stretchy tank top to form a makeshift bandage around her thigh that stopped the last of its sluggish bleeding, wincing as the fabric aggravated the myriad small cuts on her hands. The noise from above her had quieted. It would be hard for the griffins to maintain a hover to attack, especially with their prey out of sight.

Taking advantage of the reprieve, she braved poking her head up into the upper space for long enough to lay her jacket and pants in the sun to dry before ducking back out of sight. Her body was still damn cold, but she wasn't as susceptible as a human. Damp clothes would be miserable once night fell, though. Tasks complete, she rested her head back against the wall and wondered how long it would take Bast to find her. The connection to him felt more distant than it ever had. When she concentrated, she briefly felt a sensation like they were breathing in synch and warmth spread through her veins, but it faded as soon as she focused on anything around her and all that was left was a memory like a phantom limb. Closing her eyes, she let fatigue drag her down into sleep.

CHAPTER 16
BAST

When the call had come from Mica as he was still flying back from his confrontation with Aliya, Bast had almost ignored it. He'd had more than enough of the politics and demands of the council for one night. There was no way he could turn down Mica's plea for help, though.

The two elementals snuck out of the city separately under cover of darkness, neither of them keen to let the other rulers get wind of what was going on. Bast couldn't afford them knowing he wasn't there to defend his city and Mica couldn't risk one of the others deciding his perceived weakness was the perfect time to strike and make a play for power.

At least this outbreak hadn't been affected by whatever had catalysed the contagion last time before they had a chance to get to it. Bast had been worried the intelligence of the stronghold might have the same amplifying effect on it, but the darkness was relatively contained to an out-of-use storeroom on the outskirts of the limestone cave network that made up Mica's home. He hated to think what effect the contagion could have on the sentience that resided in Mica's subterranean stronghold, but he wasn't going to give away the fact he couldn't sense its emotions like every other elemental could by asking. The rulers might suspect his weakness from old stories of soulweavers, but they didn't know for sure, which meant they couldn't assume he wouldn't notice a stronghold poised to attack him.

The Earth Lord's face was pinched and tense as they inspected the pulsing shadow nestled between two stalagmites.

"She amputated this cave from her essence as soon as the contagion formed," he said, his low voice strained as he spoke of his stronghold.

Bast winced at his words and the image of Tir's severed hand on Ryker's desk from weeks ago flashed in his mind. Hopefully this disused cave wasn't too important to the stronghold's nervous system and essence. He had no way of knowing if it had been like losing a finger or like losing a lobe of her brain. From what he'd gleaned over the years, the strongholds were vast intelligences but relatively young and impressionable compared to the age of the Earth. They were often characterised as sophisticated symbiotic pets, dependent on the guidance and power of the courts they partnered with and still growing into themselves as they were shaped by their interactions with the people around them.

While the contagion outbreak itself was small, Bast was already tired from the long journey at peak speed. Both of them had poured power into their flight to get there as fast as possible. As he gathered power from the dead of the Earth Court and wove it into a new barrier, the now familiar sickening sensation of brushing against the diseased absence of reality washed over him and Bast swayed where he stood. It took longer than it should have for him to tighten and crush his containment until it was a pinprick sphere that looked like the singularity of a black hole. As Mica's power flared to anchor and supplement the protections, Bast crouched and rocked back on his heels, pushing his palms hard to his eyes in an effort to ease his throbbing headache.

"Thank you," Mica said, finally turning to him and inclining his head. Time would tell if his absence and exhaustion were worth whatever gains he could wring in return from the Earth Lord.

Bast nodded and rose to his feet. There was no time to rest. The sense he'd left his city exposed was a constant nagging panic in the background of his subconscious. He couldn't shake the sensation something was wrong at home. Every second they delayed was another second that might clue the rest of the council into their absence.

When they finally left the Earth stronghold behind them to return, Bast rode Mica's slipstream to conserve as much energy as he could. Even with that assistance, each wingbeat weighed heavy as his exhaustion threatened to slow their supernatural speed above the oceans. When he felt the Earth Lord's power bolstering his flight without having asked his permission, he was too tired to do anything but pretend not to notice. The nagging sensation something was wrong only increased the further they flew, but with every wingbeat feeling like he was pulling against the weight of a dragon flying in the opposite direction and with no power source above the wide vacant ocean to refresh himself from, he couldn't be sure the feeling wasn't just intense vulnerability.

The sunrise seemed to chase them across the harbour when they finally spied the city. Scouts called greetings as they passed, with faces showing concern. He distantly heard Mica passing on an order to one of them and he couldn't even make himself care at the over-step. The Earth Lord's voice sounded as distant as if it was at the end of one of his stronghold's tunnels. "Clear the entrance to the tower of anyone not loyal to your lord."

Bast had been steadily dropping for the past few hours and when he failed to gain enough height to land on the roof of Soul Tower, Mica landed beside him as if they'd been out walking the streets and it had always been their intention to walk in the front entrance of the building like humans. As shaky as he felt, Bast wasn't sure anyone was buying it. Hopefully his scouts had done as Mica asked and there was no one around to see.

Ra was waiting in the elevator for him when he finally staggered inside, his friend obviously realising he would only draw attention to him if he ran out to meet him in the foyer. Bast waited for the doors to slide closed before sagging against the wall.

"What did you do to him?" Ra growled at Mica.

"I got him home safely. I owe him a debt I'm not sure I can ever repay."

Bast waved his hand vaguely in Mica's direction. "Had to be done," he said, voice slurring.

"It did. But no one else would have. Thank you, Bastion." The doors opened on the floor Mica was staying on. "Take good care of him," he said to Ra as he stepped out.

"Always."

Once they were alone, Ra slid himself under Bast's arm until he was supporting most of his weight. "I hate to do this to you, but we've got a problem," he said.

Bast groaned. "I can't. I'm empty."

"You've got an hour to recharge and then we need to talk." Ra's actions belied his bossy words because he almost carried Bast out of the elevator before gently depositing him on the couch and fetching the high-energy steaming hot meal Ana must've made as soon as the scouts saw him on the horizon.

Bast groaned again and reached out to the souls around him for support. They raced to his call, flooding through his system, but even their energy could only make a small dent in how he felt. The edge of frantic anger he caught from them wasn't helping either. Whatever it was that was wrong had upset even the dead. This wasn't going to be good. They must've sensed he wasn't with-it enough to listen to them though because they kept silent as he shovelled food into his mouth under Ra's watchful gaze.

He didn't bother trying to find his bed. He just closed his eyes where he sat and stopped fighting to stay conscious. When he woke not nearly long enough later, it was to a small hand wrapped around his and soft blue feathers covering his chest.

His first attempt at speaking resulted in an inaudible croak and someone pushed a glass of cool water to his lips. He tried again. "Don't waste your energy on me, Kaia."

"You're not the boss of me, Uncle Basti."

Ana chuckled from nearby. "She's being careful. Aren't you sweetheart?" Her tone of voice said Kaia wouldn't like the result if she wasn't.

"The carefulest!"

Bast drew in a breath and risked cracking his eyelids open. It took a few breaths for the room to come into focus, but at least someone had dimmed the lights so his head didn't ache so badly.

"Ready to chat?" Ra asked, making himself comfortable on the edge of the couch by Bast's knee.

"That's our cue to leave, sweetheart," Ana told Kaia, and the two of them headed out.

Bast tried to sit up but Ra's firm hand on his chest kept him in place. "Rest while you can."

"That bad, huh?"

"Hel never came back from searching the city for Tir."

Bast surged upright and blinked hard as the room spun around him before settling into place. His heart pounded as adrenaline flooded his system. "How long's she been missing? Why haven't you found her already? What happened? Is she okay?"

"I was hoping you could tell me that last one at least. She's been gone just over twenty-four hours."

Bast realised Ra's tone wasn't matching the panic that had laced through his blood when he heard she was gone. "You think she ran."

"Ryker called and said he told her the truth about her childhood and that you'd cancelled her debt. We found her smartwatch tucked in a tree trunk near the university campus. There was no sign of blood or a struggle. Scouts searched a wide radius from the location and found nothing. All our guests are accounted for."

Bast looked inward and felt along the connection he had to his hellcat. It took him longer than it should have to sink into the places they were one. Her heartbeat was slightly elevated but her breathing was calm. He could feel a jagged edge of pain.

"She's hurt."

"Doesn't mean she was attacked. She might've injured herself when she fled."

Bast felt a surge of annoyance. "I didn't say she was attacked."

"I can hear it in your tone of voice. You're worried about her. She never wanted to be here."

"I'm worried about finding Tir without her."

Ra just raised an eyebrow and stared at him.

"Fuck. Maybe I'm a little worried about her as well. I need a drink. I can't think straight," Bast finally ground out. He was thinking back to the other day. The way the fiery woman had shut down when she'd spotted the hound on the hill. The way her body had hung in his arms limply on the flight home. How vulnerable she'd seemed. He could feel that same sense from her now in the distance and the protectiveness surging through him was enough to give him a tiny burst of energy.

"Do you know where she is?"

Bast closed his eyes and felt for the tug on his soul before pointing vaguely east. "I'm running on empty. I can't do more than follow the link right now. She's not far from the city."

"But she is outside the border?"

Bast sighed and nodded. "She's stationary right now. I would've thought she'd have made it further away in twenty-four hours if she was running for it."

Ra's phone rang before he could answer. Bast watched his face drop into a frown and he swore before hanging up.

"What's up?"

"Aliya and Ty have convened the council without you. They're starting as we speak. Mica's on his way. You need something to wear."

Ra was already heading for his bedroom, presumably to grab some clothes. Bast looked down at himself and realised he'd been wearing a fucking tuxedo for the last day and a half. He'd gone with Mica straight after his little chat with Aliya without stopping to change. He was a windswept mess.

Five minutes later he was adequately presentable and doing his best to put enough energy into his step that he wouldn't look like a reanimated corpse as he entered the chamber. Mica was just sitting down, his hair still wet from a shower and three of his top shirt buttons undone.

"We didn't ask for your presence, Bastion. You can crawl back into whichever bed you came from," Aliya said, cloying sweetness dripping from her voice like poison.

"Last time I checked this was my house and you were a guest. I'll go wherever I damn well please."

"You know that's not how the council works, Bastion," Nerida said, not unkindly.

"Then the council can do without my assistance securing the Archivist," Bast snapped.

"Excellent. That was exactly my proposal," Aliya said.

Bast felt nausea roiling in his stomach. He was too exhausted to navigate this conversation and he'd walked right into that.

"Let's not be hasty. Or are you forgetting what brought us here in the first place? The contagion is spreading. We need the answers the Archives hold. Even without that, would you willingly give up access to generations of history just because of who we need to ask for help?" Mica said.

"He's no better than the monster who forsook his duty to give us access," Tyson growled.

"Tir is no more a monster than you are, Lord Tyson. The Fire Court never could see the value in any species but their own," Nerida said.

"Speaking of which, where is the woman you peed your power on to try and convince us she was worthy?" Tyson asked.

Bast's jaw ached as he gritted his teeth to stop the challenge on his lips. He'd be damned if he'd keep playing into their hands. "Perhaps she needed a break from people trying to kill her."

"Are you accusing him of breaking guest-right?" Aliya asked, sounding delighted.

"I named no one. If you'd like to accuse him, go ahead," Bast said. As much as he would love to challenge Ty, he needed to shut down this conversation before it derailed everything.

"Enough. We don't have time for this. Bast, whatever you were doing to track Tir, you need to get on with it," Mica said.

"It's not that simple. I can only track them when they're in this dimension and they only come here to feed."

"My sources tell me the highest probability location is that island in the harbour. All isolated and full of predators. The perfect hunting ground," Aliya said. There was something in her voice Bast didn't trust. An implication he was failing to grasp with his tired brain.

"It's a logical spot. The ley lines are so knotted there we would never sense them until it was too late," Ty added.

Bast's mind whirred. What was their angle?

"They'll look for the weak and defenceless. A loner who's left the safety of the flock," Aliya added.

Bast felt his heart drop as he looked over at Aliya to find her watching him with sickening satisfaction written across her face. She wasn't speaking about Tir. Reaching inside to his connection with Hel again, he let his eyes follow the tug of their connection eastward, out across the city, across the harbour, to Matiu Island. A lone defenceless woman in a sea of predators. He didn't think Tir would eat an intelligent being, but the griffins and dragons certainly would. How had she even gotten to the island? Aliya's smirk said she knew what Bast was sensing, but he couldn't accuse her of anything based on that. According to his scouts, neither Aliya nor Ty had left the tower while he was gone.

The more he thought about it, the more he wondered if Ra was right and someone had merely helped Hel make a run for it. The far side of the island had a history of being used for smuggling. She could be waiting for someone to collect her. Either she was about to die a violent death at the claws of the island's predators or she was about to disappear along with his only chance of winning over the council and stopping the contagion.

"I'll go investigate," Bast said, jumping to his feet.

Mica was looking at him like he'd grown a second pair of wings, no doubt wondering why he was abandoning the council meeting from such a blatant ruse. He didn't have the energy or time to politic his way out of the room. Who knew how long Hel could evade the notoriously protective predators if this wasn't part of her plan. The dragons were worse than magpies when they thought you were threatening their young and the griffins were just as likely to snap into unprovoked homicide as their far-distant feline cousins. And if she was waiting for a pick-up, she'd already been gone over a day. She wouldn't stick around much longer. He was out the door and heading for the roof before any of the others had time to so much as smirk in his direction.

His foot tapped on the floor the entire length of the elevator ride up as he watched the floor numbers rise too slowly. He needed the extra height to make the flight easier. He used the time to flick a text to Ra.

Bast: *Hel's on Matiu. Heading there now.*

Ra: *You're exhausted. Take back-up,* the immediate response came.

Bast: *Can't afford to appear weak.*

The ache in his shoulders as he launched himself from the roof said he probably should've listened to Ra. He dragged power from the souls around him to make up for the fatigue that threatened to let gravity win the battle against his flight. As he drew closer to the island, even his magic wasn't helping enough and he stayed aloft through raw determination and an urgency to reach Hel he tried not to examine too deeply. There was a reason they'd abandoned the island to the predators that nested there. That tangled knot of ley lines Aliya mentioned played havoc with normal elemental senses and even his own power didn't function as it should when he was in close proximity.

When he'd tried to explain it to Ra once, his friend had decided it was their own personal Bermuda triangle—a story his friend had described from the human pre-Melding Earth. People and power went missing from the island. The former because of smugglers and predators, and the latter because of the weird characteristics of the land itself. That was why the souls that followed at his call had sheared away from him like flaking skin as he neared the island's coastline. It took every last drop of his drained concentration to project the aura that would ensure the predators saw him as too big a threat to attack. Even so, he stayed over the water as he searched the island for Hel. He didn't need to borrow trouble by appearing to threaten a nest. The connection between them was growing stronger. She was close.

His first focus was the south-eastern coastline, out of direct sight from the city proper and closest to the mouth of the harbour for any waterborne vessel. He needed to make sure no one was waiting to whisk her away. Hovering low above the water, he scanned the beach for any sign of disturbance from a boat being brought to shore, all his muscles screaming from the effort. Satisfied any potential rescue wasn't imminent, he returned his focus to the tendrils of the bond that linked him to his quarry. It took him longer than it should have, even that intrinsic sense of her a struggle in his current state. The pull was taking him toward the lighthouse on the southwest coast a little way past the pointed outcrop he was flying over. He felt a shudder of relief as he realised Hel had managed to find shelter and then realised it only reinforced the likelihood she'd planned this. Why else would she end up in the hardest place for his scouts to track her?

The shadow falling across his face was his only warning he'd let his focus on Hel distract him. He barely managed a barrel-roll to avoid the worst of the diving dragon's strike. As it was, he still took a glancing blow to his body that sent him careening down toward the rocks. Maybe if he hadn't flown for twenty-four hours straight he could've pulled himself out of it. Or if his power hadn't faded to barely a flickering ember. His only saving grace was that he was flying so low that, when he crashed into the jagged outcrop with a sickening crack, the radiating agony was confined to his wings. The rest of him could still function even if he was probably land-bound. He immediately rolled, ignoring the pain that almost sent him into unconsciousness. Stillness now would be death. A spout of flame blasted into the spot where he'd just been lying. He needed to do something. Fast. With the last of his strength, he flung a desperate shriek of power into the sky hoping to startle the predator into leaving and grab the attention of his people back in the city. He had to hope the island wasn't disturbing his connection to Ra and Ana, which had never been as strong and clear as he had with Hel.

His roll had left him on a gravelly beach, half submerged in the shallows. Staggering to his feet, he searched the skies, all too aware he couldn't move fast enough to evade another spurt of fire. He froze as he saw two hovering figures dropping toward him. One haloed in light as her white-gold wings scattered the midday sun. The other with wings of flame that matched the dragon's fire he'd so narrowly avoided.

"You're looking a little the worse for wear," Ty called.

Bast drew himself upright, calm resignation descending as he realised he couldn't defend himself against even one of them. As long as he remained close to the city and his body was intact, his souls would eventually find him and bring him back from death despite the island's vagaries.

"You don't have time to play, Tyson," Aliya chided.

"A shame," his brother replied, and then a shot of pure power struck Bast's chest and his heart stopped beating.

The world grew dim around him as he fought to will the organ to contract, but power wrapped tight around the muscle forcing it to stasis. A crunch of gravel sounded nearby.

"Goodbye, brother."

"I'll deal with the body," Aliya said.

Bast's existence was already nothing but darkness when he felt power wrap around his dying body and wrench it skyward. The last thing he heard was Aliya's soft voice, already fading as he lost his grip on life. "You look so like your father as he died."

His soul was carried into ether on a surge of helpless rage. He finally had his answer. And it was too late. Aliya was carrying his remains far from home where his souls could save him and revenge alone was not strong enough to anchor him to the world of the living.

It wasn't his rage that made him cling to the edges of the veil, though. It was the image of a woman with jade green eyes and sweeping black hair. Had she been the willing bait for this trap? He couldn't believe it of her. They wouldn't leave her alive as a witness either way. He wished he'd had time to save her. He drifted in the darkness, hoping she wouldn't join him even as he was filled with desperation to feel the touch of her essence against his own one last time.

CHAPTER 17
HEL

A soundless cry echoing through her soul jolted Hel awake from a fitful nap. She'd tried to use the cover of darkness to leave her safe haven, but the griffins hadn't given up. They knew where she was and apparently they held a grudge because they'd swooped down as soon as she tried to leave. She was lucky they hadn't waited for her to reach the ground or she'd have had nowhere to take cover. It hadn't made for a restful night and she was paying for the lack of sleep now.

The cry that had sent her surging to her feet was quickly followed by a sensation like the marks on her back were being sand-blasted by dry ice. Bast was nearby. And he was in trouble. It took her valuable seconds to silently make her way up through the lighthouse to the top where she was afforded a view of the cove below. She cursed the threat from the griffins that kept her hunched low to the ground until she could safely ease her head above the parapet to look out. Her eyes widened in shock as she took in the scene at the beach below.

A crumpled heap of black feathers and darkness lay on the ground. Broken. As she watched uncomprehendingly, Lady Aliya used her power to scoop up the unresponsive body in a net of power. Her soul ached as she watched the familiar infuriating, beautiful countenance of Bast's face fall to the side, lax and missing any hint of the energy and tension that always flowed between them.

As Aliya launched skyward, dragging the net below her, the lady used every bit of her power to become an insubstantial blur. Hel's choked sob broke through the quiet.

He couldn't be gone. She hadn't even had a chance to process what Ryker's revelation about her debt meant for her. For them.

She clung to the last insubstantial thread of connection between them, desperately holding tight. But nothing could stop it from slipping through her soul's grasp. A moment later, searing agony shot through the mark on her back leaving behind a terrifying absence. She knew without looking that the tattooed wings were now as dull and lifeless as the limp form already too small to see in the distance. The silence that followed was so much worse than before. As if every sensation in the world had been lost to her forever.

Psychic backlash dragged her into blessed unconsciousness. She welcomed the darkness for the moment's relief it provided from the agony tearing her apart and the memory of another darkness, warmer, that had wrapped around her for too short a time.

HEL WOKE to rough hands shaking her shoulders until her head smacked against the wooden floor of the lighthouse.

"What did you do to him?" Ra shouted in her face, tears streaming down his face.

Hel stared up at him blankly, distantly aware of a scout standing nearby and more elemental wings flitting across the wedge of sky she could see out the window from her position on her back. She stayed silent as she took stock of her body. The gash on her leg was still a dull throbbing ache, one that was now matched by the lump forming on the back of her head. It wasn't either of those things that were the real problem, though. It was the gaping hole in her chest like someone had reached inside and wrenched her still-beating heart out through her ribs with nothing but their bare hands. It felt like every artery and vein in her body had been torn free along with the organ—that sense of something missing ribboning through each limb and joint right down to the tip of her fingers and toes. And her back. Her back felt like it had been flayed along each line Bast had left on her skin.

"He's gone," she whispered, her voice barely more than a croak after over a day without water.

"What did you fucking do?" Ra growled again, his voice dropping low and dangerous as his fingers dug hard into her shoulders.

Hel couldn't focus on the question. Couldn't focus on anything. How had Bast infiltrated so much of who she was? His loss left her a shadow of a shadow. Drifting in shock, she tried to make sense of what was left of her without him. Images flashed through her mind. His wings as dark as a black hole wrapped tight around her, his power holding her safe from her father's hound. Her memories dragged her to the day Bast had laughed in his office as she raged against his contract and the words he'd spoken—*Even if I had died, my souls here would never have let me cross the veil.* Hope seared through her numbness like poison.

"His souls. Can they save him?" she asked, hating the desperation in her voice.

"If he was here, yes. Is his body nearby?"

"She took him," Hel whispered.

"Who?"

"Lady Aliya."

Ra swore. "Then his body is either beyond our reach or destroyed already."

"What happens if his body is destroyed?"

"Then there's nowhere for his souls to return him. He's lost forever. Dead."

Every cell of Hel's body rebelled at the thought. She wasn't done with him. She needed to tell him how pissed off she was at the way he'd stolen into her soul when she wasn't watching. She needed to find his stupid Archivist before little Kaia faced a world where she couldn't survive. That thought reminded her of the points of darkness across the city. "Is the contagion still contained?" she asked. Bast would hate it if his protections failed his home.

"The shields and the city are still functioning but who knows how long the souls will continue carrying out his last instructions. Was the price worth your 'freedom'?" Ra asked her bitterly.

Hel ignored the question, all too aware that nothing she could say would convince Ra she was innocent at that moment. She wasn't even sure she *was* innocent. If she'd just stayed in the tower like she'd wanted to, none of this would have happened. Guilt washed over the raw edges of her soul like acid. She needed to fix this. There was no point staying hidden only to have the world collapse around her. Damn Bast for getting himself killed.

Hel closed her eyes and submerged herself in the pain that wracked her soul. She drew it around herself until every nerve ending burned with shadow-fire and then she propelled her mind out into the void, careless of whether she might stray too far and never make it back. Bast's power was unique in coming from the connection between the living and the dead, but her power came from the connection between worlds. Surely, they weren't so different. The place the dead went to must be something like another world. Maybe that was why it always felt like their magic was twining together, recognising a kindred spirit.

She'd always sensed the nexuses where the two realities had melded together and the gateways where dimensions and planets were bridged by the few beings with the power to portal. Now, she drew on the memory of Bast's power to hunt down the connection between the realm of the living and the realm of the dead. Her threadbare and fragmented soul, damaged by Bast's loss, tried to shred itself in the hidden currents swirling around her but she gritted her teeth and held fast, hunting. A distant slap to her face, Ra trying to wake her, almost shocked her back to her body. She pushed the last of any physical sensation away and focused only on her search.

With a pop like a part of her had dislocated, she felt her mind slip into a space of darkness, a threshold. All sense of movement, of propulsion, faded and she hung in a space with no up or down, no beginning and no end. No way out. Waiting there, was a tiny point of condensed light that contained the essence she was searching for. Bast. A whisper of his familiar voice brushed through her mind in the silence. *No. You shouldn't be here.*

Should she be there? She couldn't quite remember. The lack of any sense of direction combined with the over-stimulus of power surrounding her was leaving her disoriented and confused, slowly losing her sense of self. She was searching for something, and she'd found it. Maybe she could rest? She started to loosen her hold on the threads of her soul she'd strung together like some raft that would carry her across the rapids of the multiverse. The point of silver light that had spoken to her stretched wide and wrapped around her, holding her together. Phantom feathers and warmth brushed against her essence. Feathers. Bast. She'd found him, but not the part she needed.

She tried to take a breath, to brace herself. But she had no body and there was nothing in this place, nothing except the memory of a man still holding her safe even in death. She held tight to that light, letting it fill the painful spaces it'd left inside her. The reminder of her pain was enough to return her sense of her distant body, still lying prone in the lighthouse. She forced herself to hold tight to the connection between herself in this gateway to death and that corporeal form. The sense of something dislocating returned and, when her vision settled, she could see a string of blue starlight stretching back to her body, a visible representation of the ties holding her to the physical world. When she turned her new vision on the light wrapping around her, she saw a similar thread of connection heading into the distance. Only this one was the silver of soul magic twined with the familiar darkness of Bast's wings. Where her own connection was as thick as an umbilical cord, this one was as thin as the finest strand of spider-web. The connection between Bast's soul and his body had faded to almost nothing.

Pulling herself free of the warm embrace she could have bathed in forever, she sent her consciousness skimming along that delicate strand, careful not to touch it lest she snap it. She clung tight to the cord connecting her to her body as she went, feeling it stretch tighter and tighter until every part of her was waiting for the moment it snapped and sent her careening into the void. At some point, she'd left the in-between place and there was no longer the protective light of Bast's essence to hold her together if she broke. Finally, she reached the end of the line. A body. She had no sense of where it was. Her mind had skimmed across the connections between worlds and the view around her shimmered like she was trapped inside a soap bubble, distorting any view beyond recognition and leaving behind a swirling rainbow of infinite realities layered impossibly thin on its surface. She held still in the place she knew Bast's body rested, soul aching with the effort of holding herself suspended. This was where she needed to be, but she couldn't retrieve his body without real hands to carry him.

Refusing to give in to the forces pulling her apart, she gathered power around herself. She was immediately flooded with a torrent of magic that threatened her precarious stability. This place between worlds was a treasure trove for someone like her. She was bathing in more power than she'd ever known, more power than she could control. Gritting her teeth, she forced her intentions to narrow the flow until she could shape it into a portal. With one final push, she used the tension of the cable she was grasping to snap her back into her own body and released her hold on the dangerous level of power that had been threatening to consume her. She had just enough time to notice the light-house floor disappear in a swirl of her power like solar flares beneath her before the portal she'd created dropped her into who knew where.

THE FIRST THING she felt after her portal immediately collapsed behind her, or more accurately *above* her, was the impact of dropping onto a hard cold surface from a height that was thankfully only about as tall as she was. The second thing she felt was the brush of a stronghold's sentience against her awareness.

She quickly erected the shields around her mind that had always worked in the past, the ones that made her seem like she was human, but that only seemed to alarm the entity even more. The casual pressure on her mind became distinctly hostile and she felt the glassy surface she was resting on grow colder. Her eyes snapped open and she staggered to her feet on limbs tingling with pins and needles where they'd lain still for too long.

She was in some kind of bedroom, but the walls, floor, and ceiling were made of clear crystal. The four-poster bed nearby was covered in blankets of spun gold and draped with a canopy of white frosted mesh that glinted in the soft light that seemed to come from everywhere and nowhere. Each piece of furniture appeared made of blown glass filled with firework colours suspended in the same crystal that formed the room.

It was ostentatious. Wasteful. Ridiculous. At least she knew she was in the right place. There was no way this was anyone's home but Aliya's. She'd portalled halfway across the world from Matiu Island to the Air Court floating above the North American continent.

The sensation of rabidly bared teeth from the stronghold was a stronger version of what she'd sensed from the shard that had floated above the City of Souls. When she glanced down, she could see through floor upon floor of people going about their business. A flurry of activity suggested she wouldn't be alone in the room for long. Far below, an image of drifting clouds screened the view of the floating rock she knew the stronghold was suspended on. And hundreds of feet below that would be whichever city it was parked above that day.

She spun in place, searching the room for the man she'd followed across multiple planes of existence to find, and a strangled cry fell from her lips. There, nailed to the wall with crystal spikes through shoulders, wings, and feet, was Bast's spread-eagled naked body. She barely noticed the shrine that'd been set up on the floor before him as her eyes traced every injury and the unnatural grey tinge of his skin. A rich golden rug was spread on the floor between them. The ankle-high padded bench stretching along its length looked like it would allow Aliya's creepy cult leaders to kneel in prayer. That fucking bitch. Of course she'd taken Bast's death and fed it into the lies she spun for the humans who followed her.

Stumbling forward, she reached for one of the spikes that held him like a moth in a museum display. As soon as she touched it, she felt another surge in the malevolence of the entity surrounding her and the spike shot outward, piercing through the palm of her right hand before wrapping around her wrist to hold her captive. She was shackled to the dead man she'd come to save.

A chilling laugh came from somewhere behind her.

"What do we have here? Is that Bastion's pet human? You're a hard lady to get alone. And now here you are, right in my lap," Aliya said, sounding delighted.

Hel tried to twist to face the threat, but a second crystal spike shot out and pierced her other hand, trapping her against Bast's cold rigid chest. Fuck this. A distant part of her knew the risk she was running by using her magic this way, but there was no point staying hidden from her father only to end up dead. Before the stronghold could get any other bright ideas about where to pierce her, she dragged power to herself, surprised at how readily it flooded her system. An anguished scream rang from the sentience as she slashed a portal right through the crystal wall holding them captive, and then she was falling forward on Bast's lifeless body, the blue tinge to his skin so much more acute in the reflective glow of her power as they crashed to a hard floor for the second time in as many minutes. Silence fell as her portal snapped close behind them. She hadn't had time to target the portal to a specific place, so much as the concept of home and safety.

Hel tried to sit up and a whimper left her lips as the severed crystal tying them together pulled against her palms, sending a shock of pain through her that kept her exhausted mind clinging to consciousness. She heard feet running toward them and her head jerked up as she tried and failed to reach for a weapon. Her eyes frantically searched the empty room they were lying in and a familiar breakfast bar and couches filled her field of vision—Bast's penthouse. A figure appeared in the entry as she struggled to maintain her hold on consciousness.

"What the fuck?" A voice said, and she eventually processed it as Ra's.

"I brought him back to you," she whispered, and then her eyes rolled back in her head and she collapsed against the stiff, cold body of the dead man she'd risked everything to save.

THE SMELL of spicy tea was what lured her back to the world of the conscious. She reached up to brush a hair from her face and felt rough gauze against her skin. Someone had bandaged her hands. She was lying on her side and when she opened her eyes, the black-on-black of feathers lying slack against silk sheets filled her vision. She reached out a trembling finger to Bast's bare arm lying near her, ignoring the pull on the IV line that ran from her wrist to somewhere behind her. He still felt cool to the touch. A tear snuck down her cheek before she could stop it.

"The souls here are drawing him back. This is the heart of his network. They're all through the structure. He's close to returning. Can you feel it?" Ra said, his voice coming from the doorway.

"All I feel is the hole where he should be," she said, too tired to obfuscate the truth.

The bed dipped behind her as Ra sat down. "If you sit up, I'll take that line out and you can have some of this tea. Or I could just put a shot of caffeine straight into the drip? You seem like you need it."

Hel let him help shift her until she was leaning back against the headboard, body cushioned by pillows. He carefully pressed the mug he'd promised into her injured hands and she closed her eyes and let the steam drift over her face, relishing its spicy scent and the sensation of warmth after the cold dark of the void and unconsciousness.

"How long?" she asked after she'd taken a sip.

"A day from when you stopped responding in the lighthouse until you pulled your disappearing trick. Two days since you magically reappeared in the living room."

"And why am I in Bast's bed?"

"Would you believe me if I said there was only one bed?" Ra teased. "It was easier to keep an eye on you both in one place. And your connection with him is far stronger than ours. We thought it might help pull him back." Clearly he was meddling again. She marvelled at the man's ability to pull this kind of shit even when Bast was dead and she'd almost followed him.

Ana and Kaia must have heard their voices because they rushed into the room before she could reply. "Auntie Hellkitten!" Kaia said, throwing herself toward the bed before Ra caught the girl in his arms.

"Auntie's a bit delicate right now, sweet-pea. Be gentle."

"I missed you," Kaia whispered in her ear, sweeping her wing over Hel's body as she hugged her carefully without disturbing her tea. That moment of kindness reinforced her resolution that she *had* to leave as soon as the Archivist was found. There was no way she could put these people at risk, put Kaia at risk. That wasn't a surprising realisation, though. The surprising part was that she didn't *want* to leave anymore.

"Thank you for saving him," Ana said, voice cracking.

"Speaking of that. How exactly did you get him back here?" Ra asked.

"Enough. She's only just woken up," Ana said, whacking

his arm. "We'll go and start prepping dinner," she said, pulling Kaia away from Hel's side.

Hel felt panic set in as Ra's question reminded her how exactly she'd got there. She avoided portalling because it was the only way her father could trace her. And now she'd led him right to the tower, right to Bast and Kaia and all their family. Could she pull off whatever trick had stopped the hounds again? It wouldn't matter if they still reported back her location. And the other hunters that followed would be unlikely to be as vulnerable to her power.

"I have to go," she said, abandoning her tea on the side table and struggling to disentangle herself from the sheets.

"Hey. None of that. You need to rest," Ra said, refusing to get out of her way.

"He'll find me," she said.

A shiver of ice-cold power across the marks on her back was followed by a barely intelligible croak from the limp form beside her—"You're safe here."

Ra dived over her body to clutch a now-conscious Bast in his arms and hug him tight. Hel would have taken advantage of the distraction to sneak out but his weight was pinning her legs to the bed.

"I have to go," she said again.

Ra finally rolled off her legs, but Bast reached out and twined his fingers with hers before she could move. He wasn't strong enough to hold her there, but she still couldn't make herself pull away. Every breath he took was reviving their dormant connection as colour returned to his face. He took a sip of water from the cup Ra offered and then spoke again. "You protected me. Now the souls around the tower are protecting you, screening you from discovery. Whoever is chasing you doesn't know you're here."

Hel froze and stretched out her awareness. Even as exhausted as she was, the effect of channelling so much power seemed to have made her hyper-sensitive. Her range was extended and she could sense details she never had before. Bast was right. There were no new portal signatures from her father's hunters, although the ones that had cornered her before were probably still in the city.

"We still haven't found the Archivist," she said, hoping to change the subject to less difficult territory.

"Give me a moment to come back to life and then we'll deal with it. In the meantime, how are you not dead?" Bast asked.

Hel glanced down at him where he lay with a forearm thrown over his eyes to block the light. She wondered if Ra had put any clothes on him before tucking him into bed. Her eyes traced down his bare chest before she caught herself. Fuck. Not relevant. She needed to think up an answer for him that wouldn't give away her identity.

"I didn't die."

"You were in the place where only the dead who don't want to leave reside, the source of my power," he said.

"Only my mind was. I was searching for you with our connection."

"It was severed when I died."

"Guess I didn't find you then," Hel snapped waspishly.

Ra chuckled from the other side of the bed where he'd pulled up a chair and even Bast cracked a grin.

"Where did you find him?" Ra asked. "His body, I mean."

Hel winced and looked away until Bast squeezed her hand gently. "I need to know," he added.

"In Aliya's bedroom. Pinned to the wall for her weirdo cult to worship," she said finally.

Hel watched the fury play across Bast's face as he fought to get himself under control. "Tyson wasn't there?" he asked.

"No. I saw her take your body and he didn't follow after her."

"We didn't even realise he was out at the island. He'd left for his stronghold by the time I returned from searching for you. Was Aliya using him?" Ra asked.

"It wouldn't have been hard to. He was always blind when it came to getting revenge. I'll enjoy telling him he was duped into helping our father's killer," Bast said.

"She admitted it?"

Bast nodded and winced as if his head pained him. Hel reached over and flicked off the lamp, throwing the room into shadow other than the light coming in from the hallway.

"Thanks," Bast murmured.

"You're really not going to tell us how you did it?" Ra asked her.

Hel looked down at her lap and kept silent.

"This conversation isn't over," Bast said. "But sleep comes higher on the list for now."

"I'll leave you to nap until dinner," Ra said, kissing Bast and then Hel on the forehead before leaving the room.

Despite her exhaustion, Hel was all too conscious of the fact she was now alone in bed with this man she could no longer bring herself to hate. His eyes were still closed and he squeezed her hand gently again as if he could sense her thoughts.

"C'mere," he said, voice slurring with tiredness as he released her fingers to stretch an arm out towards her.

Hel looked down at him in the dim light and decided to

wait until later to start acting sensibly again. Right now, she just wanted to revel in how warm and soft he felt after the shock of cradling his body when it was still stiffened in rigor mortis. She *needed* to.

"I'm glad you're okay," she whispered, before shuffling down to rest her head on his shoulder. His arm wrapped tight around her, followed by his wing. She fell back to sleep cocooned in the reassuring heat now radiating from his body and lulled by the sensation of his heartbeat pulsing along her skin through their restored connection.

CHAPTER 18
BAST

When Bast woke for the second time, he definitely felt like he'd spent three days as a dead body. His heart beat sluggishly as if it was holding the incident against him and he felt like he imagined an old human would feel, every muscle stiff and aching. The one thing that made it bearable was the soft female body nestled against his side. His body thrummed where they touched and he wished he had the energy to take advantage of their position that might never be repeated.

Who is she? he asked again of the souls who still lingered like anxious parents, worried their reanimation wouldn't stick.

That's her story to tell, the response came back.

But she refuses to tell it.

Then you need to be more convincing, an old woman snickered back, her dirty tone conveying exactly how she thought he should go about his convincing.

He groaned and pressed his fingers to his forehead. He couldn't deal with souls who missed having a sex life on top of everything else. They'd better not be watching. Dead voyeurs were the worst.

Hel shifted in his arms at the noise. "You okay?" she murmured.

He pulled her closer and kissed her hair without thinking, losing himself in the intoxication of her scent before clearing his throat awkwardly as he realised what he'd done. "Yeah. Just feeling a bit like I was dead."

She tilted her head up toward him and the silver glow that had returned to his inner wing surface bathed her face in light making her green eyes flash. "Do you do this often?" she asked.

His gaze narrowed on the movement of her lips and he rolled to face her. "Dying? This would be a first," he said, unable to resist the urge to cup her face and brush the pad of his thumb over those lips that were holding him so fascinated.

He could feel her breasts brushing against his chest as her breathing came faster and her lips parted where he touched. He was just leaning toward her, exhaustion be damned, when a sharp knock at the door interrupted.

"Dinner's ready!" Ana called, pushing the door open. "You need to eat to get your strength back and you both need to get back on your feet."

Bast groaned and pressed his forehead gently to Hel's, but the moment was lost. She was already turning away from him and he loosened his hold so she could pull free and limp toward the door. He took an extra fifteen minutes to shower and brush the sensation that something had died in his mouth from his teeth. The something being his own fucking tongue along with everything else. Aliya and Tyson had a lot to answer for.

By the time he'd eaten the meal Ana had prepared for them, he was almost starting to feel like he was actually alive. The constant casual touches from his family as they passed helped, tactile reminders that his heart was beating and he was there for the people who cared for him. Kaia went so far as to curl up in his lap as soon as he'd finished, refusing to let him up until he sat holding her wrapped in arms and wings.

"Don't ever die again, Uncle," she whispered in his ear. "I need you to be here when mama's gone."

Bast's heart almost broke at the quiet words. Obviously, Kaia knew her mother was human, but this was the first time he'd ever heard her state so clearly she knew Ana wouldn't be there for her through the centuries like an elemental mother would've been. She would live longer thanks to his mark on her, but no one knew how much longer. "I'll always be here for you, baby girl. Not even death could keep me away."

Kaia sniffled and hugged him even harder. Hel was watching them and Bast wondered what thoughts were hidden behind her calm expression. What did he really know about the woman? And yet their connection had grown like an invasive weed through his power. He frowned at the thought. He'd been too distracted by everything to notice his magic wasn't the only thing holding them together. What kind of power did she have that it could mesh with his so deeply and allow her to travel to the place of souls? He would've known if it was soul magic. If this was some previously unknown to elementals branch of human magic then it would upset the balance of their world.

The anger he'd felt for her for so long had all but disappeared. She'd put herself at risk to save the people of his city when the contagion hit and she'd done the impossible when she brought him back from Aliya's stronghold. He'd misjudged her when she'd refused to help at first. She obviously cared. And he could no longer remember the reasons he shouldn't act on the compulsive attraction that had grown between them right from the moment they'd met. But that didn't mean he didn't need to figure out exactly who and what she was. The more he thought about it, the more he wondered if she was even human at all. The only other person in their world who could portal was Tir, and he was pretty sure Tir wasn't from their Earths. They were an utterly unique species here.

Hel disappeared to her room while he was lost in thought, conveniently avoiding any further questions, and Kaia's body had relaxed in his arms, her breathing deep and even.

"I'll take her off to bed," Ana said, scooping the girl out of his lap without waking her.

"Who's still here?" Bast asked Ra, accepting the glass of whiskey he'd brought over.

"Mica and Lady Nerida both decided to stay long enough to figure out what was going on."

"Good. We can meet in the morning and sort out this mess."

"You need to rest and rebuild your strength."

Bast shook his head. "No time. They won't stick around for long. At least I'm only dealing with physical tiredness now. With my body still half held to life with magic while I heal, I can draw on that power to compensate."

Ra looked incredulous. "Fuck, man. Don't say that like it's a good thing. You mean you're still half dead."

Bast shrugged. "It's better than the alternative."

"What are you going to do about Hel? Do you trust her?"

"Nothing's changed. We still need her. And she saved my life. Again."

Ra raised an eyebrow. "Uh. Everything's changed. Don't think I can't see how different your connection to her is compared to ours. And none of that is a reason to trust her. Who knows why she did it. Maybe it was guilt for betraying you. And, just as importantly, who knows *how* she did it. We don't even know how she ended up on the island."

Bast pushed aside the irrational surge of protectiveness he felt for Hel at Ra's suggestion. It was a perfectly logical concern and Ra was right to raise it. That didn't mean he had to listen to it, though. "Like I said. We still need her."

"Would you let her go if we didn't?"

Everything in him rebelled at the thought. "That's a pointless hypothetical," he said after too long a pause.

"You never answered my question. Do you trust her?"

Bast thought back to all the unanswered questions, the mysterious hounds that hunted her, the unknown source of her power. He weighed that against the few potentially self-less acts that had unbalanced his opinion of her and found the scales were not where he wanted them to be. "No," he sighed.

"Then for fuck's sake, start holding some of yourself back. She hasn't noticed how much power she has over you. Don't let her."

Another night's sleep did wonders for Bast's body. He no longer felt like he was fighting his joints to make them function and the ever-present ache in his muscles was starting to fade. Of course, that could have been because the rigor mortis would have been wearing off anyway. He could still feel a constant thrum of power through his blood as the souls flooded his system with magic to keep it functioning. It accelerated his healing. At least he should be able to leave the tower before the day was out without setting back his recovery.

His first stop was an impromptu meeting of the city's leaders so early the skies were still dark. "Where are we at?" he asked Morrigan.

"Rumours were starting to circulate about you dying, but if you show your face somewhere public today I'm sure we can quash that. There's been an increase in random predator attacks. Several dead bodies have been found on the outskirts of the city in places they wouldn't usually venture. We've upped our patrols, but something doesn't feel right about them."

"Have you identified the species attacking? Could it be the hounds?"

"The wounds have all been too mangled to tell. Which would be understandable once, but this is three bodies now that have all been left in a state that we can't identify what killed them. It's not normal."

"Keep doing what you're doing. See if you can find a pattern in the locations and redistribute some of the surveillance cameras."

Morrigan nodded, still looking troubled.

"What about the humans? Was there any unrest after Aliya's stunt at the ball?" Bast asked Niko.

"The usual posturing. I'm worried about how she got the word out without us noticing earlier, though. I've got people looking into it. It's possible we have a leak in the tower."

Bast winced. The last thing he needed was one of Aliya's people in his domain. "Ana, can you help get to the bottom of that?"

"On it."

"Anything else urgent we need to deal with?"

The room fell silent, everyone already focused on what they needed to do to keep the city functioning.

Mica and Nerida were breakfasting on the roof terrace when he searched them down, the wind calm enough that it wasn't causing havoc with the heavy brocade table cloth. The two elementals looked up in surprise as he strode out to join them. Apparently his people hadn't warned them he'd returned.

"Bastion. It is good to see you. When Ty and Aliya disappeared, I feared the worst," Mica said, standing to grip his hand.

It was Bast's turn to be surprised when Mica drew him into a half-hug, clasping his shoulder with his free hand. Nerida watched the interaction with interest, remaining seated.

"I don't know about the worst, but Tyson killed me and Aliya decided I would make a good game trophy on her wall," he said when they were all seated, taking great pleasure in the shock his statement inspired as he poured himself a coffee.

"It doesn't seem to have held you back," Nerida said drily, despite her obvious discomfort at his revelations.

"It was enlightening at least. Aliya admitted she killed my father."

The lack of surprise in his companions was telling.

"Does Tyson know?" Mica asked.

Bast shook his head and Nerida chuckled. "That will be a fun conversation. If you don't kill him first?"

"I hadn't really thought ahead to the family reunion."

Nerida was watching him with her head tilted, judging. He ignored her to take another sip of coffee.

"He'll do," she said finally, addressing her words to Mica. "You're right. Things have progressed too far if your stronghold has been breached and the power he showed in coming back from the dead should suffice."

Mica nodded. "It helps that he is not the murderer we thought."

Bast blinked and struggled to follow the change of topic. "What exactly do you think I'm doing?"

"Nerida and I are agreed there's no point in standing on tradition with things the way they are. We need four of the most powerful magic users to hold Tir to this dimension. If you stand in, we only have to convince one more ruler. So, take your pick. Are we going after the woman who framed you and hung your dead body on her wall or the brother who killed you thinking you murdered his father?"

"Does this mean you're accepting me on the council?"

Nerida threw her head back and laughed. "Don't get ahead of yourself, boy."

Bast narrowed his eyes at the woman but it wasn't like he had much leverage. This needed to happen and he wasn't going to risk further deaths by delaying as a negotiation tactic. It was a first step closer anyway.

He considered Mica's question. Realistically, blackmailing Aliya with the threat of telling Ty who killed their father was probably the easiest option. She was nothing if not a pragmatist. It didn't sit right with him though. He could understand why Ty had done what he did but Aliya's actions spoke to a cruel self-interest he didn't want anywhere near him, especially in such a volatile and delicate undertaking. Tyson, on the other hand, would stand by his word if he committed. He might be a vengeful, murderous, arsehole. But he was an honourable one.

"It has to be Ty," he said, voicing his conclusion aloud.

"I agree. The trick will be how to win him over. If you can convince him of Aliya's guilt I think he will come round, but he's been out of communication since he left and he's not likely to believe anything that comes out of your mouth," Mica said.

"Would you enter a truth spell with him? And can you actually deliver the Archivist?" Nerida asked.

Bast pressed a finger to his temple where a migraine was starting. How had this morning spun out of control so quickly? Would he submit to be locked in a truth spell? It was the only way Ty was likely to believe his story about Aliya killing their father, but once it was set he would be compelled to answer whatever Ty asked until he was released. He could be forced to reveal anything.

"Let me talk to my people."

HEL LOOKED UP WARILY from where she was playing cards with Ra when he returned to the penthouse as if she could sense his agitation, which she probably could. By the time he'd explained the outcome of his morning's conversations, Ra was just as concerned.

"It's too big a risk. We don't even know if you'll be able to corner Tir. It's not like you've had any luck so far even when they've been in this dimension."

Hel shifted in her seat and Bast felt her heartbeat speed up along their connection. "Something you'd like to share?" he asked.

"I think Aliya was tipping off the Archivist to our search

through someone in the tower. A human," she said, keeping her eyes fixed on her hand.

"And why do you think that?"

Hel cleared her throat. "Because I overheard her giving the order."

"And when were you planning on informing me of that, incredibly pertinent, fact?" Bast growled.

"Now. At this incredibly pertinent moment," she growled back.

Bast's wings flared out as he tried and failed to control his annoyance. "Is there anything else you'd like to share?"

"Ummm ... I think I can get you to the Archivist's dimension using his hand?"

Bast very carefully lowered himself onto the chair across from her because, otherwise, he was going to lose his temper and pick up the infuriating woman, throw her over his shoulder and do something he regretted. "Again. Wondering why you're only telling me this now."

"I didn't know it could be done before. But I think I can use the same method I used to find your body," Hel said, but something in her tone said this wasn't all the truth. He glared at her as if he could peel back her deception by sheer willpower.

"You can create portals," he stated, sick of dancing around the truth.

Ra looked stunned as Hel placed her cards on the table with the slightest tremble to her hands, not making any attempt to deny his intuitive leap. "It's ... dangerous. Complicated. I can be tracked that way, but if your souls can keep my location hidden then I could try."

"The hounds sniff out portals. That's why they were at the tunnel."

"And they travel by them. The fact they haven't appeared inside the tower by now means whatever your souls did is working."

Bast frowned in thought. He didn't know what exactly the souls had done, but he suspected it was location-specific. There was layer upon layer of warding and magical infrastructure around the tower, all seeped in his power. It was unlikely to work elsewhere. He reached out to the ever-present community of the dead around him. *Can you hide Hel away from the tower?* He waited while a buzz of inaudible debate resonated through his senses.

We can interrupt the trace in a small radius around her, a wingspan only, if she keeps your mark. Her hunters would still be able to trace the portal's residue once she left the vicinity.

What do you mean IF she keeps my mark? Bast growled at them. A thousand variations of chuckling laughter echoed through his mind. He rolled his eyes.

"What did they say?" Ra asked, well used to his silent conversations.

"They can hide portals within the bounds of Soul Tower or within a small radius around my mark on Hel, but once she moves away from the portal it will be traceable again."

"Huh. So this mark does have a use after all," Hel said and Bast gritted his teeth in annoyance.

"That thing is the highest honour our people can bestow."

"It's a glorified fucking leash and you know it," Hel snapped back.

Ra groaned. "Will you two give it a rest? Where does this leave us?"

"I fly Hel to Ty's stronghold with Mica and Nerida and

convince him I'm not the bad guy. Hel portals us all to the Archivist and stays very still in the gateway until we contain them. We find the cure for the contagion in the Archives. Hel portals us back to the tower where she can't be traced. Job done and we have the added bonus of leaving Ty to deal with the hounds that will come sniffing after her around his stronghold once she's gone."

"The parting gift he deserves," Hel said with an evil grin that matched his own.

"All you have to do is convince him not to kill you a second time on sight," Ra said.

CHAPTER 19
HEL

"Tell me that's not your whole plan," Hel said as she waited with Bast on the rooftop, all too conscious of the weight of the carefully wrapped severed Archivist's hand hanging in one of her belt pouches.

"The best plans are the simplest."

"I'm not sure that 'Fly to Ty's stronghold. Build a truth spell. Lure him into it.' even qualifies as a plan. It's barely a rough outline. Where are you building it? How are you going to get close without his scouts raising the alarm? Why would he knowingly step inside a spell?"

Mica's laugh sounded from behind her, pausing her tirade. "I like her, but I still don't understand why she's coming along," he said to Bast, sparking a poorly hidden glare from the her in question.

Nerida emerged from the doors behind Mica. "Tyson can't risk offending me and Mica. So we two can fly openly and cast an illusion on you and young Bastion," Nerida explained. "It should last until we pass the boundary of his island and the stronghold realises what's going on."

283

"There's a beach near the human-built settlement on the coastline we can use as the spell location. It will be difficult for the stronghold to cause any major disturbances there without harming the locals. That should buy us enough time for Tyson to come personally. He won't want to delegate killing Bast," Mica added.

"Difficult because the 'stronghold' is a fucking volcano and lava is just a little bit destructive?" Hel clarified.

"I'll keep you safe," Bast said, pulling her into his arms in preparation for flight.

Hel remained tense, fighting her body's natural reaction to his embrace, which was to sink into him until she was pressed close to every part of his muscled form she could reach. "I stand by my earlier statement. That barely qualifies as a plan."

"It's the best we can do with the time we have. If we wait and he gets wind I'm still alive, he'll be alert for attack and we won't make it past the Tyrrhenian Sea without sheets of lava filling the sky," Bast said. And with that cheerful thought hanging unanswered, he propelled them out into the open air, setting a course for the far-distant Fire Court Stronghold off the coast of what was once human Italy.

Bast was holding Hel chest-to-chest and she quickly wrapped her arms and legs around him so she had some semblance of control. From her position, she could watch the two older elementals flying behind and to either side of them over his shoulder. She could also feel every ridge of his abdominal muscles pressing against her core. Why did the wingbeats of flight have to feel quite so much like a certain other driving rhythmic activity?

It took Hel a few minutes to steady her breathing after the adrenaline rush of watching the city disappear far below.

This wasn't like any of the previous times she'd flown in his arms. The three elementals were flying as fast as the combination of their bodies and power could take them, using their magic to weave a tailwind that flung them not unlike a targeted hurricane towards their destination. Bast's shielding counteracted any wind resistance, leaving them travelling in a private bubble of negative air pressure that had Hel's ears braced for a sonic boom that never came while the volume around them, somewhat aptly given Bast's soulweaving, remained as quiet as a graveyard in the dead of night.

"Have you spent much time in the Fire Court?" Hel asked when the silence grew too much.

Bast took his time gathering his thoughts and she almost thought he wouldn't answer. "I grew up on the coastal mainland nearby. The distance was too far for juvenile wings to fly, but I tried to steal a boat to visit the island when I was nine. I didn't even make it halfway. That was the one time I remember my father setting foot in my foster parents' house. He told them if they couldn't keep me in hand, he would take one from each of them to motivate them. I wasn't stupid enough to ever try again."

Hel swallowed hard and squeezed her own hands tighter around his neck. "And I thought my dad was a dick. I'm sorry," she said.

Bast let loose a bitter laugh. "By rights, he could have left me to die when I was born. He would've been insulted my whole childhood for his choice to let me live. He *was* a dick. But I owed him my life."

"We all owe our life to our parents. You were his child. The bare minimum of decent parental care is not actively murdering you," Hel argued. She should know. Her father had hunted her like a sacrificial deer from the moment her guardian had stolen her away to this world as an infant at the dawn of the Melding.

Her indignant response had drawn Bast's focus and when she tilted her head to look up at his face, his rich black eyes ringed in silver almost glowed with suppressed emotion as he watched her. "Anyone would think you care," he murmured, his lips so close she would barely have to move to meet them.

"No child should be abandoned."

"Even an evil necromancer?" he asked, his voice twisting on the would-be insult she'd thrown at him so many times to shut him down.

"Especially a necromancer."

"I want to kiss you," he said, making her startle in his arms.

"Shouldn't you be watching where you're flying?" she asked as her heartbeat started to race.

"Later, then," he promised, but there was a question in his voice, the tiniest hint of vulnerability she didn't know what to do with.

"Once we've dealt with that whole winning over the homicidal brother and saving the world thing," Hel said, leaning closer despite herself until their breath mingled in the thin, cold air of the upper atmosphere they were flying through. What she didn't add was her silent *if I haven't already had to run away.*

The brief moment of vulnerability was replaced with his familiar charisma as a cheeky smile spread across his face and one strong hand firmly stroked down her back. She couldn't help but groan as the move massaged muscles tense from the effort of clinging to him. "I'm not waiting that long. Once our feet are back on solid ground," he said, nuzzling her cheek before tucking her head back into his chest and making up the lost speed the distraction of their conversation had caused.

Not for the first time, Hel wondered what she was doing. Her father's hounds were drawing too close. She needed to get Bast to the Archivist and then find somewhere new to hide, somewhere far away from where the hounds were searching. *But the tower was the only place she'd ever been safe,* her traitorous inner voice pointed out, which was not entirely true because in Bast's arms was the other only place she'd ever been safe.

Round and round her confused thoughts went until she drifted into sleep.

Despite his teasing words, Bast didn't chase a kiss from her at their only stop en route—a safehouse on the outskirts of Mica's territory, the surrounding streets rife with Hel's childhood memories. They both needed every second of sleep they could get and it wasn't like they had the time or privacy for anything that kiss might lead to, Hel reminded herself. She pushed aside the unwanted feeling of disappointment and then immediately harangued herself for feeling it in the first place. She didn't need him. The fact she could sleep soundly nestled in his arms when she'd never been able to truly rest without a locked door between her and anyone nearby meant nothing. With his soft feathers brushing her cheek and his distinctly clean masculine scent evoking the cold gusting winds of the harbour city of home under a star-strewn sky filling her every breath, she slipped back into the blissful simplicity of unconsciousness.

The second leg of their marathon journey took the better part of twelve hours and they crossed the toe of Italy's boot at nearly midnight. A large moon lurked above them, so yellow it was almost orange as if the lava from Ty's volcano strong-hold had reflected into the sky and stained its face.

Bast had dropped to the ground to let her stretch her legs every few hours, but her muscles were cramping unbearably after so long suspended in his grip with limited ability to move. Even the distraction of his body so close to hers was no longer making up for the discomfort. She shifted in his hold, tensing and untensing her limbs as she tried to ease the ache.

"Not long now," he whispered in her ear.

The silence around them had deadened even further as Mica and Nerida reinforced the illusions cloaking them from sight. With the dark sea below them and the night sky above, it reminded Hel of the place of souls she'd found Bast drifting in when he died. She shivered and hugged him tighter.

The first glimpse of Tyson's stronghold was a red glow on the horizon that slowly grew in size. As they drew closer, it resolved into a coalescence of heat and light dripping rivulets of fire in a meshwork of lava flows down the volcano's sides, which were all but invisible in the darkness. She couldn't see it, but she knew Ty's residence was punched into the side of the conical landmass, a marvel of magically shaped and reinforced floating volcanic stones that wouldn't have looked amiss alongside Frank Lloyd Wright's Fallingwater house. That is, if you replaced the water with lava and expanded it by an order of magnitude that made it clearly visible from the coastline they'd just flown over. The comparison of the two buildings was one of many iconic images people shared in online forums to show the mirrors and echoes between the history of the two Earths that had melded.

Hel could imagine a young Bast staring longingly out

over the water, forced to face the constant visual reminder of the family who'd declared him outcast. Had he tried to spot his little brother launching from the family home as he learned to fly? She'd never laid eyes on her family, but she knew what it was like to watch from the outside wishing you could have something you would never receive. She squeezed Bast a little tighter and felt a surge of warmth in response down the connection between them.

Between one wingbeat and the next, they crossed over into the stronghold's bounds. The familiar questing presence brushed against her mind, this one carrying with it the sense of heat and pressure that formed its physical core. It surged around them and Hel felt its confusion at this man who felt like family but couldn't talk to it.

"The stronghold recognises you. Maybe this will work better than I thought," she whispered.

Bast's movements hitched and they dropped lower in the sky before he recovered. "You can feel it? Is it alerting Ty?"

"Wait. You can't?"

Bast was silent for a moment as if he regretted his words. "No. Another eccentricity of being a soulweaver. Don't share that with anyone."

"How the fuck will you know if it's about to attack then?"

"You'll tell me. Hush, now. We're nearing the settlement."

Hel clenched her teeth so hard her jaw started to cramp because it was the only way to avoid shrieking at him. Did he value his life so little he would enter enemy territory half-cocked and exhausted with no way of knowing when the situation turned deadly? She hoped at least Mica and Nerida knew what they were doing.

The three elementals landed on a beach near a pier strung with glittering globes of suspended lava like volcanic fairy lights that dimly lit their surrounds and reflected in the lapping waters of the sea.

"He knows we're here. We don't have long. We'll draw the spell out on the sand. He shouldn't notice in the darkness. You'll just have to get him to step in front of you," Mica said.

Hel watched in silence as the two rulers each grabbed a stray stick from the tideline and started sketching an intricate design around the space where Bast stood. Elemental magic generally didn't need such diagrams but this particular spell, often used in trials to contain and compel, needed a frame to channel the magic through. In courtrooms, it was inlaid permanently into the floor and activated as needed. Out here, the sand would have to do.

They were only partway finished when the first dragon swooped over them, close enough that the downdraft from its passing sent Hel's hair flicking across her face. She was watching it climb back into the air when it jerked around in a harsh turn as if some external force had taken control. As it banked down toward them, she felt the nearby sentience's eager-to-please curiosity turn to growling anger, a guard dog set on intruders. The ground rumbled beneath her feet and the stars were blotted out by a patch of darkness as ash shot into the sky from the volcano's crater.

"Incoming. I'll run interference," Nerida said.

Bast shifted his feet, but Mica was gripping his shoulder and hissing in his ear. Hel couldn't make out the words over the screeching of dragons and the sounds of the volcano's rage. Drawing her baton from its sheath, she untwisted it into its dual knives.

"Nice blades," Nerida muttered behind her as she put her back to Hel's and drew forth a spout of water from the nearby ocean to shape into a dome over their position.

"That's not going to do much against a volcano," she replied.

"Let me take care of Vella. Ty's got her all worked up and she's hurt that Bast's ignoring her."

Another dragon swooped down on their position. The impact of its claws dragging across the water shield sent sparks flying across the beach that kept burning where they landed in flames as blue as the ocean Nerida had drawn from. Their position was now lit like a runway.

"Ugh. Look at Ty being all fancy from the safety of those dragon's minds," Nerida complained. "I could really use one of your lover's shields about now so I can focus on offense, but he'll mess up the spell if he tries anything from inside it."

The next assault came from three directions at once. An amorphous blob of burning magma the size of a small car slammed down from above at the same time as two dragons crashed at the sides head-first. The shield flickered under the combined weight and the larger dragon breached its side as Nerida was forced to divert the water of her shield to the point where it was being steadily steamed away. The dragon, sporting a large collection of fangs at the head of its sinuous body, was heading straight towards Bast. If it got any further it would erase the damn spell-work from the sand.

"Hey! You fucking coward! Come down here yourself instead of sending these poor creatures to die!" Hel yelled, 90 percent certain Ty would be using the dragon's senses and would hear her. She launched one of her blades at the same time as her cry, aiming for the soft tissue where the dragon's back leg met its body. They weren't made for throwing, but they were perfectly balanced regardless and Hel put all her considerable inhuman strength behind it. The blade hit its mark with a dull thwack that left a forearm's length of sharp metal impaled in the creature.

The dragon swung its head around to the threat and, as it watched her, the fiery lava of its eyes faded to burnt amber. Ty had left it. Which meant it was now far more interested in the annoying person sticking holes in it than the prey its master had set it hunting.

She heard Mica curse as the dragon's tail swept over the edge of the design he'd been drawing. He'd have to fix it before Tyson made his entrance. Nerida was totally engaged in deflecting the shower of volcanic meteors that was now raining down around them and Bast couldn't do anything without messing up the spell. That left Hel to deal with the big angry flying lizard. Shit. She darted to the side as it half slithered, half pounced toward her on its weird melding of clawed limbs and serpent body. Staggering as its scaled side slammed into her ribs, Hel winced as the clawed tips of its folded wings tore shreds through her leather jacket.

The metal grip of her knife flashed in the darkness beside her, reflecting the red glow of the volcano's continuing assault. Shoving her other blade into her thigh sheath, she grabbed onto the one sticking from the dragon's side, using it to haul herself up its body and out of reach of those lethal claws and jaw. Her fingers scrabbled for purchase on the slick surface of its scales and she grasped the edge of a wing to haul herself onto its back using that same trusty knife hilt as a footstep to push higher.

Riding a dragon was nothing like riding a griffin.

There were no soft feathers or fur ruff to cling to. The edges of its scales caught at her hands and left them criss-crossed with slices like papercuts. She was grateful for the small protection of the light bandaging that still covered her palms. She'd thought she'd be out of reach of its jaws once she was on its back. She was wrong. Its body was far more flexible than a griffin and its neck stretched long past its wings, meaning the only thing stopping it from snapping her head off right at that second was the fact she was hunkered down close to the join of its membranous wings. She'd also forgotten about the whole flame thing.

"Hel, move!" Bast yelled.

Luckily, the creature had decided to launch into the sky while it toasted its prey. As its wings raised high and its body stretched upward, she used the momentum to throw herself back to the ground. The angle of its attack and its surging flight meant that its own wing blocked the worst of the flames from reaching her. The sand an arms-length to her left turned to glass and a wave of heat scalded her exposed skin as its misfire landed. The now airborne dragon banked around to face her and she scrambled back, knowing she was out of options.

"Leave," Nerida's voice cracked out from beside her, and the dragon shot past them and back to the looming mountain, responding to her sheer dominance.

"I don't suppose you could have done that a little earlier? Like as soon as it fucking attacked!" Hel panted, fuming.

"I was busy and you seemed to be managing well for a human," Nerida said, her curiosity clear.

Had she been testing her? She could've been killed! Hel rolled her eyes and staggered to her feet. The sky seemed to have stopped raining magma and the lack of movement in Bast's direction suggested Mica had completed the spell. Either that or he was dead. She peered into the darkness and saw Bast still standing, his barely visible black feathers rustling in the low breeze. Nearby, Mica was leaning on a low wall, his face lit up with the blue glow of a satellite phone. Not dead, then.

Tyson's voice broke the silence as he dropped down out of nowhere to the beach near Bast. "I knew I should have burned your body to a crisp when I had the chance."

"Why didn't you, brother?" Bast asked.

"Aliya wanted to play. It seemed like a good idea at the time. I won't make that mistake again."

"And what if Aliya was playing *you*?" Nerida asked, moving closer so she and Mica each flanked Bast's position, their movement distracting Ty from looking down and seeing the patterns drawn in the sand.

"If you take his side, I will consider it a declaration of war," Ty warned.

"All we're asking is that you listen to him," Mica said.

"Or we could settle this the old way. Unless you're too scared to fight me hand-to-hand?" Bast said.

Tyson took a step forward, fiery wings flaring wide and fists clenching at his sides. Hel's breath caught as she waited. Two more steps and he'd be in the circle.

"I was never the one who ran scared, *brother*," Ty said.

Mica was watching Bast with a look of concern. "Let's not say anything we might regret," he warned.

"No. You just hid safe in your little castle while your creatures hunted me down," Bast said.

"I didn't hide the day I killed you."

Bast took a half-step forward and barely jerked to a stop in time to avoid breaking the circle he was standing in. "Did you not? You couldn't even dispose of my body yourself. Coward."

That did it. Tyson charged forward and a flare of light raced across the sand, enclosing the two men in the spell and trapping them each out of reach from the other. Bast was speaking before Tyson even had a chance to process what had happened. Hel knew he had to get the words out before Ty realised he held the upper hand. As the one standing in the questioner's circle, only Ty could break the spell now it had been triggered. Anyone else who crossed the lines would be caught right along with Bast, forced to speak only truth.

"It was Aliya who killed our father. She told me as I lay dying in her grasp," Bast said.

"Liar," Ty spat back, but his eyes were tracing the spell-work on the ground and he froze as he realised where exactly he was. "You're totally vulnerable to me right now. Why would you do that?" His face was a study of confusion that turned to shock as he belatedly processed Bast's revelation.

"Because it was the only way."

"Ask him if he can really find the Archivist," Nerida said.

Hel's head whipped around to the woman. What was she playing at? This wasn't the plan.

"Can you?" Ty asked.

"Yes," Bast said through gritted teeth.

"Ask him how," Mica added.

"What the fuck? I trusted you," Bast said.

"And you can still trust me. This is too important for you to be keeping secrets," Mica replied.

Ty grinned. "Not the allies you were hoping for, brother? Welcome to council politics. I think I'll ask a few questions of my own as well, though. How do you regenerate?"

Hel watched as Bast strained to keep his mouth shut. Sweat beaded on his brow and his body shook from the effort of keeping silent. Ty was going to make him tell them how to kill him. He would destroy Bast's tower and the reservoir of souls who'd saved him so he couldn't come back from death ever again.

She shouldn't care what he said in that circle. She didn't owe him anything. There was no way to get to him other than a portal. She didn't have to expose herself like that. She could just let this play out. Nausea flooded her at the thought and every instinct screamed at her to *do something. Save him.*

The first words of an answer dragged forth from Bast's mouth, each one catching as he tried to pull them back. "The ... source..."

Fuck this. She couldn't let it happen. She was ten paces away. All four elementals spun to face her when she launched into a sprint from a standing start. Bast's speech paused for a breath, but then his shock destroyed his focus and his words came faster.

"...of my regeneration..."

Four paces away. She reached into her belt pouch, grabbing Tir's severed hand and desperately feeling for the withered connection between it and the rest of the Archivist's body.

"...resides in..."

Two paces away. She was drawing down power without care, flooding her body with the energy from the connection between worlds where Ty's stronghold grew through, between, and below the human settlement, each supplementing the other. The roots of a volcano run deep, and the power that shunted her out into the vastness of possible dimensions burned hot and fast.

The elemental rulers looked more confused than

anything. Ty's face was twisting into a scornful smirk, probably anticipating questioning her when she entered the circle. Dick. She put on a burst of speed that was nothing compared to the speed with which her consciousness was flying towards her target.

"...my..." Bast's voice hitched again as the spell adjusted to her presence.

The magic didn't get a chance to kick back in, because her destination had finally locked in place. She careened into Bast, tackling him, and it was a measure of his shock that he fell as she intended instead of catching her. The two of them tumbled through the still-opening portal she'd just forced into being behind him. A sensation like the searing heat of a sun flashed across her mind as they crashed through the gate between dimensions.

Her physical fall was cushioned by Bast's fairly solid chest, but the snap of her consciousness back where it belonged after such a precipitous use of her magic left Hel feeling like her mind had collided with one of the stone walls of the room they'd landed in. She groaned as she rolled clear of Bast and thumped onto a hardwood floor. She was never using her power like that again. She would've crawled off into a corner to die or vomit or something, but his arms wrapped around her as she started moving.

"You have to stay next to the gateway," he reminded her, voice urgent.

She groaned again, flopping back to the floor.

"I wondered how long it would take you to show up. To what do I owe the pleasure, little cousin?" a rich tenor voice called from nearby, just as the rest of the elemental rulers emerged through the gateway after them and all hell broke loose.

CHAPTER 20
BAST

The discomfort of multiple boots tripping over him as three-quarters of the elemental council made a somewhat inelegant entrance into Tir's dimension was nothing compared to the roiling guilt Bast felt at Hel having exposed herself. How the fuck was he going to protect her now?

Mica was the first to recover, always the calm general, and had looped a noose of raw power around Tir before his wings had even flared to halt his stumbling fall.

Tir's tentacles shot toward them in retaliation and the refined voice that had greeted them shifted to an animalistic shriek of fury. Bast tried to shield himself, but there were no souls in this pocket dimension. It may as well have been a desert for the power it offered him. Instead, he shifted his body between Hel and Tir, shielding her the only way he could.

Tyson, hot-headed idiot that he was, had used his momentum to charge the Archivist, sheathing his body in flame to avoid their attack while he tried to pin them to the wall. Tir's jaw had unhinged into five wide petals in response, each lined with razor-sharp teeth that snapped toward the Fire Lord as they wrestled.

Nerida circled the room, observing from the side-lines, but quickly added her noose of water to Mica's when he glared at her.

"Do something. They're hurting them," Hel said from behind him, voice desperate.

He turned to her in surprise and when he looked back, he processed what she'd already seen, what he should've seen himself, given his history—a person pinned to the wall and thrashing in pain as three elementals ripped their freedom away.

"Stop!" Bast called out, his voice booming through the space. But no one paid him any mind and Tyson was already wrapping his own leash of fire around Tir's neck.

"Shield them," Hel hissed.

"I don't have any power here."

Hel reached out and took his hand, her calloused grip strengthening the shock of connection between them. "Use me."

This time when he sought his power, he sent his mind reaching through the network of entanglement that joined him to the woman beside him. His nerves thrummed as he sunk into the sensation of her. He wished he could pause and just exist inside her, but his magic drew him onward. She was part of the gateway she'd created and, through her, he could sense their world on the other side, the world that contained the power he needed. Hel became a channel for him in the same way the dead usually did.

Drawing forth a shining cord of magic from the adjacent world, he sent it shattering across the room. All movement froze. Crystal droplets of his power drifted toward the floor like petals in a spring breeze. When they reached the ground, the spell would break. What could he say to make them listen? Hel squeezed his hand from behind him and an idea formed that might save Hel and Tir both. He just hoped the Archivist was as canny as they seemed.

"Perhaps we could take a second to breathe. Tir let us enter the Archives through their portal. Shall we ask them why?" Bast said, laying the foundation of the deception that it was Tir's portal instead of Hel's that'd given them access.

The Archivist's swirling nebulous eyes flashed with pinpricks of light and colour. He just hoped that didn't mean they were about to keep trying to eat Tyson. The first of Bast's drops of power hit the ground with the sigh of a body's dying breath and the elementals were released from his hold.

"You agreed to help us, Bastion. Are you backing out?" Mica asked, his arm muscles straining where he'd ended up holding back one of Tir's arms from clawing at Ty's face.

"No. I'm calling a truce," Bast said, directing his words to the Archivist.

Tir tilted their chin in acknowledgement, the movement sending the tentacles undulating from their head like braids susurrating downward while their horns glinted in the fading sparks of Bast's power. "I will listen if they release me." Their voice had resumed its rich tenor, strangely refined in contrast to their earlier shriek and the violence they were capable of.

"You'll run if we release you," Ty said.

"I will hear you out."

"This will go much faster if we have their willing assistance," Nerida said.

Mica nodded and released Tir, stepping away slowly.

That was a good sign. Mica and Nerida were old enough that they would've dealt with this strange person many times in the past. Whereas Ty was even younger than Bast and he doubted the Fire Lord had ever visited the Archives before they lost access after the Melding. Ty swore under his breath and followed suit. None of the rulers had released the bands of power they'd leashed Tir with, though.

The Archivist laughed bitterly. "I suppose that's about as much as I could hope for from an elemental ruler," they said.

"Is what Bast said true? Did you open the portal to let us enter?" Mica asked.

Bast held his breath as Tir's eyes met his and then flicked to the woman behind him. "I let you enter," Tir said finally, carefully skirting the truth. Their species' inability to lie was part of the reason they'd been press-ganged into their current role centuries earlier. Technically, Tir *had* welcomed them before the fighting broke out and Bast certainly wasn't going to argue semantics. The important thing was that the council believed Tir was responsible for the portal. He took a calming breath.

"Why?" Mica asked.

"Because there is only so long I can run, and my sanctuary has already been defiled."

As one, the elementals swung their heads toward the archway that led to the Archives proper. The chaos of the previous minutes meant none of them had noticed what was now painfully evident. The precious archive of their people's history, so carefully stored in this empty dimension to keep it safe, had been sacked. Broken furniture and scorch marks abounded and the scent of charred parchment drifted in the air.

"Who did this? Why did you let them in?" Ty growled, lunging forward to press his forearm to Tir's throat.

Tir smiled in response, or at least Bast thought they smiled; it was hard to tell with the number of lips and teeth in question. "If I was infallible, you never would have succeeded in enslaving me in the first place. They came while I was out hunting in your dimension. I never saw them."

"Is anything left?" Nerida asked, and Bast was surprised to see a tear leaking down her cheek as she stared toward the empty room beyond.

"Only my memories," Tir said.

"Do you remember anything that could help us with the contagion?" Mica asked.

"Perhaps. What are you willing to give for that?"

Surprisingly, it was Ty who responded. "Your freedom."

"You cannot make that decision alone," Nerida chided.

"There's nothing left for them to guard. What does it matter?" Ty asked.

"The boy has a point," Mica sighed and the two older elementals seemed to hold a silent discussion between them.

"Very well," Nerida said, finally. "If you make a record of all the information you recall from the Archives, we will set you free."

Tir's eyes glowed with satisfaction at the concession as he spoke. "I've been searching the Archives since the contagion first appeared. The only possible reference I could find was on a slip of paper tucked into a first edition of 'Dawn' I collected from a second-hand bookstore on the outskirts of Lord Mica's court. It read: *I thought we were leaving him to burn, but the contagion's darkness slipped in behind us through the gate. Watch for his vanguard and the shards of stasis. He is the self-proclaimed Emperor of Suns. The Melding was his firebreak, do not let him repeat it. When there is no choice left, call for my atonement."*

"Well, that's fairly cryptic. It's a start at least. I want every text you've memorised recorded before we release you. We need to preserve our history and we may notice something you've missed," Nerida said.

"That will take months," Tir said, their tentacles thrashing like angry snakes.

"What is months compared to the rest of your immortal life?" Mica asked.

Tir's nebulous eyes glared at the elementals, every single one of their teeth bared in a horrifying rictus. "Fine. I will do it at *his* home," he said, pointing at Bast. Before any of them could react, a shimmering veil brushed over Tir's body and they disappeared through a portal they'd somehow wrapped around themself like an impossibly thin cloak slipped between their skin and the loops of power around their neck.

"I guess that saves us the debate of where to keep them. We're lucky they left us an exit," Nerida said drily, picking her way back across the room toward Hel's still-open portal.

When Bast looked down at his hellcat, she still looked shell-shocked enough from whatever it had taken to portal to the Archivist's dimension that he risked scooping her up into his arms from her position slumped on the floor.

"Twisted her ankle," he said when Mica raised an eyebrow in question, the excuse allowing him to wait for the others to pass.

"You can't portal home or they'll realise it was you," he whispered once they were alone, unsure how much of a sound barrier the gateway was.

"I couldn't anyway. I'm tapped dry," Hel said, and he

could feel the truth of her words in the way she hung limply in his arms.

"I'm going to get us away from here as fast as possible. No chance for the hounds to follow."

Hel just nestled her head into his chest and he was floored at her trust. He squeezed her closer, protectiveness surging inside him. He was careful to only take one step through the portal, pausing on the other boundary to let his power seep back into him. When Hel's body had crashed into his and carried him over the first time, the breaking truth spell and physical impact had lessened his awareness of crossing the gateway. On the return trip, his brain felt like it somersaulted in his skull in some sort of synchronised swimming move with his stomach and he shivered as the portal's power played across his feathers, Hel's power. It felt like a miniature sun. Life-giving despite the searing heat. That part wasn't actually unpleasant, although it did heighten his awareness of her body pressed against him and he couldn't afford the distraction.

The other three rulers stood several paces away on the beach talking as the portal snapped closed behind them. He wasn't going to risk delaying their exit by joining them. Sending a plea to the souls of those who'd been lost to the volcano's vagaries over time, he shaped his request without words but instead communicating only the feel of his intense need to keep the woman in his arms safe. Power surged through him in response and he drew it tight around himself like a coiled spring.

"Follow quickly if you don't want to be left behind," he called to the others. The less they saw, the better. He hoped they left before Hel's hunters arrived and sparked more questions.

When he launched himself into the air, it was a straight vertical take-off that shot him skyward so fast the stars blurred to white lines across the sky. The glowing centre of the volcano's crater below them was only a distant speck as he curved his trajectory homeward.

"Thank you," Hel said, her words just audible over the wind rushing past his ears.

"The least I can do is get you home." He breathed deep, inhaling her scent. Home. He'd grown used to having her sullen presence filling the penthouse. She'd made a place for herself within his inner circle, within his chosen family.

"Not just for that. For finding a way to keep my portalling hidden from the council. And for giving me back a piece of myself I thought was lost forever. Before this, I hadn't used my power since I was thirteen."

Interesting. What had happened back then? That would be around the time her guardian disappeared and Ryker had bought her indenture. They'd dug into her past when she'd first caught his eye but there were no records before the indenture auction, no sign she'd existed at all. "Well, you've saved me three times now. It's only fair."

"Careful. Your contract might land you in debt to me," Hel teased.

"You're only one ahead. I saved you from the hound as well as tonight."

"The hound who wouldn't have found me if you hadn't dragged me out to chase portals in an abandoned tunnel!"

Bast grinned against her hair. Sometime in the previous weeks, their bickering had become a comfort. A sign the danger was not imminent enough to stop the tension that always ran between them.

"Who's hunting you, Hel?" he asked, and he immediately regretted the question as the silence turned sharp and her body stiffened against him.

"It doesn't matter," she said.

"I can't keep you safe if you don't tell me what the threat is."

"It's not your job to keep me safe," Hel snapped.

But I want it to be, he thought. *And even if I didn't, we're so entwined now that I don't know what your death would do to me.* He didn't say that, though. She was skittish enough as it was without sparking her flight reflex with that kind of revelation.

Tir was waiting for them on the roof terrace of Soul Tower when they landed, still ahead of the other rulers. The Archivist's tentacles undulated with the city's winds like a child making waves with their hand out an open car window.

"I can feel the flow of souls through the air currents here. They feel ... content," Tir said.

Bast gently lowered Hel to her feet and kept his hands on her hips as he looked at the strange creature in surprise. He'd never met anyone not connected to him who could sense the ocean of souls that washed over the city.

"Can you speak to them like Bast can?" Hel asked.

Tir shook their head and the swaying tentacles settled down. "No. That's not my nature."

"We appreciate your discretion about our entrance to the Archives," Bast said carefully, searching Tir's face for any sign they would give them away.

"And I'm sorry about your hand," Hel added, wincing as she glanced down at their damaged arm.

Tir looked at Hel and smiled that terrifying smile again. "It was my choice to sacrifice it. It will grow back. We three understand what it is to be predators made prey. I won't share your secret, little cousin."

Bast's eyes flicked back and forth between them. "You're related?"

Tir laughed. "A figure of speech only. Our powers are different, but with a similar result. Distant cousins if you will."

Bast wondered if that were all the truth because Hel had stilled beneath his hands, and her heartbeat that was now an ever-present background song to his existence had kicked up at Tir's words. The only people he knew who could form portals were Tir, the mysterious master of the hounds hunting Hel, and Hel herself. It was entirely possible the Archivist was related to his hellcat. He couldn't explore the question any further though because a series of thumps behind him marked the arrival of the three other rulers.

He raised a hand in greeting. He'd wondered if Tyson would make the trip back, but the lure of Tir's knowledge must've been enough to drag him along.

"Come. We could all use some rest. We can reconvene in the morning," Bast said, leading the way to the entrance to the Tower.

By the time they'd made it inside, Ana was there to whisk their guests away to their quarters. Bast kept his arm wrapped around Hel's waist as they headed to his penthouse.

"I guess that's my contract finished, then," Hel said.

He inhaled sharply as they stepped into the penthouse, adrenaline and raw possessiveness flooding through him at the thought she might try and leave. The intoxicating contrast of her jasmine and steel scent filled his lungs. Her shirt had come loose during the flight and his fingers slipped underneath to trace against the soft skin of her hip. His lips curved in satisfaction when she leaned into him, soothing his agitation. Energy surged down their connection despite the fatigue that wore at him. The power dancing between them expanding and twisting through their bodies until he could feel each breath she took, each beat of her heart, each shiver at his touch, as if they were his own. They were both silent as they passed through the living area and headed to the hallway. When they reached her doorway, he paused and bent his head to rest against hers.

"Stay with me?" he asked, and he wasn't sure anymore whether he meant this one night or something more. This was the woman who'd chosen to save him every time, even when she'd hated him. The woman who'd trusted herself to him when the world told her he was a monster. The woman who made his body burn with need even when he couldn't stand her, and it was so much worse now he could. He knew nowhere near enough about her and yet he knew everything that mattered. He wanted her. She belonged with him.

She tilted her head up to look into his eyes and he ached to ease the vulnerability that flashed there. He almost pulled back as the echo of her mental state played along their connection. Something had left her reeling under a raft of complex emotions he struggled to identify, but before he could back off she'd wrapped a hand behind his neck and was kissing him. As her mouth crushed against his in a motion that was more desperate need than seduction, a wave of lust swept between them that washed both their thoughts away. The time for rationality and barriers between them was past. Now, they were nothing but need.

Spinning them around, he pressed her body hard to the wall, hoisting her up to wrap her legs around him as he took control of their kiss. Her moan sent a shiver through him that had him struggling not to rip her clothes off and take her right there in the hallway. He'd never been so hypersensitive to each touch and every stroke of his tongue against hers. Hel raked her nails through his hair and he could swear he felt each individual line of pleasure sink down through his body to the throbbing erection he was grinding against her.

"How the fuck does this come off?" she gasped, tearing at his jacket.

He grinned and kissed her again, nipping at her lip as he freed a hand from under her shirt to stroke along the magicked tailoring at the collar of his shirt and jacket to make the fabric drop away from his wings. As he pulled his hand away, he dragged the disassembled garments with it and threw them to the floor.

"Smartass," Hel murmured, as she scraped her nails down his now bare chest.

He groaned as she caught his nipple and he sent his pleasure surging back down their connection to her only to have it reverberate back at him as his hands explored her body.

"That's cheating," she panted.

They were fast losing themselves to shared sensation. Bast could feel the nervous systems of their interwoven power becoming ever more tangled, reaching deep inside him where nothing had ever touched. He felt a moment of concern, but his malfunctioning sense of self-preservation flickered out as Hel moved her body against him, sending more of his blood careening south. He was desperate to rip her clothes off and feel her skin to skin, but he didn't have enough free hands as he kept one gripped tight to her ass, supporting her to keep up that exquisite friction.

"Bed. Now," he said, reluctantly removing his hand from

her breast to wrap her in his arms as he carried her away from the wall's support.

He was barely watching where he was going as he kissed and bit his way down her neck, finding the door to his bedroom by instinct. He stumbled as Hel took advantage of his distraction to run her hand down the sensitive inner surface of his wings making his whole body shiver. They flared open in involuntary response as her fingers sent sparks of his silver magic drifting into the air to settle against her. He could feel every point where his power sunk inside her and combined with the erotic torture she was sparking with her touch, his control snapped at the sensory overload.

Her sultry laugh as he threw her onto the bed had an edge to it, inflamed by the now throbbing connection between them that was fast making it difficult to separate whose pleasure was whose.

Even submerged in hedonistic obsession, he still couldn't help but pause and take in the picture she made spread out on his bed for him. As he watched, she kicked off her boots and wriggled out of her tight jeans. His eyes traced a path up each perfectly sculpted calf and thigh, taunting himself with the thought of exactly where he would place each kiss. He felt her energy turn darker as a wicked glint entered her eyes. Turning, she rose onto her knees facing away from him as she shrugged off her jacket and tossed it aside. He was captivated by her every movement as she reached down to the hem of her tank top.

She'd swept her shadow-black hair over her breasts as she turned her head to watch him over one shoulder. He was so lost in her deep green eyes that it took him a heaving breath to notice the agonisingly slow reveal of his mark on her back as she drew her top up over her head. The sight ratcheted his lust impossibly higher and his control short-circuited. Every muscle grew rigid as he fought to remain in place while she tossed the cotton fabric to the side and knelt there before him like an offering. His wings had flared out to fill the room and the only light in the space was the glowing silver of his power that reflected off her skin until she looked bathed in starlight. The black lines of the feathers he'd imprinted into her body trembled under the pressure of their shared desire.

"Say yes," he said in an almost unintelligible low growl that she would probably only understand through the intent he was sending where their power joined. He couldn't wait. Couldn't be gentle. Couldn't seduce. He needed to be inside her. A quiet note of alarm sounded deep in his subconscious, but he was too far gone to care. If he moved, it would be to take her. He forced himself to verbalise the thought, needing there to be no doubt what was about to happen. "Now is the time to leave if you don't want this. I have no control left."

Hel licked her tongue across her lips and he almost lost it, using his own power to leash himself as his muscles strained to take what was his. He immediately regretted it because his power now tasted of her and the sensation drove him even closer to the edge he was teetering on.

"Yes." The whispered word hung between them and time froze for an infinitesimal moment.

"Condom?" he asked, whatever strange compulsion that was driving him flaring in objection to the suggestion. He managed to ignore it. Barely. A distant part of himself knew he should be worried by the reckless force that had hold of them, but there wasn't room in his thoughts for anything but Hel.

"No," Hel said, her vehemence matching his own

instinctive need to have no barrier between them; both of them seemingly reduced to one-word sentences.

Then she reached down and ripped the last scrap of material that stood between his eyes and her body away. The tearing sound of the lingerie's destruction and the shot of pure lust spearing out from her smashed his last thread of restraint and he lunged forwards, barely aware of the drop of power he sent to his remaining clothing to leave it trailing on the floor behind him. He'd never been more grateful for elemental tailoring.

His wings were still spread wide and his lunge sent him briefly airborne. When he dropped to the bed behind her and his hands finally gripped around her hips, it felt like coming home. She dropped to her elbows and knees, arching her back as he pulled her closer. Somehow, he managed to stay aware enough that he paused his motion to make sure she was with him as he pressed against her soaking wet core. She wasn't any more capable of patience than he was, though. The knuckles of her hands turning white where she grasped the sheets was the only warning he got before she drove herself back against him in a sharp movement until he was fully sheathed inside her. The sensation of finally slipping into her warm, tight body was too much. The world disappeared. There was nothing but Hel and him and the pounding rhythm between them. He could feel Hel's power opening to his as they moved together and he pushed forward with every part of him until she welcomed him so deep inside her that he could never let go. The silver of his magic twined with the blue of hers until they were inextricably woven together. Her heartbeat was his heartbeat. Her gasping breaths were his gasping breaths. Her soul was his soul.

He froze in place for a split second, ice chilling his veins even as his cock throbbed in protest at the lack of movement and his arousal demanded he keep chasing such exquisite pleasure.

What the fuck had they done? That was a fucking mating bond.

CHAPTER 21
HEL

Hel moaned at the deep satisfaction of Bast stretching inside her until she felt so full of him she didn't know where he ended and she began. She'd felt his moment of fear, but she couldn't deal with that right now. Right now she needed him to *move.* She was stealing this one night of pleasure before she was forced to keep running to keep him and his family safe and she was going to damn well enjoy it.

She tightened her inner muscles around him, ignoring the way the action was mirrored in the less tangible connection between them—their entwined power settling ever deeper inside them both. She was rewarded with his tortured sounds followed by strong hands clenching even tighter on her hips. Every time he drew out of her, he slammed back inside a little faster as if he couldn't bear even that slight separation. She moaned again, every thrust hitting just right as it wound them tighter and tighter. Her power was pulsing in time to their movements, threading around the now-familiar silver of his magic in an erotic reflection of what was building between them.

One of his hands shifted to the marks on her back and she jerked back against him in sensory overload as the caress made it feel like she'd grown phantom wings he was stroking with his fingers. A lock of her sweat-soaked hair fell across her face and she flicked her head to clear it, distantly wondering why it seemed to be shining too bright in the glow from Bast's feathers that curled tight around them. His wings brushed against her sides, shaping to her form like he needed to touch every part of her with every part of him.

A strong arm wrapped around her torso and his fingers crept lower, his touch exquisite as he pulled her closer with his other arm until his mark on her back rubbed against his muscled chest with every driving motion. It was too much for both of them. She felt his surging need through their connection a moment before his throbbing release inside her sent her splintering into a soul-deep pleasure she hadn't known was possible. Power flared between them and she felt a draw on her essence and a moment of sharp heat where his heart rested against her back. Wave after wave of shuddering aftershocks swept between them, suspending them in a haze of intense endorphins that self-reinforced as the feedback loop of their connection held them captive.

She had no idea how much time passed before the clenching surges of pleasure started to abate. If Bast hadn't been holding her upright, she would have collapsed to the bed long before. She could feel the tremor of effort in his arms as sated exhaustion began to replace the driving need that had supplanted every thought and her own body trembled in sympathy.

Bast gently lowered her to the bed but didn't move to

join her. The loss of their physical connection as he drew away left her frowning.

"Sleep," he said, cupping her cheek and running his thumb over her forehead to smooth away her frown.

She could feel something was wrong, but exhaustion was pulling at her. Her eyes slipped closed despite herself. The last thing she heard before drifting into unconsciousness was his whispered words—"I'm sorry. This may be the worst thing I've ever done."

THE SENSE of betrayal those words sparked followed her into sleep and her dreams were plagued with half-formed memories.

She was six years old and she'd been watching a family feeding doves together in a public garden. Earth sculptures of wondrous creatures lined the space and a little boy was playing chase with his mother around them.

"Mama, Mama. You can't catch me!" his cry rang out.

Her guardian had told her stories of her father from her youngest days, stories to inspire fear and keep her running. But it was the first time she'd ever noticed the lack of the other parent in her tales.

The scene shifted and she was standing in a dark cellar with Amira, her knees covered in grass stains and her cheeks stained with tears as the woman who'd raised her continued to harshly berate her for sneaking off.

"Am I your daughter?" she asked.

Anger flashed across Amira's face. "You are my atonement."

This may be the worst thing I've ever done.

The scene shifted again. She was staring out a window. Hidden. Paralysed by poison. Her friend had tripped on the rooftops they played tag on and was falling to her death. Hel had portalled her to safety by instinct. And then the hounds had come. She'd watched as Amira ignored the fact her friend was bleeding out on the ground, instead using her power to shift her friend's shape until the human girl she'd snuck off to play knucklebones with in dirty alleys was replaced with a mirage of something else—a boy with twisting horns rising through pale hair that glittered silver in the morning light where he lay slumped unconscious on the ground with some kind of strange wings crumpled against his back. Amira had changed as well. Still the same familiar face, too stern, too broken. But now she had horns, too. And ... a tail? One that whipped out to score red lines across the hounds as they lunged in attack until one managed to catch her hamstring and drag both figures through a shining portal that had burned against her magic sense like the molten cores of a thousand suns even through the numbness of the poison.

Hel was all alone and staring at a pool of blood too large for any human child to have survived.

When the local enforcement elementals finally found her in the empty home, she could still barely move. They told her to come. She waited for them to use the codename Amira drilled into her. If they could be trusted, they would call her Dawn.

They asked her what her name was and her world fell out from under her.

She could have fought the light compulsion that wrapped around her to draw her name forth, but she'd been trained from birth not to give her power away like that. So, she told them. "I'm Helaine. I'm alone."

This may be the worst thing I've ever done.

SHE JERKED awake who knew how many hours later with Bast's words still ringing in her mind. She was alone in the bed. He'd never returned. What the fuck?

Struggling to push away the haze of her dreams, she shoved the covers off. Her subconscious was having a field day with that note Amira had left Tir. How long before she died had she left it with them? And why had she left them the only words that would have called her out from hiding? She'd concealed the message in a book titled after the code-name her so-called guardian had never bothered giving to anyone who might've cared for her when Amira died. If they'd sent out a public call for people with information about atonement and a book called the Dawn, Hel would have exposed herself. Amira's message was clear—Hel should be sacrificed to her father to stop the contagion. Fuck that. At least the old lady had been cryptic enough that the elementals might not realise.

Hel shook her head and grabbed her clothes off the floor. One thing at a time. First, she needed to deal with the man who'd run off the second he pulled out of her. Then she needed to get the fuck away from him before she brought any more destruction down on them. She'd find somewhere nice and *alone* to hunker down while she figured out what to do. Glancing in the mirror as she left the room, her stride hitched. A streak of her hair above her temple had turned the silver of Bast's soul magic and her skin had the slightest shine, like starlight catching on grains of glinting golden sand on a beach. The damn soulweaver had a lot of explaining to do.

Her hand stroked the baton at her side as she followed the pull of his presence out to the living room. That was new. She'd never been able to find him like that before without deep concentration but now it was like her sense of him was constant background noise, always there on the edge of her awareness. That wasn't the only background noise either. There was an incessant whispering of voices she couldn't quite make out, like a party happening on the other side of a well-insulated wall.

She found Bast asleep in an armchair, his wings draped awkwardly over the sides and his head tilted at an angle that said he'd be waking with a killer headache. She slipped closer, intending to kick the chair and send him crashing to the floor. She needed to let this anger out. It was the least he deserved. Unfortunately, some sixth sense had his eyes flicking open as she drew near and she froze in place at the surge of guilt from him along their bond.

"What the fuck did you do to me?" she asked.

Bast rubbed a hand over his face and she noticed the deep shadows under his eyes. He hadn't slept well either. Good.

"You mean what did *we* do," he corrected.

"We fucked Bast. I'm well aware. And I know you've fucked plenty of people before so I very much doubt it was that fact alone that made you say *I was the worst thing you'd ever done.* I haven't fucked *quite* as many people, but I can assure you that at no point afterwards have I *ever* woken up with my body and my power changed. Now, *what the fuck did you do?*" She hated the way her voice was rising to a scream, but she couldn't stand it. Her anger and shame at her poor judgement were mixing with his guilt and fear, which she *should not* be able to feel, and the combination was driving her to distraction.

"You weren't the only one who changed. It went both ways. We bonded."

He'd stood up and his fingers brushed over his heart as he spoke. Hel's eyes flicked to the bare skin below his collar where his top shirt buttons were undone. She could just see the edges of silvered blue markings that hadn't been there last time she'd looked. When he was naked. And hard. Ugh. She needed to focus. An unwelcome surge of possessive lust shot through her and she resisted the urge to step closer and rip his shirt undone to bare her mark on his chest.

His eyes smouldered as that irritating bond transferred her moment of distracted arousal to him. She frowned, letting her anger burn it away. "What do you mean, we bonded?"

"A mating bond. My power reached out to yours, and yours reached out to mine, and we bonded. It's not something I could do *to* you. We did it together."

Hel's jaw dropped. "I didn't ... That's not ... How is that even possible?"

"You tell me. It's not supposed to be possible between an elemental and a human. Was there something you forgot to mention?" Bast said, anger now slipping into his voice past the guilt.

"What does the bond do?" Hel said, ignoring his dangerous question. Every secret let loose was another line her father could tug to reel her in. The last thing she needed was the elementals getting wind she wasn't human. They didn't have a great track record with unique species. Look what they'd done to Tir when they'd found them—enslaved to guard a bunch of dusty books. They'd throw her to her father's hounds in a second if they thought it would save them, and if they ever deciphered Amira's note that's exactly what would happen. *But Bast wouldn't. He'd protect you*, the devil's advocate inside her said.

"Our souls and our power are intertwined now. Forever. It can't be broken. If I die, you die. If you die, I die. It's not something elementals generally do anymore for that reason. Especially with a soulweaver because you'll probably go mad from my magic and drag me with you. That's how I killed my mother. She hid what I was until it was too late. My umbilical cord infected her with my magic. They had to cut me from her dead body. The soulweavers who aren't killed at birth generally die before adolescence for the same reason." His voice was flat and emotionless as he gave the explanation but the guilt she was feeling from him suddenly made a horrible sense.

Empathy warred with anger inside her. She shouldn't feel sorry for him. He'd just told her she was probably going to die. And all she wanted to do was take his hurt away. She let a trickle of the protectiveness she was feeling flow down the bond to him and he jerked his head up in surprise, searching her eyes.

"Don't worry about it," she muttered. "I'll probably die before that happens and then I'll have killed you, instead. And I need to leave anyway so we can just pretend it never happened."

A surge of familiar frustration came down their bond. "You can't fucking leave. The tower's shields are the only thing keeping you hidden from whoever's chasing you. If you're caught outside you probably *will* kill both of us," Bast said, but his harsh words were belied by the depth of concern she could feel tempering his anger. It wasn't a selfish concern either. He was worried for *her* safety. The emotion was unfamiliar. No one had ever cared about her like that before.

She wasn't sure she could make herself give that up. Nor could she ignore the driving need to protect Bast and his family from the danger that followed in her footsteps. She'd thought she would do that by leaving, but this mating bond changed everything. If Bast died because of her, how would the courts deal with the contagion? What would happen to Kaia? What would happen to the city?

"Fine. I'll stay," she said.

"What did we do to deserve each other?" Bast sighed, his tension easing at her agreement.

"Must've been something pretty bad," Hel agreed.

Through their connection, there was no hiding their now desperate need for each other, the matching holes inside them the other filled. They might not have wanted or chosen this bond, but now it had formed they were as essential as air to each other and the physical attraction that had flared between them the moment they met was exponentially more acute.

The two of them leaned toward each other without conscious thought, like moths drawn to each other's flame. As their lips were about to meet, Hel's magical sense flared in alarm and she felt Bast stiffen against her as their new bond transferred the sensation to him. On the very edges of her sensory range, the largest portal she'd ever felt was forming and it tasted of the molten core of a sun and the vastness of an empire that spread across worlds.

The vanguard had arrived.

T*HANK YOU FOR READING!*

If you'd like to hear about my new releases and read the prequel short story of how Bast came to the City of Souls during the Melding and met Ra, sign up to my newsletter through my website and I'll send you the free ebook From the Ashes.

ACKNOWLEDGEMENTS

This was not the first novel I've written, but it's the longest and steamiest! It's also the first I've ever published. I dedicated it to my wingpeople and while I definitely meant my fellow winged romance fans, I also meant the amazing people who've supported me along the way.

First and foremost, thank you Amber and Marie. You were my gateway to this genre, my greatest cheerleaders and supporters, and this book wouldn't exist without you.

Thank you to my wonderful beta readers—Rebecca, Toni, Cassie, and Priscilla. And to my awesome editor Madeleine Collinge.

Thank you to the communities of writers and readers I belong to, especially my Speculative Collective who help me in countless ways every day, the FaRo authors, Romance Writers of New Zealand, and Jared Gulian via the Fans of Urban Fantasy Facebook Group who gave The Crypt its name.

Thank you to my ARC reviewers and to all the readers who take a chance on a debut author.

And last, but not least, thank you to my family, friends and colleagues who are endlessly interested in my writing (or at least pretend to be) and excited for me. Maybe don't read this one if you don't like steam, though? I guess it's too late if you're reading this.

ABOUT THE AUTHOR

Mel Harding-Shaw is a paranormal romance and urban fantasy writer from Wellington, Aotearoa New Zealand. Her debut novel *City of Souls* won Agent's Choice in the RWNZ Great Beginnings Contest.

She's also a widely published award-winning writer of short speculative fiction as Melanie Harding-Shaw and has published five books under that name: the Censored City trilogy of near-future novelettes, a short story collection *Alternate*, and a witchy urban fantasy novella *Against the Grain*.

Mel won the award for Services to Science Fiction, Fantasy and Horror in the 2020 Sir Julius Vogel Awards. You can find her at www.melaniehardingshaw.com and on social media.

Manufactured by Amazon.ca
Bolton, ON